Loya

HOPE E. DAVIS

DEDICATION

To every friend who has ever had to listen to their author friend's insane book ideas while sitting in a bar on Monday night. (Thanks, Maggie!)

Author's Note

This book is based loosely on Incan culture and myths. I say loosely because I have made several changes to their myths, legends, and cultural aspects in order to make them fit my artistic purposes. While I use real Incan words and lore, none of this should be taken as fact or history. Any relation to real people, places, or things is pure coincidence.

That being said, the Incans did engage in human sacrifice as a common practice, and the idea of human sacrifice will be discussed on the page. Additionally, this book contains adult depictions of sexual content only intended for audiences 18+. For a full list of triggers, please see my website at hopeedavis.com/buy-books/

You will find several words in Quechua in *Qoya*. Quechua is a modern, indigenous language still widely spoken in Peru today. However, the words may be taken out of context or mixed with Incan words that don't exist in modern Quechua. Please check the reference in the back of the book if you need to know the meaning of a certain word or phrase.

Rurac's
Home

Sacred
Valley

Sun
Temple

Bridge

Palace

SIPAN

Prologue

AZUCENA

I had known since my sixth Inti Raymi that I would eventually become empress, I just hadn't expected that moment to come so soon.

Sometime after my first menstrual cycle, while I was in one of my many lessons, my father fell ill with a cough that wouldn't leave. It only dug its talons deeper into his lungs with every hack until he began coughing up blood.

When my fourteenth solar-path rolled around, he took his last breath.

There were no rules in Sipan that prohibited women from ruling, and my mother stepped in when my father went to join the gods in Hana Pacha.

Until a few solar-paths later when the same mysterious cough came to collect her too.

On her deathbed, my mother beckoned me to her side. When I kneeled, my ear pressed close to her mouth, she whispered, "Remember where you came from, Azucena Katia." My full name sounded unusual coming from her lips, but I didn't have time to dwell on why she used it because she had begun coughing non-stop, and I had to send for a healer immediately. By the time she was settled down to sleep, her odd emission had evacuated my mind entirely.

It was just after my twenty-fourth solar-path that I was named empress, and I stepped into the role with ease. I had trained for my entire life to be empress—spending my days watching my mother in the throne room as she spoke to villagers instead of spending time running in the woods with friends.

Listen to the villagers intently, but don't let them think you are on their level.

Smile, so they think you care, and never, ever, cross your legs. It's rude.

The rules were endless, and they often popped up in my memory—in my mother's voice—at the most inopportune times. Usually when I was doing something I shouldn't. But it didn't matter, I was the empress now.

Despite the copious amount of time I had spent in my parents' shadows, I had always been used to the finer things in life, and now that I was in control of every aspect of the empire, and everyone was at my beck and call, life was even better for me. When I did occasionally remember those strange last words of my dying mother, I couldn't ever figure out what she had been talking about, and why she had used my full name. It hadn't affected my life as far as I could see though, so I carried on with my empress duties—managing land disputes between different high-ranking officials in the empire, overseeing trade regulations, and collecting the tithe from all citizens of Sipan. Of course, there was the occasional grumbling of the neighboring peoples who were not part of my spectacular empire, but I would send my guards to smash any attempted breach of our borders, and that was that.

Sure, the peasants complained they didn't have enough food, and the upper class complained that my taxes of spices and goods were too high. But how was that my problem? I had an empire to run; I couldn't stop the progress of the masses just to save the few bits of food for those who whined.

Because I was just twenty-four when I began spending my sun-cycles sitting on the gilded throne and listening to the problems of the peasants, I was required to have advisors by my side for the first several solar-paths of my rule. Since I was now approaching my thirtieth Inti Raymi—the magical age where I was suddenly "fit to rule" on my own under the law—most of them had finally stepped down. All except one by the name of Yezema.

Yezema and I had honestly never gotten along—we were just too similar. Yezema was perpetually upset over the fact that I had been chosen to succeed my parents. She had also come from wealthy parents, and if I died, would be next in line for the throne. We had discussed it in many heated debates over the last five solar-paths, but the truth of the matter was, in the Sipan empire, rule was handed down by blood whenever possible—the blood that ran in my veins, not hers.

Besides, most of my job was just delegating anyway. It wasn't *that* hard.

I couldn't possibly be doing as poor of a job as she often insinuated.

A tingle on the back of my neck had always warned me that this particular dynamic between myself and Yezema could lead to darkness, so I watched what I consumed in her presence and always placed at least two guards at my door when I slept at night. Some days, I wondered if she had indeed been the cause of the cough that took my parents, but there was no proof, so if she had somehow poisoned them, she had gotten away with it.

I just wish I had been more careful. Maybe if I had been less distracted by the shiny aspects of being empress, I would have foreseen what was to come. Maybe I would have been able to stop the chain of events early on, or maybe I would have even been able to prevent them from happening altogether.

But now, as I sit, locked in the dark and damp room, wondering how I will ever get back to being the rightful ruler of my people, I know that it is too late. I made a grave mistake, one that will cost me my people, and maybe even my life.

How did I get here, you ask? Well, as I already mentioned, it is all the fault of Yezema and her deplorable attitude. But it's probably better if I show you exactly what happened. That way, you can have the entire story, and you can make your own decision about who the villain is in this tale.

I'll give you a hint though, it's not me.

One

AZUCENA

I shifted the small, painted llama, ensuring it was in a pristine line with the other seven.

Stepping back, I put my hands on my hips as I observed the clay ledge where they lived. Although I now had seven of them, the ledge still seemed a bit empty. I would need to commission another, or four, and soon.

"Empress! Empress!" Nania, my yanakuna, called from the hall before swooping into the room and nearly passing out. I pushed a gilded tree stump in her general direction, which she collapsed onto with a huff as she began fanning herself with her plain, but colorful, apron.

"I—he—you—"

"Catch your breath first, then try telling me again." I rolled my eyes as I inspected my nail beds—they weren't in the best condition, something I would need to remedy soon. I glanced back up at my yanakuna to see her still panting, so I went back to looking at my llamas. I think the next one I commissioned would need to be blue with green flowers. Satisfied, I glanced up to see if she had caught her breath yet.

Nania was always running from place to place in my massive palace, which was perched on a hill overlooking the metropolis that was Sipan. So much so that I wondered if she even had a speed that was below jogging. As a result, she always showed up panting, which, though annoying, built anticipation as you waited for her to catch her breath and spill the tea.

"Sorry, Empress. I—"

"I've told you a million times, call me Zu," I snapped. Although Azucena was my full name, it was too much of a mouthful for frequent use. Unless, of course, you were a peasant or a guard and weren't worth my time, then you could struggle over my name all sun-cycle long. Not my problem.

"Sorry, Sapa Inca," she started again, reverting to my true title instead of the name I had just reminded her to call me by. "But I needed to tell you. The torture cells are at capacity again."

I mentally ran through all the punishments I had divvied out in the last few sun-cycles. Space in the basement of my palace—the torture chambers—always seemed to be running low. Not to mention that punishing someone for not paying their tithe only went so far, as they couldn't farm or harvest with their hands damaged, but that was beside the point. I counted mentally. "But I only sentenced four people to the chambers this moon."

"I know, Emp—Sapa Inca. It's Yezema. She sent over twenty people there today."

I let out a groan at my wayward advisor's name. "Not again."

"Ye—"

"It was a rhetorical question, Nania," I snapped before realizing how harsh it sounded. "Sorry, I didn't mean to snap at you. I just can't believe this is the third time this moon cycle she has overloaded the holding cells when I specifically told her not to. We need that space for real crimes, not whatever petty reasons she keeps sending people there for."

Nania began speaking, likely explaining some of the cases Yezema had heard in my absence, but I tuned her out as I pulled on my brightly colored robes and placed the golden sun crown on my head, brushing my dark hair to the side. Try as I might, I truly attempted to oversee all the proceedings in Sipan, but the population had grown so prolifically that, in recent solar-paths, I had been unable to sit on the throne long enough each sun-cycle to see all the individuals who wished to present themselves to the empress. As a result, Yezema, my only remaining advisor, spent a short period of time in my chair each sun-cycle, collecting tithes, and issuing punishments while I was otherwise indisposed.

Nania was still prattling on as I slipped my gold bangles over my wrists, admiring my light brown, blemish-free skin, and pulled my gold collar over my neck. Glancing about the room, I wrinkled my nose, making a mental note to ask Nania to clean up in here this afternoon. Last night I had summoned a man from the village to share my bed, as was my right as empress, and the scent of his perfume oils still lingered. That just simply wouldn't do.

I had no idea what Nania was still blabbing about, but it didn't seem that important, so I turned toward the door, and headed down the hall to the throne room. It wasn't too far of a walk as my chambers were located nearby on purpose so I could step away and rest when I needed to. I didn't feel like we were moving at too quick of a pace, but all too soon, Nania was out of breath again as she attempted to keep up with my long strides. The noise of her panting caused me to grit my teeth.

Stopping in my tracks, I spun to her. "Nania, you can walk slower and catch up with me later if you're going to pant like a dog."

"It's not that . . . Empress . . . it's just this drama gets me so excited, and you know my lungs are weak." She reached out a hand, likely looking for something to lean on.

I took an exaggerated step back. "You know you are not to touch me, under any circumstance," I reminded her as I simultaneously rolled my eyes up to look at the ceiling, which I noticed had a rather large brown smudge. I would need to request that it be cleaned later.

Now, where were we?

Oh yes, going to the throne room, locating Yezema, and

finding out why there were twenty people added to the holding cells since midday, when I had left my throne for a brief nap.

Picking up my pace again, I arrived at the door to the throne room in just a few moments, Nania panting at my side, despite my request that she walk slower. She tried to brush my robe free of dust, as is customary before my entrance, but I motioned her away and did the brushing myself. I didn't like when people breathed on or touched me. Ever.

Once I was ready, I tucked my dark hair behind my ears and nodded to the guards, who slammed the door open, forcing everyone to watch as I entered the room in style.

"Yezema!" I shouted, taking note of her position on my throne, her thin and wrinkly legs crossed to cause her dress to ride up (which she wasn't supposed to do), a bored look occupying her face.

"Azucena!" She snapped to attention, her sickly-sweet voice making me cringe. "I mean, Sapa Inca. I didn't realize you would be back so soon." She bowed her head, but not enough for it to actually be considered respectful.

She always did this—play dumb. But I wasn't an idiot. I brushed a hand in the direction of the peasant kneeling at the base of the throne and the guard swiftly carted him away so my advisor and I could speak in private.

"Yezema, what is this I hear about twenty people being added to the holding cells?"

"Well, Empress, see they . . . uh . . . committed crimes and I, uh—"

I held up my hand to silence her. "We've talked about this. One, we have limited holding cell space, so you can't just tuck every Laka, Zoila, and Pahuac in the dungeons whenever you feel like it. Two, we need working citizens in good physical condition to collect tithes. If they're constantly being tortured, they can't work. And three." I held up my fingers. "It makes people angry, and that's how you incite a rebellion. We don't have the time, or resources, to deal with an uprising this solar-path, especially with the guards we have to keep on the border—"

"But, Empress—"

I cut her off again. "No, Yezema. Go get every one of those twenty people out of the holding cells and send them home—free. And give them a packet of food to smooth things over. Tell them there was a name error. Unless one of them murdered someone, then they stay."

Yezema moved off the throne, grumbling to herself, and she moved down the few steps to the floor, but I could hear every word as I stood there tapping my fingers on my arm in impatience.

"This is why you don't give a child the throne."

"Yezema."

"Hm?" She turned back toward me.

"I am not a child."

She slapped a hand over her mouth. "Oh, Empress, I did not mean for you to hear that."

I smirked, not fooled by her fake blunder. "Clearly."

She continued her path toward the dungeon, beckoning an ancient finger at two guards to follow her, likely to help her unload the prisoners without issue. I rolled my eyes at the blatant disregard of the fact that I had just delegated that task to her, only for her to re-delegate it.

They shouldn't let someone a million sun-paths old be an advisor.

My internal thoughts brought a sly smile to my face as I brushed off the throne and took my rightful seat. In Sipan, we did things how my parents had always done them and there was no time for Yezema's dumb ideas. I motioned to the guard who brought the man who had previously been removed, back in to present his case.

He was a scrawny little thing, with leathery skin that showed he worked under the sun all day. At that thought, I couldn't help but glance at my reflection in the gilded throne. My skin was smooth, and light, beautiful even. Nothing like this . . . worm's.

As he spoke, I watched the air above his head. Many of my subjects believed me to be cold-hearted, because I would not meet their eyes as I heard their plight. But what they didn't know was that I held a secret magical power—passed down through my family lines as a direct gift from the gods.

I could see when someone was telling the truth or a lie.

It wasn't quite as simple as it sounded—it wasn't like the answer appeared above their head, but rather a color would appear there. Over the solar-paths, I had learned that red signified a lie, orange a partial lie, and white was a lie, but a harmless one. Green, blue, and purple all signified various ranges of truth in their words. And if gold appeared, the color of the late sun-cycle sun as it sank below the horizon, well, that meant they were blessed by the gods with a gift of their own. At least, that's what I had discerned up until now. There were so few with magical powers left in the empire that most of what I knew I had taught myself.

This peasant, as he explained his tragic tale, was haloed by blue, meaning I would likely grant what he needed. Unless it was more time to pay his tithe, because everyone in the province knew I didn't grant extensions. Ever.

My magical gift appeared sometime around my sixteenth path around the sun. Meaning I'd never gotten the chance to speak to my father about it. But later, once I realized the colors weren't just my imagination, or a fever, I went to my mother with concern. My mother explained to me that it was a magical gift that only passed through the female line in our family, and, in fact, my father wouldn't have understood had he still lived.

Not that it made me feel any better. I shifted in my seat, uncomfortable as I remembered that my parents had left me alone to rule an empire all too soon.

When the peasant finished his story, I motioned to my guard. "Take care of it."

He dipped his chin and then followed the man out to help him at home with a field border dispute. I didn't know the guard's name, but I'm sure he could figure out a good solution for everyone involved.

Brushing another invisible speck of dust off my shoulder, I dipped my chin to the guard, indicating to send the next person in.

By sunset my head throbbed with all the problems the peasants had poured out. But the moment I stood up from the throne, I let them fall off my shoulders. At the end of the suncycle, I lived in the palace, away from their petty poverty problems. I could only do what I could to solve them, and that was that.

Making my way back down the hall, I stopped to snap my fingers outside the throne room doors and Nania ran to my side to assist me back to my room.

"Did Yezema empty the holding cells?"

"Yes, Empress."

Again, with the title. I was too tired to address it again today, though, so I continued on. "And there are cells available again?"

"Yes, Empress."

"Very well. Have my dinner brought to my room."

She nodded, completing the escort to my door before dashing off in the direction of the kitchens, assumably to collect my dinner tray. Hopefully she wouldn't pant all over my dinner.

As I pulled my crown off my aching head to set it on the holder in my room, changing from my throne room robes into my dressing gown, I had no idea of what was to come.

I had no idea that the dinner currently en route to my room would be the last I ever ate here.

Two

AZUCENA

T he dinner Nania delivered was a specialty, known all around the province for its delicious taste and unique name, but I couldn't care less as I picked at it with my flawless fingernails until Nania finally came to collect the nearly-full dish and return it to the kitchen. It was made from lizards, which was supposed to be a delicacy, but I much preferred the basic alpaca to the tough lizard meat.

The door snicked shut behind her, and I threw myself across my llama skin bed with a sigh. Being royal was much harder than one would expect, and it stole so much of my energy. I closed my eyes, not sleeping, really, but taking a much-needed silent pause to recenter myself, giving my gift a chance to cool after a long day of judging the peasants in court.

Just as I was about to drift off into a dreamland, there was a knock at the door.

I sat up, rolling my neck and shoulders. "Nania, just come in for crying out loud." Sometimes, I thought seriously about replacing my handmaiden with a different yanakuna; I was that tired of retraining her. But then I remembered I would have to completely train someone anew, and the task just seemed too insurmountable to tackle, and so, Nania kept her position another sun-cycle.

I looked up from my thoughts, only for my jaw to drop at the sight of Yezema, not Nania, peeking around my doorframe, a green aura floating around her head.

"Sapa Inca?"

I rolled my eyes. I wasn't going to correct her. "Yes, Yezema? What can I do for you?"

She cleared her throat and stepped fully into the room, revealing her hands, one of which was clenching a clay pitcher and the other two cups, colorful bracelets lining her thin arm. Some of the bracelets had symbols stamped on them, but I couldn't get a good look due to the fact that her hands shook slightly, probably due to her advanced age. She braced her elbows against her dress, which was almost as colorful and ornate as mine, revealing how heavy the pitcher was. Why she didn't have a yanakuna follow her with it was beyond me. My eyes automatically returned to the air above her head, where the green aura was still present.

"I thought we might have a chicha morada together." She set the two cups on my table, filling them with the purple liquid from the pitcher. Chicha morada was my favorite beverage, and she knew it.

"What's the occasion, Yezema?" This wasn't the first time she had brought chicha to my rooms over the course of my rule. In fact, this was a normal occurrence, especially when she had bad news to give.

"No occasion," she quipped, lifting a cup to hand to me. "Just wanted to thank you for all of your guidance over the years, and I know how you like chicha."

I arched one of my thin eyebrows. She had never thanked me before—or ever, really—and something about this situation felt odd, but I wasn't about to turn down a glass of my favorite beverage.

Accepting the cup from her hand, I decided we better discuss the events that had occurred earlier. "Yezema, I wanted to thank you for correcting your mistake, and remind you to be more cautious of how many people you send to the holding cells going forward."

"Yes, Sapa Inca," she said, but her actions didn't match her words, as I noticed the slight, almost imperceptible, roll of her eyes.

Silence settled between us as I mentally counted down the sun-cycles left with her as my advisor. "You know your position here is almost finished. Have you considered what you will do in your final solar-paths after you leave my employ?"

Yezema's eyes widened. "What do you mean my sun-cycles here are almost done?"

It was my turn to be surprised. I had always assumed my parents had instructed her as to when her last sun-cycle would be. I tapped a finger on my clay cup as I replied. "You were only to be my advisor until my thirtieth solar-path, which is in a few sun-cycles, don't you recall?"

Yezema grimaced, her eyes darting from side to side as her hands fidgeted with the edge of her skirt. "No, Sapa Inca, I did not."

"Very well then, now you have a few sun-cycles to consider what comes next for you."

"I can't stay here?" She sounded almost shocked by the revelation, as if she really expected me to keep her around or something.

When my other advisors had finished their tenure, I had allowed them to stay in the palace until they could find family to return to, but Yezema and I had never gotten along, and there was no way I wanted her around any longer than what was absolutely necessary. "I'm sorry, but I would prefer you leave the premises as soon as your tenure is complete. You understand, I'm sure."

"All right then," she replied. But she didn't smile, and her eyes didn't meet mine.

Something felt off, but this was how interactions almost always went with my wayward advisor, so I brushed away my apprehension. I was the empress, and I was almost free from

Yezema. No more having to constantly fix her mistakes, or monitor the number of peasants she sent to the torture chambers. I couldn't wait.

Desperate to avoid the continuing awkwardness, I stood from the bed, tapping my cup against the one she held in her hand. "Bottoms up then!" I called out before tilting my head back and taking a small and cautious sip. I never emptied my glass fully when she was around, even when her aura indicated she was telling the truth, like it did now.

When I looked back at Yezema, she was grinning, but in an odd way that almost looked like she was in pain. "Are you sure you are okay?" I asked, my eyes narrowing. Her aura was still green.

"Of course, Sapa Inca, of course." She motioned to the pitcher. "Would you like another glass?"

"Sure!" I replied, a bit too enthusiastically, hoping she wouldn't notice that I hadn't had more than a delicate sip of my current glass, before I turned to my vanity to slip my gold earrings and necklace from my body and lay them on the small table which held my sun crown on a pillow.

When I turned back around, Yezema once again held out my glass, and same as before, I tapped mine against hers, said a cheer, and tossed a single gulp back. With a satisfied sigh, I moved to set my glass down only to see Yezema's face swimming.

That's odd, I thought—I didn't think my eyes were watering.

I tried to move my mouth to tell Yezema that something was wrong, but it was too late, and my world suddenly went black.

Three

AZUCENA

S unlight was streaming through the window when I cracked open one eye before slamming it shut again. For some reason, the first thought on my mind had something to do with Yezema, which, trust me, was definitely out of the ordinary. But I couldn't help this lingering weird feeling about her after last night.

As memories of the night before trickled into my mind, I realized that I didn't have any memory of taking off my clothes or preparing for bed.

I cracked open one eye again, just enough to take notice of the wood ceiling above me and red bedspread tucked beneath me.

Red?

I hated red, it was the color of lies.

Panic pulsing through my body, I shot up to a sitting position, quickly taking inventory of the room. The walls were made of stone, with mud caked in the cracks. There were no decorations, and where my vanity had been the night before was now an empty, crooked wooden tree stump.

What the Mictlan!?

Further investigation revealed this was not my room at the palace. Actually, I was reasonably sure this wasn't even a room *in* the palace, which was constructed of beautiful, mud-plastered stone walls and painted with a variety of ornate colors I had commissioned myself, including gold. That's when I glanced down and noticed I was still in the dressing gown I had changed into the sun-cycle before.

As my breathing quickened, I ran through the events of the night before for the second time, forcing myself to come to some conclusion as to how I ended up here, in this small excuse for a room.

The longer I thought about it, the more I realized I was absolutely wasting time. Instead of waiting for whatever Yezema had done to me to come to the surface of my mind, I rose from the straw bed (nothing like my llama skin one at home), taking immediate notice of my bare feet.

Well, walking around without my slippers was about to be a chore, but I didn't see them located at the end of the wooden bed frame.

Ugh, Yezema had stolen my slippers. That bitch.

Whatever. I could handle this. If my backward advisor truly thought stealing my slippers would break me, she was wrong.

Without waiting a moment more, I moved to the door, swinging it open to reveal a small sitting room and kitchen combo that reeked of peasants and looked nothing like the palace interior. But the good news was, the door to whatever this Mictlan was, stood open, revealing a field of lush green grass bowing in the wind.

Now, I wasn't much of an outside person (too dirty and too many peasants), but I was about to make an exception to that rule.

Glancing around the living/kitchen area one final time to deduce it was, in fact, empty. I dashed out the door, my arms pumping as I flew off the small plaster porch and into the grass. I had to get away from here, and back to the palace as soon as possible.

I'm not going to lie (it's not really my thing anyway) the grass had looked much softer than it actually was, and the soles of my feet immediately started to get cut by the sharp blades. Not only that, but the ground beneath the grass was far from soft, and the small pebbles and rocks were waging their own war on my poor, palace-pampered soles. Regardless, I ignored the pain, pumped my arms harder, and ran on.

My dreams of escape were cut short, however, when only a few strides from the porch, something large and heavy hit me from behind, causing me to tumble roughly to the ground, face-first, my mouth filling with grass and dirt. Whatever the weight was, it remained on me, even as I tried to push it up and off. Desperate for air, I was able to lift my head at least and spat out the rocks and dirt. Around that same moment, I heard a grunt, and realized that the weight on top of me was actually a rather large man

"What the—" I cursed, trying to twist to see my captor.

My struggling did nothing, however, as the man barely moved, even as I twisted harder and spat curse after curse at him.

"You might as well save your energy."

I paused. The voice was smooth, earthy . . . and deeper than most of the guards I was acquainted with at the castle.

So, who was on top of me?

"If you want to keep your head," I countered, "you better remove yourself from my body, immediately."

"Keep my head? Seems like my head isn't going anywhere," the voice taunted back, pulling me to him so my back was flush with his muscular chest, one massively muscled arm around my midsection, the other holding my delicate neck in place so I couldn't turn to see his face. Just who in the Pacha Mama did this rogue guard think he was?

"You should know better than to attack me," I tried again, with authority, digging through my brain to think of the worst possible insult. Weirdly enough, I had never been in this position before, and previously, threatening someone's head had been enough to get them away from me . . . so why was this guy still here?

My thinking distracted me to the point where I missed the next words out of his mouth. But then he began to stand up, so I readied my body to make a run for it.

"I wouldn't try anything if I were you."

"Why not?" I quipped, an idea blossoming in my mind.

"I'll just tackle you again."

"So?" I countered.

"You're built like a twig. I might snap your back this time."

I huffed. I had never been referred to as a twig before, and despite this awkward situation, it kind of felt like a compliment.

Without revealing who he was, he spun us around, facing the small stone hut I had just escaped from. On the outside, it looked like it was barely being held together, and one strong windstorm would be the end of the straw-thatched roof. But I had to admit, with the forest in the background, it did look kind of quaint, all things considered.

"Fine, just tell me where we are, and I'll work on getting a pickup arranged."

He laughed and started forcibly moving me back toward the hut.

I fought harder—as much as I could, with my arms pinned at my sides, held in place by his impossibly large biceps. I dug my heels in, but he just pushed them forward with his unnatural strength. I tried to make myself dead weight, but that didn't faze him either.

Now I wished I had learned to fight as my mom had suggested when I was in my adolescent solar-paths and preferred swimming lessons to spending more time than was necessary with the guards.

"Let . . . me . . . GO!" Changing my tactic, I moved my head back just enough to sink my teeth into his forearm, right in the middle of some fancy tattoo he'd gotten there.

He screamed.

The taste of salt and dirt filled my mouth; I gagged and almost vomited.

Okay, that was a bad plan.

I threw myself back into fighting as much as I could, trying to twist and thrash while also kicking my legs.

It didn't work, however, and the hut grew closer.

"STOP FIGHTING!" he yelled, his voice gruff.

But I was never very good at listening, so I continued my struggle until suddenly, something firm collided with my head, my vision became fuzzy, and then, everything was black again.

WHEN I OPENED MY EYES, I recognized the red woven blanket, and the terribly-thatched stone walls immediately. A quick glance around confirmed I was alone in the room in the small stupid hut once again.

Didn't he learn anything last time?

I smirked to myself, rising from the bed to make another run for it. But before I could push open the door, I realized there was something heavy around my ankle. I looked down only to see a circle of hewn stone surrounding the base of my leg.

Not just that, but the circle was attached to another circle. And another after that.

It was some sort of chain of stones.

Like a rabid animal, I crouched to the ground and began following the chain on my hands and knees, only to discover it led under the bed to an open square where the dirt was visible—a stone pike in the center of the dark mound.

I was chained to the ground underneath the hut.

Well, this is just great.

Needing some time to re-group, I crawled back onto the bed, the chain making scraping sounds as I got myself situated. The red of the blanket burned my eyes, and even though I knew I probably wouldn't get another, I couldn't help but rip it from the straw bed and toss it as far away from me as possible.

There was a thin white blanket covering the straw at least, but now I would have nothing to cover myself.

Oh well, that was future Zu's problem.

I took a moment to investigate the stone chain better. Even in the palace, I had never seen stonework like this. It was etched perfectly and must've come all from one stone the way it was chiseled as one continuous piece. The part around my ankle wasn't fully stone; some of it was made from bronze—a metal I recognized from my less-liked jewelry collection. And there was a hole in it that looked like it could fit a tiny rod.

Just as I was getting acquainted with my chain and sub-par lodgings, the wooden door swung open to reveal the man who had grabbed me earlier. At least, I assumed it was the same man; I didn't really get a good look before—but I did now.

He was tall, much taller than me, and his head was covered with a dark mess of black hair, which pointed every which way before ending just above his ears. His skin was a deep brown, darker than mine, likely from days spent in the sun, though I could still see the black lines of the tattoo I bit into earlier, two pink welts in the middle causing pride to swell inside my chest as I followed it up the length of his arm to where it disappeared beneath the sleeve of his white shirt.

Ha. Take that.

As my eyes roamed up the rest of his body, which was covered in an ill-fitting shirt and pants—common peasant clothes—before moving up to his sharp and angled jaw, and then finding his dark eyes staring me down, malice in their depths. "Are you done?"

I shrugged, noticing the clay bowl in his hand for the first time.

"What's that?"

"Food," he replied, pulling the stump over to the bed, which creaked in warning as he sank his weight into it. I cringed, certain it was the last sun-cycle for the stump with his massive body weight on it, but for some miracle, it held.

He stirred the bowl with a wooden spoon, holding it out in my direction. I peered at the mound of mush on the end and raised my eyebrow.

"What is that?"

"I told you, food."

"What kind of food?" I had always been a bit picky, especially with textures.

"Just eat it."

"No."

"Fine." Without waiting a moment more, he rose from the chair and headed for the door.

"Can't I have something else?" I asked, though I knew he probably didn't have much else in his puny peasant kitchen.

"No," he snapped, the door slamming shut behind him.

I sank back on the bed with a sigh, noticing the light fading from the window over the bed. It was official, I had been here almost a full sun-cycle, and I was no closer to figuring out where I was and what happened last night with Yezema. Hopefully, this was just one bad nightmare that I would wake up from tomorrow. But as time dragged on and the room was eventually fully immersed in darkness, I started to realize a horrible truth.

I, Azucena Katia, *might* have been kidnapped.

Four

RURAC

The girl was already more trouble than she was worth.

When Kuntur had dropped her off, with specific instructions to keep an eye on her and ensure she stayed alive until the next sacrificial moon, I had assumed she would be happy to stay in the cabin eating the meals I prepared for her every so often.

But no. She had been here for only one morning and had already wreaked so much havoc I'd been forced to pull out the stone chains and my mother's special healing potion for bite wounds. Both of which I hadn't used for many solar-paths.

Now that I was thinking about it, I couldn't even remember the last time my father and I had been responsible for wrangling an animal that required the use of both the stone chains and the bite wound potion. Go figure.

As I rubbed the fowl-smelling potion over the raised puncture wounds on my forearm, I heard the sound of the chains dragging across the floor again. Tilting my ear toward the ceiling, I waited for the telltale sign that she was about to attempt something nefarious, but after a few shuffling sounds, all was quiet. She must've finally decided to get some sleep.

I had no idea why my boss had wanted me to hide this

woman, and on such short notice too. She didn't seem like the type to commit the sort of crimes the criminals they brought to my father were known for, but she must have done something worthy of the punishment coming. Maybe she was scamming nobles—something that was on the rise, according to my friend Kuntur, a hunter who lived in town, who told me about one particularly harrowing burglary attempt by an assumed enemy the last time he had come to visit.

Walking over to the window, I used the side of my finger, which was not covered in goo, to pull the curtain back. It was my favorite time of sun-cycle, with the sun sinking low enough to light a rainbow of colors across the sky—the shadows of the trees stretching across the meadow, but not so much that they became terrifying. Once it was fully dark, not even I would venture into the woods surrounding my home.

I had grown up here, in this house, under the care of my father after my mother died in childbirth. My father, like myself, had been the Prison and Game Manager for the emperor, prior to his death. After my father died, I had taken on his role, though it seemed that modern Sipan society didn't have much use for a Prison and Game Manager anymore. Or, if they did, they must have had a second one I didn't know about, as one glance at the large, wooden sun-cycle and solar-path tracker on my wall told me that we hadn't heard from the emperor, nor been delegated a prisoner, in nearly ten solar-paths . . . until now.

It didn't really matter though, as the forest itself had been changing as of late. While it once used to be teeming with large animals and creatures that needed taming and managing, I hadn't seen some of the larger beasts in several moons. Even before his death, my father had mentioned that they had begun receding further into the hills, venturing less close to our cabin, and as a result, less close to society—giving the emperor less of a reason to keep us on their payroll.

A few sun-cycles ago, I had been sure I was about out of a job. Though I was still receiving regular allotted rations from the palace via Kuntur, I figured it was only a matter of time until my boss showed up and told me I was done as large animal manager.

Which is why, when Kuntur had shown up yesterday, with the female prisoner, I hadn't questioned it. Sure, imprisoning future tributes wasn't technically in my job description, but it was something my father had done from time to time as a favor to the emperor, and it looks like he hadn't forgotten. Though none of the individuals we had held before looked like this one.

The woman was definitely beautiful, with dark features and smooth, light brown skin. She was smaller than me, but clearly well fed, and was much taller than any of the women I had met in the village. She was curvy—something that made me glance twice, even though I knew I shouldn't. And though she wasn't anywhere near my height, she had fought like cat in heat when I'd grabbed her. Not to mention, she was quite rude and ungrateful, and did this strange thing where she watched the air above my head as I spoke. But, well, that's about what you can expect of a prisoner. Although something about the way she had looked bothered me, but I couldn't quite place what it was.

Regardless, it wasn't my job to get involved with matters of the emperor. If he wanted me to keep this girl, fine. I just hoped she would settle down. Otherwise, I would be making an unscheduled visit to the palace, something I had only done once with my father as a small boy.

I much preferred it here, in my quiet hut, away from judging eyes.

I had always gotten along better with animals anyway.

People . . . well they were quite complicated. Even when my father was alive, we hadn't ventured out much, and now that he was gone, the sun-cycles I left my hut were few and far between. Usually, only when I couldn't grow enough of my own food and was forced to venture into town to trade. Although, I rarely went past Kuntur's home, which was on the edge—instead trusting him to do my more difficult trades for me.

As I cleaned up the remainder of the tools I had used to cook dinner and treat my wound, I debated checking on the woman. But after a few moments of debate, I figured she would just try to escape again or demand something else from me. She would be fine in her chains until morning.

At least, I hoped so.

I wished my father was here. He was always so much better at this than me, which is why I hadn't minded the fact that I hadn't been given work in nearly ten solar-paths—even if it meant my measly rations I received in payment would have eventually stopped altogether.

Reaching down, I pulled open the trap door, which led to my suite of rooms below ground. When the previous emperor had commissioned my grandfather to live out here, he had provided just a one-bedroom hut, not suspecting he would ever have company or a kid. And when he serendipitously met my grand-mother, and they had my father, they'd had to expand in the only way that wouldn't raise questions—building several rooms beneath the ground, into the depths of the Pacha Mama.

Besides expanding the number of rooms at their disposal, the below-ground rooms gave them a place to hide if political issues arose—though things had been peaceful for a while—as well as a space that was temperate all solar-path, despite the moody seasons these hills were known for.

Currently, the dugout held a second sitting room and food storage area, as well as two additional bedrooms and a bathing chamber, leaving the above-ground bedroom for guests or prison-ers, as needed. As I stripped down to my undergarments and extinguished all of the lights besides the candle on my bedside, I couldn't help but be thankful I had such an amazing father who prepared me for such a peaceful life.

Even if the next few sun-cycles were sure to be tough with this brat of a prisoner, I would fulfill my duty to the empire. Just as my father would have wanted.

Five

AZUCENA

My stomach woke me the next morning, growling its disdain for my having skipped dinner the night before. But still, when the burly, yet attractive, man came to the door with another unintelligible bowl of sludge, I shooed him away with insults, my eyes focused on his aura, rippling with the colors of deception.

I was going to make it harder than that to drug me again.

On his way out, his gaze found the blanket I had tossed in the corner of the room. Admittedly, it had been cold last night, but not cold enough for me to swallow my pride and use the red blanket. No way.

"It'll be cold here soon. You might want that." He didn't even turn around to deliver his message.

"No thanks. I'll freeze," was my retort, my arms coming up to fold across my chest. "Unless you have a different blanket I could use?"

"No," he snapped again, yanking the door open with his large fist while trying to balance the food he had brought in the other.

Apparently, he didn't understand that I was the empress and that my word was law in pretty much the entire southern half of the continent. "Don't you know who I am?"

"No."

My eyes widened, and all words escaped me. Everyone knew who I was—murals of my entire family decorated large portions of the many small villages under my rule. Plus, there was a shrine in the center of each village outside of the main metropolis to ensure they could pray to the gods for my continued safety.

Who was this man, and had he grown up under a rock?

Lucky for him, I was a gracious empress. "Don't you *want* to know who I am?" I was giving him the option to correct his horrendous mistake.

"No."

His abrasiveness caused me to practically choke on air. So, he was just holding me here, for fun? "Is that the only word you know? No?"

He opened his mouth, his lips clearly about to form the word "no" when he realized the trap he had just walked into. His eyes narrowed. "I'm not going to answer that."

"Fine." I slumped back on the bed, the chain around my ankle making noise as the stones rubbed against each other. "Can you at least tell me why I'm here?"

"No idea." His voice was gruff and muffled as he turned away. "Emperor's orders."

With that, the door slammed shut, leaving me more confused than before.

There was no emperor of Sipan—just me, the empress. So, who was giving this man orders then? I scratched my chin, looking around the room for any sort of clues as to where I was and who the man was, but the room was terribly bare. There were no statues, paintings on the wall, nor a loom to glean a Quipu from as I clunked around the room, the chain dragging behind me. If he really had been ordered to detain me, it was an order that originated outside of the area of Sipan. I ruled over the entire kingdom, which included several provinces. The closest people not under my rule were the Alcahuasis and Canas, both small tribes with no known emperor. Or at least, they hadn't had an emperor when my trusted spies had last reported back.

Sinking back on the less-than-comfortable bed, I began to ponder the options.

I eventually surmised that I was being held by mistake. There must've been some confusion about one of my orders. But I hadn't ordered anyone to be kidnapped recently . . .

Looking at my bound leg again, I sighed and began trying to work my fingers under the bronze, looking for any sort of weak spot. But no matter what I did, or how hard I pulled, it refused to budge.

At least the chain was long enough for me to visit the clay waste pot in the corner, I just hoped this issue, whatever it was, would be worked out swiftly so I wouldn't have to continue to do so. I missed the royal toilet rooms already. How could the peasants live like this?

Giving up on my fabricated task, I sank back onto the bed, closing my eyes to try to bring the memory of my brief moments outside to the front of my mind. But nothing about the field, or the forest that flashed behind my eyelids seemed the slightest bit familiar.

For the first time in probably my entire life, I realized that the fact that I had never left the palace, until now, could very much be my downfall. After all, who knew what this brute of a man wanted with me? Knowing my luck, I would be murdered in just a few sun-cycles, or perhaps tortured, or worse.

If this man was working for the Canas, and planning to turn me over to them, this could very well be the downfall of the empire my parents left in my stead. And we can't have that—it would be simply disgraceful.

Which meant that I needed a plan.

ONE SUN-CYCLE BLED into the next, and then another one after that. Each morning the burly man brought me a bowl of sludge, and another one in the evening, and on the fourth day I caved, shoveling my mouth full of food as fast as possible to calm the rumbling in my stomach.

The burly man, of course, tried to slow me down with, "careful, you'll make yourself sick." But I didn't listen, continuing to shovel until I felt my stomach starting to revolt, then, admitting he may have been right, I stopped my shoveling and took a moment to breathe and rub my stomach.

"Told you." He rolled his eyes. "They never listen."

I narrowed my eyes at him, but he didn't seem to notice, moving to empty the clay waste pot as I continued eating at a much slower pace than before, mentally cursing his existence.

"You know, if you just took me back, you wouldn't have to clean up after me," I mumbled around the bite in my mouth, motioning to the chamber pot with the wooden spoon.

"As I said before, orders are orders," he grumbled, carrying the chamber pot out the front door and returning a few moments later to place it back in the corner.

In the meantime, I had finished the sludge and then clanked the spoon into bowl, loudly.

He didn't seem bothered, simply sweeping the bowl from my grip and turning to leave.

I don't know what compelled me to ask the next question, but it flew from my lips before I had the chance to hold it back. "What's your name?"

The question appeared to surprise him just as much as it did me, his eyebrows shooting up nearly to his hairline. He seemed to ponder the question a moment before deciding it was apparently harmless to reveal his name. "Rurac."

"Hm." I rolled his name over my tongue, testing it out. "Rurac." I would need to remember that name so I could order him to be tortured later.

"Yup."

30

"That's a nice name."

"Sure is."

The conversation stalled. After all, he was still my jailer, and there was still some horrible mistake as to why I was here. The colors in his aura shifted and mixed, but red and orange were still prominent. He was lying about his name.

"I'm Azucena," I told him, watching his face for the inevitable sign that he recognized who he had kidnapped.

He didn't so much as flinch. "That's a nice name."

Wow. He was dense. I opened my mouth to tell him that I was, in fact, his empress, but then quickly realized that if he was Canas, that would be a bad idea, as then he may try to trade me for ransom. I couldn't have that, not with Sipan's currently precarious spice situation. The number of farmers seemed to be in decline—something I attributed to Yezema's idiotic ways. I had tried to explain to her time and time again that if she locked up all the farmers, the empire wouldn't have any food or income, but she just didn't seem to get it.

Pulling my thoughts back to the present, I realized that I needed to escape from this peasant, and he would need to be none the wiser. I closed my mouth again, and he said nothing, silence stretching between us.

We stared at each other across the room, the clay bowl still clutched in his fist, his other arm resting on the door jam.

"I'm going to try to get us something different to eat tomorrow." He motioned to the bowl. "I'm not much of a cook."

I tilted my head to the side. Now he was volunteering information about himself? What a strange man indeed.

I rolled my eyes, my fingers coming up to play with the ends of my black hair. "Don't look at me. I don't cook either." There had just never been a reason to learn to cook, living in a palace filled with yanakuna at my beck and call and all.

"That's interesting." He rubbed his chin. "Aren't all women supposed to learn to cook from their mothers?"

I felt the fury building in my chest, and out of habit, I began looking around for something to throw, but of course, I was still in this barren room. I settled for letting out a low growl and a "No."

"No?"

I had managed to keep the fury in once, but now it exploded. "NO! Just because you're a woman doesn't mean you have to learn how to cook. Cooking is beneath me." I swore.

That had his attention, but rather than battle it out with me, he gave up, shrugging his shoulders and closing the door behind him.

"COWARD!" I called through the wood. He could hear me, I knew it.

The silence in the room grew, as did the shadows. Reclining back on the bed, and lifting my chained foot from the floor, I breathed out a huff.

Over the past four sun-cycles, I had thought all the thoughts, dreamed all the dreams, and there really wasn't anything else to do. I had been hopeful that I could ask Rurac, or whatever his real name was, for some sort of activity to occupy my boredom, but my short temper had ruined that.

As the room got darker, I swallowed what was left of my pride and grabbed the red blanket from the corner. As much as I hated the color red, Rurac hadn't lied about it getting colder with each passing night.

I tucked myself under the offensive blanket as well as I could with one ankle chained and realized I would need to start planning an escape, and fast. Since brute force and my name hadn't gotten me anywhere, it was time to try the last thing I was used to, but that I knew would work:

Being nice.

Then, when he trusted me enough to release my chain, I would make a run for it.

It was foolproof, and hopefully, based on today's conversation, I could count on it working quickly.

Yes, it was all coming together.

Six

RURAC

The woman, Azucena, was right about one thing: If I could snap my fingers and return her back to wherever my boss had gotten her, I probably would have at this point.

But that was part of the problem—I knew little of where she came from.

Seeing as she was the first human prisoner I had been delegated to handle on my own, I was really unsure as to how this was all supposed to work. When I had been given animals to care for in the past, the job was always to feed them to ensure they were plump for sacrifice . . . but I wasn't sure whether or not the same would apply to humans. While human sacrifices had been common when I was growing up—my father was given a prisoner once per solar-path to hold for donation to the gods—things had changed since his death, and the emperor had stopped sending humans. My father had spoken about visiting the emperor to find out more regarding why things had been changing, but then he got sick and well . . . I wasn't much for travel.

Brushing away those thoughts, I pushed open the prisoner's door to find that she was sitting on the bed, smiling at me, her legs crossed demurely. Her dress, which had been quite ornate for a peasant when she arrived, was looking worse each sun-cycle, though today it appeared as if she had at least tried to brush off the dirt.

I narrowed my eyes immediately, sensing the something was off. "What did you do?"

She raised her eyebrows. "Nothing, I just thought I would be up and ready for breakfast when you came."

I didn't trust her one bit, and with my eyes still narrowed, I thrust the bowl at her. "Here."

"Thanks," she replied, smiling at me sweetly, her teeth still looking beautifully white though I hadn't provided her with a toothbrush.

As she quickly demolished the measly breakfast I had handed over, I scoured the room, looking for any sign she had gotten into something that she shouldn't have, but everything was in its place. Including the red blanket, which was back on the bed for once.

"I was thinking." She spoke between bites. "After breakfast, maybe I could help you with the food preparation for the day? I'm not much of a cook, as I mentioned last sunset, but I don't think I can be any worse than this." She motioned to the bowl of mush in her hands.

I raised an eyebrow and crossed my arms. This was all very strange. I debated for a moment in my mind, trying to remember if my father had let the prisoners help around the house, but for some reason I couldn't picture how things had gone with the last one. All I could remember was the sad look in his eyes as he said, *"We must make their final sun-cycles as comfortable as possible."*

"I'm serious," she insisted, interrupting my journey through my memories.

"What do you want?" I pushed, not trusting her at all. There was no way she was being this nice and didn't want something.

"Nothing," she replied. "I told you last night, I'm bored. Anything is better than being in this room alone for another sun-cycle. Especially if this"—she motioned around the room—"is long term."

"Hm." I thought for a moment. "Okay," I relented, "you can come and see what you can make of what I have in the kitchen, I suppose."

She beamed at my words, clearly excited. Maybe she thought I was going to release her stone chain, but there wasn't a chance in Mictlan. I wasn't going to let her be *that* comfortable.

Grabbing her empty bowl and dropping it in the kitchen, I made a detour on the way back to grab another one of the large chains I had on hand. Before returning to the room, I snapped one side of the second to my ankle, quickly snapping the other on her own before she could object.

"Wha—" she started, but her eyes quickly followed the trail of interlocking links to my ankle. "Oh."

Without deigning to reply, I leaned down, pulling the bronze key from my breast pocket and unlocking the chain that restrained her to the bed, smirking to myself. Apparently, she had thought I was unprepared to deal with prisoners.

Standing back up and returning the key to my pocket, I held open the door. "After you."

The smile was no longer on her face, but she also didn't curse or say anything mean as she made her way to the front room, the chain dragging on the dirt floor between us. I pointed to the kitchen. "You can look through my stock. I was planning to grab some more herbs later."

She shuffled about, peering in each storage jar, likely looking for the tools used to prepare meat. Little did she know, I had a second food preparation area below her feet, and that was where I kept all the sharp items.

"Looks like a kitchen to me," she finally replied with a shrug, glancing around the room. "So, what do you do all sun-cycle?"

Her question threw me off at first. Was this really the woman I had dragged into the house, kicking and screaming, just a few sun-cycles before? She almost seemed . . . friendly. It was odd.

"Eh-hem." She motioned with her hand.

I had drifted in my thoughts, forgetting to answer her question.

I shrugged. "I mostly gather food, occasionally hunting it from the woods. I also make weapons." Her eyebrows shot up. "But nowhere near where one of my prisoners would be able to get them," I added quickly.

"So, you have other prisoners?"

I debated for a moment whether or not what I was about to say would give her an advantage, but I decided in the end, it wasn't much information. "Sometimes I have a few at a time. Right now, I just have you."

Her eyes squinted, and I swore she was looking at the space above my head rather than at my face, but she didn't call me out on my blatant lie.

"So, you gather food all sun-cycle and maiz mush is the best you can make?"

I shrugged. "Gathering food takes a lot of time and effort, believe it or not," I snapped before adding, "My dad wasn't much of a cook either, and my mom died in childbirth."

Her eyebrows raised at that. "A brute like you actually had parents?!"

"A father, yes," I pointed out, fighting not to laugh at her joke. "But please, tell me more about how you came to the conclusion that I was a brute."

"Are you serious?" She motioned around the room. "You kidnap a woman, chain her in your bedroom after she tries to run for her freedom, and you're asking me why I decided to call you a brute?"

She did have a point, on all but one thing. "I told you already, I didn't kidnap you. Also, the room you're staying in isn't 'my bedroom,' it was specifically designed for prisoners."

"Sure, sure." She brushed me off and began wandering around the small living area of the cabin, her pace slow due to the heavy chain as she lifted the blankets on the bench I used for sitting.

Realizing that maybe I should be a slight bit nicer, seeing as there was no sign of my boss, and she had already been here for several sun-cycles, I sighed and asked her a question. "What do *you* do all day if you don't know how to cook?"

She opened her mouth, and I prepared for a tirade like she had given me the night before, but to my utter surprise, she tossed her head back to the ceiling and began to laugh.

Not just a chuckle either, a full-bellied laugh that went on and on to the point where tears leaked out of the corners of her eyes.

I looked on as she wiped them away with one of her delicate fingers. I didn't understand what was funny.

Her laughter finally slowed, and she caught her breath, wiping the moisture from the edges of her cheeks. "You did not seriously just ask me that."

Annoyed at myself for my attempt at being nice, I rolled my eyes before answering. "Clearly, I did."

"Well . . ." She brushed a stray hair out of her face. "Before this portion of my . . . existence . . . I had a rather prestigious job. I made laws, oversaw yanakunas, and sent criminals, like you, to the torture chambers."

My eyebrows rose at the last part. So, she was a corrupted noble then—or the wife of one.

"Do you think your husband is missing you?" I asked, trying to get the answer to my question in a less obvious way, my gaze following her every move as she continued to poke around the sitting area.

"I'm not married." It didn't even look like my question surprised her. Instead, she just studied her nails. "No trial marriages, either."

Now that surprised me. The woman appeared to be about my age, perhaps around thirty solar-paths, and it was odd that she was unmarried. Though I had been on the outside of society for most of my solar-paths on the Pacha Mama, even I knew that most women married by their twentieth solar-path. And if, for some reason, they hadn't, they had most certainly had at least one trial marriage by then, even if it hadn't worked out. Luckily, if a trial marriage didn't work out in Sipan, you were allowed to separate from your trial partner—as long as children weren't involved.

I was so surprised by her answer, the next words slipped out of my mouth without permission from my mind. "I'm not surprised."

As soon as I said the words, I wished I could take them back. Her mood fell—any hint of her previous laughter slapped from her features. Her shoulders even slumped slightly.

What was worse, I wasn't even sure what to say next. My father hadn't really taught me the ways of women. Or people.

An awkward silence settled between us as she didn't even deign to look my way, instead lifting the corner of the curtain to glance outside.

I suddenly came to the conclusion that since she was here, and wanting to help, I might as well take advantage of the free labor. "So . . . shall we gather herbs?" I offered, knowing I should probably apologize immediately for my previous comment, but also not really knowing how to without displaying weakness.

"Sure," she agreed, following like my shadow as I grabbed my herb basket and opened the door to the hut.

As she stepped out, I debated grabbing a larger weapon than the small, short sword hidden in my worn pants, but immediately thought better of it. Based on how she fought me before, I didn't want her getting her hands on any weapon. Plus, I hadn't seen a truly threatening animal in the woods in many solar-paths. I likely wouldn't need it.

I led the way to the edge of the forest, kneeling to collect the leaves off the red uchu plant. She watched me silently, her brown eyes appraising my movements.

Trying to break up the awkwardness I pointed to the plants. "These are uchu plants."

"I know that," she replied with a huff, crossing her arms over her chest.

"You said you didn't know much about cooking—"

She cut me off. "I don't know anything about cooking, but I do know all about the spice trade, and what spices are valuable and used for which purposes. I'm not an idiot."

Her words caused me to raise my eyebrows. It was rare that women were well-versed in trade unless—

I didn't get to finish that thought as a low growl came from the underbrush.

Seven

AZUCENA

I had been staring shamelessly at Rurac, watching his biceps flex as he gathered the dainty herbs when the growl snapped me out of my reverie.

Although I hadn't spent much time outside as a child—or as an adult—I knew immediately that sound came from a puma.

Quickly, I dove into the recess of my memory, flipping through the lessons from my tutor about what to do when there was a puma attack.

"AHHHHHHHHH!" I yelled at the top of my lungs. "GAAHHHHH."

A hand slapped over my mouth.

"What in Inti's name are you doing!" Rurac whisper-yelled in my ear. My eyes quickly spotted the knife held aloft in his other hand.

Unsurprisingly, my shouting worked, and the puma immediately darted out of view.

I pushed his hand away. "Pumas are scared of loud noises," I said in a normal volume, gathering my wits to scream again, only for Rurac to stop me.

"I know that."

Okay, now I was confused. "Then why are you stopping me from yelling? Do you want to be dinner for a puma?"

Rurac rolled his eyes, an action I was starting to notice he performed frequently. "No, but puma pelts are worth quite a lot at the market."

I crossed my arms over my chest, properly forgetting about the large cat. "Oh, I'm sorry, I didn't realize you wanted to battle for a pelt *while chained to someone without a weapon!*"

He examined our chained ankles, and although he didn't say it, I could see his eyes softening, the colors of his aura shifting. He knew I was right.

"You could unchain me and chase the puma solo you know," I suggested on the sly, trying to keep the notes of eagerness from infiltrating my voice. If he made a single mistake, I was going to bolt. He was attractive, but not attractive enough for me to stick around as a prisoner. After all, I had other options for male companionship that could be brought to me at my will, in the comfort of my palace.

"Not a chance," he snapped, leaning down to gather the basket, which was half full of uchu. "He's probably halfway to the summit of the mountain by now anyway. I'll have to try again another sun-cycle."

I didn't say anything as we walked back toward the hut, a bit disappointed that our outing for today had already ended while simultaneously trying to find an excuse for him to release me from the chains and give me the opportunity I needed to run.

As we stepped through the doorway into the hut, the sound of the chains dragging across the doorstop made me cringe. Rurac didn't seem to notice as he stopped in the kitchen, shaking his basket before sorting the spices into small jars.

"What are we making with the uchu?"

He tossed the now-empty basket to the floor before replying. "Well, it would be much better if we could use it to season a piece of meat, but someone scared off dinner."

"You eat puma?" I knew for a fact that wasn't normal. Llama; yes, qwui, on special occasions, but not puma.

He shrugged, pulling out another clay jar. "I eat whatever meat is available. Puma's okay honestly, it's qwui I don't like."

I shivered as he named the small animals that ran around Sipan in large herds. While they were widely available, I, too, did not find them to be all that tasty. "That's something we have in common then."

I nearly slapped my hand over my mouth for giving this brute that type of information about me, but at the same time I filed that little detail away for later.

Rurac does not like qwui.

He didn't say anything about my observation and instead began to scoop what had to be mealed corn from the jar. "Well, tonight it will be maiz again."

I let out a huff. "You don't have any potatoes? Or maybe some quinoa?" Though I didn't eat much of either myself, I knew they were staples peasants relied on. Meat was mostly reserved for those who lived and worked in the palace.

"Nope," he replied, closing the jar and chucking it back onto the shelf.

I surveyed his small kitchen. "Why not? Can't you just . . . I don't know, grow something better that maiz?"

"Overnight?" He spun to look at me. "Shows how little you know about farming."

"I know they grow everywhere here." I inspected my nails. *Idiot peasant.*

Pulling an adorned cloth off a clay pail in the corner, Rurac poured a bit of water into the clay pot with the mealed corn, before stepping around me to grab some wood leaning against the wall to place under the large stone oven in the corner.

"They grow where the soil is fertile. Everything surrounding my hut has been leached of nutrients." I opened my mouth, but he anticipated my next words before I even said them. "We can't just steal other villagers' crops."

I wrinkled my nose, crossing the distance the chain allowed me to traverse as I peeked out the window. "How? It looks fine to me. Seems like a you problem."

"The gods punish stealing harshly, you know. Not to mention, most people are just struggling to feed their families."

I rolled my eyes; I wasn't that dumb. "I meant why is the soil leached of nutrients?"

"Overuse," he spat before I even finished my sentence. "My parents grew potatoes on this land, and their parents before that. As a result, the soil is empty of whatever makes the potatoes grow large. The ones from last harvest were too small to be worth planting again."

I peered back out the window, my eyes perusing the edge of the trees where we had collected the herbs. "And why don't you grow them in the forest?"

He didn't even look up from the pot as he stirred. "Tried that. The animals get to them if I'm not there to watch them."

"All of them?" Inti, this arguing was *so* beneath me.

He sighed. "No, not all of them, but I didn't harvest enough to make it worth it to plant more. I ate pretty much everything I harvested."

I inspected him up and down. "Have you considered maybe eating less?"

That did it. His face reddened. "Have you tried being slightly more understanding?" he snapped.

I tilted my head to the side, considering his words. I was anything but understanding, but he did have a point. This was new to me, so I took a moment to think back over our conversation. Everything he was saying made sense, and I knew that most of the peasants in the village survived on potatoes. So, how did they do it if it really was as difficult as he was making it sound?

Never having been one to hold my tongue long, I asked, "How do all the other peasants have so many potatoes then?"

"I don't know. Better soil, I suppose."

"Hm," I replied, the wheels in my mind turning, trying to

remember something, anything I would have heard in the palace that would have revealed how the peasants did it. There had to be something I was missing that I could use to make him swallow his attitude.

Before I could say anything else, he was pushing the pot into the clay oven and motioning to the sitting area. I followed his motions, taking a seat on the straw-topped stone bench, which had probably been made by hand, several solar-paths before. He sat across from me on an overturned clay pot, and silence settled over the room—other than the faint noise of the crackling fire from the oven in the corner of the kitchen.

Although there was still a chain around my ankle, and I was currently mentally updating my escape plans, I had to admit, there was something a little peaceful about the near silence as the light of Inti faded from the window.

That's when I remembered that I was supposed to be nice today—convince him to let me go. Our argument a few moments before had been anything but nice. Trying to figure out how to repair our conversation, I mentally went over all the ways my mother used to address the peasants during her time on the throne. I had to have learned *something* useful.

"So . . ." I broke the quiet at last. "Did you build all this?" I motioned to the straw-thatched roof and stone walls.

"My grandfather did, I just maintained it," he answered, his gaze downcast.

"And the chain under the bed?" I had to ask.

"My father installed that. We used to keep much . . . larger... prisoners."

"Oh." I struggled to keep the conversation going. "And where is your father?"

"Hana Pacha."

Maybe if my own parents hadn't died, leaving me alone in this world, I would have felt bad about asking after parents who had passed on. But I was me, and I had ample experience discussing death and the afterlife during my tenure as empress.

44

"Mine too," I replied with a shrug. "Think they've met over there?" The edges of my lip quirked at the joke I was making, but he didn't so much as blink.

"Probably not."

"Oh."

Defeated, I let the silence grow this time as Rurac stood and moved to stir dinner and stoke the fire. My ankle lifted off the ground at the distance. When he returned to his seat he spoke again. "You're clearly from a higher class. My parents were just average peasants."

To be fair, I had never considered the class system of the afterlife. While the classes remained separate in life, I had never wondered as to whether or not that carried on into the beyond. But then I remembered my father's tomb, which was still guarded to this sun-cycle—or at least I assumed it was.

"Do you think our class rank continues to matter after death?" It was an honest question, one I had never deigned to consider before . . . well, until now.

This time, Rurac didn't even hesitate. "Absolutely."

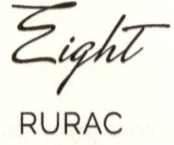

RURAC

The peace of my dinner continued to be peppered by the girl's questions about the different social classes, and what happened to them after death. Although I answered her with certainty, the more we talked, the less certain I was about my own information on our journey after death.

While my father had been religious in teaching me the ways of Inti, he had been less strict as I had gotten older, and until now, I hadn't really discussed much about death beyond the basic questions of an overly curious child.

"Do you fear going to Hana Pacha?" she asked, distracting me from my thoughts.

Before the last few sun-cycles, I would have said no immediately. But now, with the light outside extinguished and a fire still crackling from the oven behind me, I didn't know what to say. So, I settled on the truth.

"I don't know."

I felt the odd urge to explain, and I didn't know why. Maybe it was the way her hair glinted in the firelight. Or the way she bit her lip between questions. Maybe it was the fact that she was even asking me questions at all. I began to mentally delve into my father's brief lessons about wooing a member of the female species—

No.

She's a prisoner, I reminded myself.

No thinking she was beautiful allowed.

Returning to the present, spoon scraping the bottom of my bowl, I nodded my chin to hers. "Finished?"

She propelled a last bite between her lips before shoving the bowl my way. "Yes."

I stood from the sitting area, chain dragging across the floor as I returned the bowls to the counter only a few steps away. I swore this hut had never felt this small before.

Motioning for her to follow me, I led her back into her bedroom, taking the time to lean down and switch the chain connecting us to the one attached to the floor beneath the bed. She didn't hide her distaste, letting out a huff as she lay on the bed.

"If you would stop trying to escape, I wouldn't need to use these," I offered.

"Like I'm ever going to allow you keep me here willingly." She snorted in return, mischief glinting in her eyes.

"At least you're honest," I told her as I slipped the key back into my breast pocket and headed for the door.

"Unlike yourself."

Her words cut like a knife, and I'm not sure why. I never cared what anyone thought of me before, but something about the way she said it made me feel ashamed. "What do you mean?" I turned around to ask her.

She did that weird thing where she looked at the space above my head and shrugged, not offering anything further.

Not wanting to ruin what might have been an okay sun-cycle, I closed the door without another word, waiting a few moments to ensure she wasn't trying anything before heading to my portion of the house below the ground.

Once I was enclosed in what I liked to think of as my lair, I let my shoulders fall, not realizing how close to my ears I had let them rise. The girl made me so tense—I had never had this much of an issue controlling my emotions before. Then again, I'd never held a prisoner on my own before, either.

Not knowing what else to do, and nowhere near tired, I pulled out the Quipu my father had been weaving close to his death. It was unfinished, and I had yet to figure out how to finish it. Quipu's, the ancient way of storytelling, could be beautiful when finished, but this one was starting to look more like a mess.

The Quipu was knotted and tangled a bit, as it had been tossed aside for a few solar-paths now, but as I carefully separated the strands, letting my eyes rove over the knots, I wondered where my father had been going with this particular message.

It had started as a story of a young boy, one who was headstrong and determined to kill a puma that had been plaguing the village. As the boy grew, he developed more complex traps to ultimately capture and kill the puma. But none of them worked.

Until one sun-cycle, after having fallen in one of his own traps, the boy lay hurt in the woods, and the puma came to help, pulling him out gently by grasping the material of his poncho with her teeth. Once he was out, she disappeared into the woods but didn't go far. So, when the village people came to rescue the boy, she was there and subsequently killed by one of the warriors.

After this happened, the boy went home and cried, and then the story came to a sudden stop.

It didn't make any sense. The puma was dead just as the boy had wanted, so why would he cry? My father hadn't tied an ending knot to the story, indicating it continued, but I had no idea how it was possible, as the puma was dead.

With a frustrated growl, I tossed the Quipu aside, deciding to shuck some maiz instead. I hadn't told Azucena, but my stocks of that were low too, and we would have to venture for more tomorrow, especially since Inti was beginning to set sooner than before, and the cold season was coming.

I hadn't planned to have a captive this winter—there hadn't

been one for so long, and usually when there was one, they were never here this long. When Kuntar had dropped her off I had assumed the next sacrifice was near, but apparently my tracking of the sacrificial moon cycles was further off than I anticipated.

Despite my knowledge of Hana Pacha, I hadn't been active in the local village for solar-paths, avoiding almost all meetings and religious ceremonies. It just didn't seem to matter.

But now, peering at the measly supply of corn remaining in the basket, I knew I would likely have to barter for some additional supplies and find out the exact number of sun-cycles until the next sacrifice . . . otherwise, we would both starve.

THE NEXT MORNING, I chained her to me again, much to her dismay, before heading deeper into the woods in the hope of gathering some more substantial food items. I stopped first by the sad potato fields I had tried to plant the solar-path before, grumbling as I brushed my heel over the despairingly empty dirt.

I leaned back against a tree, debating on where to go next, when I heard a giggle behind me. Scrunching my brows, I turned around to find Azucena rolling around in a bed of flowers. When she spotted my glare, she stopped rolling, but the smile didn't flicker from her face.

"What in Inti's name are you doing?" I growled, annoyed that she was treating this like some sort of fun outing.

"These flowers are so nice Rurac." She ran her hands over the flowers on either side of her legs. "How can you not roll around in them?"

Now that was a new one. Not sure how to answer her rather odd question, I simply blinked in her direction. As soon as my shock wore off, however, I was furious. "How can I resist rolling in the flowers? Easy. I'd like to be able to eat this cold season. But if you'd rather starve and roll in the flowers, be my guest."

Her face fell, and for a moment I thought I was about to see her display empathy, but then she just shrugged. "Doesn't sound like that's my problem."

I couldn't contain the anger which bubbled in my gut as I turned to yell at her. "I know you don't feel like this is *your* problem, but it's about to be because I don't have enough food for you either. So, if I'm starving you will be to!"

She didn't even react to my outburst, scoffing, "You're assuming I'm going to stay with you."

That did nothing to quell my anger. "*Look around*! No one is coming for you." I motioned to the chain. "And I am not letting you go. So yes, you will be here, and you will starve with me if it's the last thing I do."

That did it. Something I said finally sunk in as the smile was swept off her face. "Hm." She cocked her head to the side, biting her lip in a way that is almost cute, which made me angrier. "Maybe you could go to the em-emperor and ask for more food?"

The way she stumbled over the word told me she likely knew the emperor personally, but either way I shook my head. "Won't work. He's cruel and cold-hearted. He doesn't care if his people starve."

"He doesn't?" She seemed genuinely confused. "Have you ever tried?"

"Well . . ." She had me there. "Not exactly."

"Ahhh." She smirked. "So, you are once again talking about things too difficult for your peasant brain to understand." She paused. "Well, since I'm here now, why don't we try it?"

I shook my head. "You didn't let me finish. I haven't been, but my father tried to get extra rations several solar-paths ago and was denied. You forget, I work for the emperor, he provides all the seeds and everything I used to grow the food we've eaten."

Confusion flickered across her features. "But there wasn't enough yield?"

I dipped my chin in affirmation. "Now you understand. I can't go to the emperor about my lack of yield, I'll be blamed for not using the seeds I had been allotted correctly."

"Hmm." She stood from the flower bed and brushed herself off. "I suppose that is a conundrum then." The chain dragged on the ground as she walked to stand next to me. "So, you've never met the emperor?"

"No. But I've been to the palace."

She jerked, like I've slapped her. "When?"

I shrugged. "Solar-paths ago; I was just a boy. I didn't get to speak to the emperor myself—I was too young. But my father did."

"And this was *many* solar-paths in the past?"

"Yes."

"Hm." She didn't say anything more, all the joy on her face from rolling in the flowers wiped away. For a moment, I felt almost guilty for the things I said, but then I reminded myself that she was just a prisoner.

"So, back to the task at hand. This is where I planted potatoes earlier this solar-path. I thought we could check to ensure I hadn't missed any." I launched into a brief explanation of the signs of potatoes growing, the plants to look for, and the tell-tale indents in the soil. Before long, she was on her hands and knees beside me, searching.

"I'm still shocked you've never harvested potatoes before," I said at one point, breaking the silence that had been blossoming between us.

"Get used to it," she snapped back as she brushed the soil from one particular location.

The range of this woman astounded me. One moment she was rolling in the flowers like she was floating in the clouds and the next she was snapping at me about a harmless comment I tossed her way.

"I didn't mean it to sound rude," I tried.

"Well, it did." She didn't look up. "I meant what I said, I'm not good for much beyond giving orders. I don't really know how to farm or prepare food, so you'll be surprised by a lot."

Now I'm the one confused. "Your parents didn't teach you anything about how to grow and procure food?"

She shook her head, moving to a new spot in the dirt a bit further from where I was looking. "They had other concerns."

"Like?" I really couldn't fathom a parent who didn't teach their child survival needs in this world.

"I was taught the ways of the gods and the ways of man. How to settle disputes, make things fair. How to give orders and appear strong. That's the knowledge they wanted me to have."

I didn't meet her eyes right away, confused by the position she was describing. Though I didn't leave my hut often, I had been to the nearby village a few times over the solar-paths and I had never heard of a job like she described.

"Does that make you uncomfortable?" she asked, a glimmer sparkling in her eye, perhaps sensing that I wasn't planning to answer her.

"No, just confused. I—" At that moment, my hand encountered something round and hard in the soil. I pulled it out, a triumphant smile on my face.

Azucena's face brightened, and she immediately moved closer to the spot where I was digging, finding a second potato a moment after. It didn't take long before we had a nice little pile in front of us.

Azucena sat back on her heels, crossing her arms over her chest. "Rurac . . . is it possible you just forgot where you planted the potatoes? Or perhaps returned to harvest too soon?"

The way she said the words was condescending, immediately bringing up my rebellious nature. "Why don't you just mind your own damn business? You're the one in trouble with the emperor, not me."

Instead of getting upset, or feeling hurt by my words—which I immediately wish I could take back—Azucena just smirked, rising from her position to go back to her flower bed. "Since I'm just a prisoner, I guess you won't mind if I spend my time in the flowers instead then."

I squinted, not because of what she said, but because she was right. "Fine, starve then," slipped out before I could stop it.

"Fine, I will," she snapped back as she lay down in the flowers. "At least I'll be happy when I starve."

"Trust me, you won't be," I grumbled under my breath, but she didn't answer, encouraging me to glance over to where she was lying. Her hair was splayed out over the ground behind her, creating a beautiful contrast with the light and colorful blooms. It almost made it appear as if she was wearing a crown, something which caused a niggle in my memory, but I quickly shoved it away.

Realizing I was staring, I quickly snapped my focus back to my task, but the image of her lying in the flowers was imprinted behind my eyelids as I finished my gathering and turned to walk back to my house, only giving Azucena a yank on the chain and an indication with my chin as to my plans.

She stood from the flowers, her eyes raking over me in a way that made me feel as if I was standing before her naked. Then, with a huff, she turned and waited for me to pass so she could follow me back the way we had come.

Despite the occasional eye roll, we didn't talk again for the rest of the sun-cycle.

Nine

AZUCENA

The next morning, our spat over the potatoes seemed to have blown over when Rurac came to fetch me for breakfast, swapping my chains and leading me into the sitting room. Which was good, because, honestly, my plan of being nice was failing miserably. I just wasn't built for a friendly demeanor.

The smell of potatoes immediately filled my nostrils and my mouth began to salivate. I spotted them on the hearth, nearly roasted. Rurac must've gotten up early to start the roasting process.

Yester sun-cycle, even though I hadn't helped much in the end, we had left the forest with a large basket of potatoes—the amount I would normally accept in tithe from a single peasant. I had no idea if this would be enough to last us the cold season, as Rurac seemed so worried about it, but there was definitely plenty. If only I could have convinced him to visit the palace and ask for help. That would have really helped this whole prisoner situation.

Rurac sorted the small purple potatoes into bowls before shoving one in my direction. It was incredibly rude, but I was so hungry, I let it go—just one time. Lifting the bowl to my nose, I inhaled before taking my first, steaming bite.

It was so hot I almost spit it out, but I knew Rurac would be angry then, so I rolled it around my mouth, trying to keep it directly off my tongue as I practically breathed steam.

We ate in silence, giving me time to do some quick mental math and realize what sun-cycle it was. "It's Inti Raymi," I whispered, a smile spreading over my face and my eyes drifting closed as I pilfered through my fond memories of this particular moment in the solar-path. Inti Raymi was also the sun-cycle the empire celebrated my birth. Though I wasn't actually born on Inti Raymi, the shortest sun-cycle of the year, as empress—a fellow god in the eyes of the gods—it was a festival both for the sun god, Inti, and for my continued rule. However, I felt my smile turn to a frown as I wondered what they would do this solar-path—in my absence.

When I opened my eyes, I immediately spotted Rurac, who was eating casually, a confused look on his face. "What's so great about Inti Raymi?" he asked without any joy in his voice.

The memories passed behind my eyelids again, as I remembered the procession of last solar-path, and I began to describe it to him, fighting to control my natural instinct to be snarky. "I love when the people dress in colorful clothes and pass through the village and palace on their way to the sun temple. There's so much singing and dancing, not to mention the delicious foods of the harvest." Rurac frowned. "You've never experienced it?"

He shrugged, his gaze not meeting mine. "They don't really do it that far out from the capital. It takes a while to arrive in the main portion of the city, and once you're there it's so crowded, most choose to stay home."

I had never considered that the villagers themselves didn't enjoy the festival as much as I did. After all, I didn't even have to leave my palace to enjoy it. But in that moment, I also realized he had inadvertently given me more information about our location. The fact that we were a long distance from the main city told me we were likely on the other side of the sacred valley. I filed that information away for later.

"It's okay if you like it, though. It sounds nice." He broke my bubble of thought with his comment. His facial expression was unreadable.

"It's also the sun-cycle we celebrate my solar-paths. I'm thirty solar-paths today." I frown as I realize this had also been the sun-cycle I had planned to release Yezema from her employ—causing something to niggle at the back of my mind about the night she had come to my room with chicha morada, right before I lost consciousness.

But Rurac had indicated his boss was a man, meaning there was something else at play here that I wasn't seeing, beyond just Yezema's suspicious behavior.

"Congratulations," he replied without any joy.

This was certainly not the treatment I was accustomed to having on my solar-path celebration, and my mood immediately soured. "You could at least say it like you meant it," I quipped.

"But I don't," he quipped back, still eating calmly, his biceps flexing with each bite. Meanwhile, my blood was boiling. I briefly looked down at the clay bowl situated in my hands and considered throwing it at his head, but I desperately wanted the purple potatoes still resting on the bottom. Which meant I had to talk this issue out and ignore my anger. Not to mention I was supposed to be nice—something that was growing harder to maintain with each passing moment.

"Why don't you mean it?" I pressed, trying to keep my tone even, but my voice fluctuated in the middle, giving away my emotional state.

He didn't look up, his gaze still centered on his bowl. "Because soon you will go back with my boss, and I will never see you again. Why would it matter to me that you had thirty solar-paths on Pacha Mama?"

I swallowed the bite in my mouth, my appetite evaporating. "So that's it then? I'm just a prisoner to you?"

His eyes remained on his bowl as he answered. "Yes."

I don't know why that phrase hurt me so badly when he said

it. It wasn't supposed to; he was just some lowly peasant. I guess I had previously thought, that though he was my jailer, he at least enjoyed my company like everyone else in Sipan, but apparently that wasn't the case.

I stood from the bench, setting the bowl down in the spot I had just stood from. "Take me back to my room, please."

He paused, and for a moment, I thought he was going to say something more, but instead, he relented, standing, and walking behind me to the bedroom. Once there he switched my chain before turning his back and closing the door behind him, his face devoid of emotion.

I SAT THERE for most of the sun-cycle, determined to hold on to my anger, even though it had pretty much evaporated shortly after he had deposited me back in here. The emotions that replaced it were odd, and I was unable to name the sourness that seemed to seep into my very being.

I had come to a terrible realization.

He was right.

I wasn't going to tell him that, of course, but I was *just* his prisoner.

It was true that I was also his empress, but I was smart enough to come to accept that he didn't know me as such, and even if he had, he was too worried about surviving the winter to worry about the celebration of an entity that wasn't a fixture in his sad excuse for a life.

Not only that, but there were so many people back in the palace who were happy about Inti Raymi, that it shouldn't matter what one man thought about my special sun-cycle.

So why did what he said still hurt?

I gulped and pushed the emotions that swelled up away.

There was no room for those here. I needed to stay focused and keep waiting for him to make a mistake. I couldn't afford to be distracted. Even though he was handsome, I needed to ignore that. He was the enemy.

The door opened, interrupting my thoughts, and Rurac entered with a bowl that was most assuredly dinner, which he handed to me before taking a seat.

I watched as he took his seat, trying to keep myself focused on my anger. But by the time he was arranged on the small stool, elbows resting on his knees and chin in his hands, I was calm once more, ready to keep acting nice to convince him to return me to the palace.

Swallowing over the lump in my throat, I glanced at the food in my bowl then raised an eyebrow at him.

"Figured you didn't want to be alone on your special sun-cycle. It's the least I could do." He didn't look up from his food, but his aura flickered from green to blue.

My heart warmed—he cared about my special sun-cycle after all. I fought to keep my lips from smiling though. I didn't want him to know how much I appreciated this. Not to mention the fact that my master plan was working. If he was convinced enough by my behavior to celebrate my special sun-cycle, then I could definitely work toward convincing him to take me home.

As we both dug into the bowls of purple potatoes, I decided to ask the question that had been hanging on my mind all afternoon. "Did your parents ever do anything special to celebrate you, Rurac?"

"No," he answered quickly, shaking his head. "My presence was hard on my father. He loved my mother very much, and I was the source of her end. I don't think he ever came to terms with that."

I rolled that thought through my head. "He cared for you, though, during your childhood, so he must've loved you, right?" I knew I was grasping at straws. I had nothing to compare it to, as my parents had made me the center of their universe.

He took another bite, chewing slowly before replying.

"Maybe. But I'm not sure if it was just out of obligation, or if it was love."

The sound of eating filled the room as we were both lost in our respective minds.

To this sun-cycle, I don't know what possessed me to say this, as it was so unlike me, but as I scraped the last bits of purple potato from my bowl, I looked up and Rurac and said, "I'd like to celebrate you for a sun-cycle since I won't be here long. Maybe we can do it tomorrow?"

He started coughing, appearing to choke on his potato, before pounding on his chest with his closed fist. When he caught his breath, I continued. "We could do something you like all sun-cycle. And even though I don't cook, I'm sure I can roast some potatoes for us." *Inti, I was so good at coming up with bullshit.* "I don't usually perform any of the Inti Raymi songs or dances, but maybe I can try—"

"Why?" he snapped, his eyes wide.

To be honest, I wasn't exactly sure why myself, so I said the next thing that came to mind. "Because, Rurac, it sounds like you need someone to be your friend, and I think we can be that at least? I haven't really had a friend before, but I think I would like to try—" I was so sure he would be happy at the prospect of being my friend, I nearly dropped my bowl at his next words.

"I don't think that is a good idea." He glanced down at his bowl, his face stoic.

"Why?" I pushed, my lips quivering. I didn't understand this emotion I was feeling. Was he really rejecting me? No one rejected me . . . *as empress,* my mind reminded me.

He ran his hand through his unruly hair, which, for some reason, I couldn't take my eyes off of, despite the harsh words coming from his lips. "Because, like I said, you're just a prisoner, and when your time here is done, we have to say goodbye."

I bit my lip. He was right, but I also knew that if I wanted to make my escape, I still had to be as chummy as I could with him, so I shrugged and said, "Friendships don't end just when you don't see someone anymore, just as your relationship with your parents didn't end when they went to Hana Pacha. We can be friends for now and even if we don't see each other again until Hana Pacha, that's okay. We can be friends when we both get there." I wanted to add that as soon as he realized I was the empress, everything would be cleared up, but I restrained myself, mostly because of the red whisps flickering over his head. He was lying about something.

He thought on my words for a long time, both of us just staring down at our empty bowls until he said, "No. I don't think us being friends is a good idea. We should remain enemies."

Then, without waiting for me to say anything more, he stood, snatched my bowl, and left the room. Leaving me alone with the realization that I probably wouldn't have been a good friend anyway.

Ten

RURAC

I nti, she was spoiled. My father had warned me about women like her when I was young—women who wouldn't be happy no matter what I did for them. At the time it had seemed like a wild exaggeration. I was barely fourteen solar-paths and there were no women around to compare to. There weren't even other people around to compare to.

But now that I had met one, I knew.

I scoffed as I reenacted our most recent conversation in my mind. How dare she suggest we be friends? Friends didn't help you survive the winter. Not to mention she was going to be a sacrifice, which was the entire reason she was here.

That didn't curb my thoughts about how badly I wanted her to like me, though. Which was stupid, because I shouldn't want her to like me.

Something about her was just so . . . alluring. And I couldn't stop my brain from picturing those plush lips of hers pressing against mine.

I shook the image free again. She was spoiled, damnit. And complicated. The last thing I needed in my life. I needed to focus on making it through the winter, and keeping my position as the Game and Prisoner Manager.

My heart wanted her though—the traitor.

I had told her no and said it wouldn't be a good idea for us to be friends, but she couldn't see the war my brain was currently fighting with my heart. My heart wanted to listen to everything she was saying—cherish the happiness I felt when I saw her experiencing something for the first time. My heart desperately wanted us to be friends—no, more than friends. I wanted to see her laughing and smiling, and wanted her body pressed against mine. But my brain knew we couldn't let that happen. Not if I wanted to keep my quiet, peaceful, and secluded life that I loved.

Mictlan, it was hard, though. Hard to say no to those beautifully expressive brown eyes.

Fighting to maintain my anger at her, I stormed outside instead of down to my living spaces, my eyes roving the hills glittering in the evening sun. Though the hill where my home sat was mostly untouched, I could see the marks of greed marring the beautiful hills beyond—fields of stumps where the trees had been chopped down to make spears and other weapons. Between them, the barren dirt which hadn't born crops for many solar-paths.

I didn't go into the nearby village much, but Kuntur, my friend, had mentioned that the village was struggling to sustain itself and would likely need to relocate in the future.

They were supposed to rotate their crops and live with the land, but with the rising tariffs placed by the emperor, that was no longer an option.

And she, whether she admitted it or not, was part of that—part of the nobility that took us, the underlings, for all we were worth. She was part of my suffering.

Yes, it was better that she died come the full moon.

At least that's what I continued to tell myself.

Though the thought of her being a sacrifice made me cringe.

Despite her willingness to learn, I felt in her words that she had the potential—

NO!

Those thoughts needed to stop here and now. I would not

betray my position—which the emperor paid me for in food and goods that could be traded for food—for one spoiled noble-woman who made my heart beat faster with just a flip of her hair.

Mad at her, and at myself, I turned and stomped back into my home, pulling open the trap door and descending into my rooms. She wasn't going to get the best of me. No way.

Needing something to keep my mind and hands busy, I grabbed my carving knife and a piece of wood I kept for times like these and began gently carving a swirl pattern into it. Glancing up, I took a quick inventory of all the carvings I had made in the past—the puma and the boy from the Quipu, several small statues of the gods, and an especially large carving of Inti. Without think-ing, my hands began to move over the wood, drawing the delicate flowers from the field. In the middle of the flowers, I pictured Azucena lying there, her arms spread out and her chin tilted to the sky.

Without realizing it, my knife had started to move in a different direction, and when I glanced down again, I could see the delicate curve of her cheek carved into the edge of the flowers.

Great, even my mind was starting to betray me.

No matter how cute and funny she may be, she was still a prisoner.

With a huff I tossed the wood carving to the side and stomped into my room.

Maybe some sleep would help scrape this incorrigible woman off my mind.

───

THE NEXT SUN-CYCLE, I barely acknowledged her as we ate breakfast, and I transferred her to the chain attached to me so we could venture gathering once again. Surprisingly, she didn't seem to want to speak with me either, mostly remaining silent as we made our way to a different spot in the forest than the place where we had harvested the potatoes.

I knelt down, placing a basket by her feet. "We need to gather herbs, but if you see any berries, grab those too."

She didn't move, instead just crossing her arms over her chest. "I'm not your yanakuna, you know."

My lips twisted into a silent groan. So, she wanted to be even more rude today. "No, you are not. I am simply asking you to help ensure we both have enough food to survive the next few sun-cycles. Life is hard, and survival is everyone's responsibility. If you want to survive, you need to contribute, so get down here."

My words were harsh, but they did the trick, and she lifted the edge of her dress to lean down and begin digging through the underbrush to look for the herbs I pointed out to her. She did glance at me in anger every so often though—something I tried to point out to my traitorous heart—but it just kept reminding me how cute she was when she was mad.

There weren't a lot of herbs in the area we were in, so after a few moments, I lifted the basket, and we moved on to another location.

The silence . . . well it was a bit eerie, I suppose. I hadn't real-ized it until now, but Azucena always had something to say, even if it was snarky. And if she wasn't talking, the auxiliary noises she made, such as her snorts at my stupidity or the giggles as she rolled through the flowers, had always seemed to fill the air.

Now it was just . . . empty.

"Enemies can talk to one another, you know." I didn't intend to say those words, but suddenly my mouth said them—as if it had a mind of its own. I glanced over my shoulder, waiting for her reaction.

She gathered in silence a few more moments, almost making me assume she hadn't heard me. But then she looked up, her eyes meeting mine. "Do they now? Please inform me more about rela-tionships with enemies. Last I checked, us Incans do not talk to ours whenever possible."

"I wouldn't know." I shrugged. "The military dealings of the empire are none of my business."

"Conflict is everyone's business," she argued. "What are you going to do when the Chanka take over, hm?"

I smirked. "Won't matter. Whether I'm a peasant for them, or a peasant for our current emperor, I'm still a peasant. Maybe their tariffs will even be lower, and I'll get to keep more food each harvest season." I was nearly laughing now. "I mean, unless they come and kill me, I suppose. But that's unlikely. I'm able-bodied and they need me to work for them once they're finished with their conquest."

She turned back to herb-gathering but her eyebrows were furrowed. "But doesn't the emperor pay you as part of his employ?"

"Yes, but I am still subject to tariffs. Part of my payment never reaches me. And the courier who brings it also takes a portion for their time."

"Hm. I never thought about it that way before."

"That's because you rarely think of anyone other than yourself," I snapped, my repressed emotions getting the better of me. I don't know why, but I volunteered even more information. "My pay from the emperor is quite low, it isn't enough to feed me the whole solar path. I've always had to supplement with hunting and gathering anyway, and I assume even if I didn't work for the new emperor my situation couldn't be any worse than it is now. Not to mention I didn't receive anything extra when I was tasked with holding you."

Azucena said nothing, her eyes focused on the task at hand.

"What, you ran out of words?" I don't know why I kept antagonizing her.

She shook her head. "You're right, I don't know what it's like to be a peasant, so I shouldn't comment on something I know nothing about. But did you ever think it was weird you didn't receive extra food for holding me?"

She was right. I couldn't remember the last time my father had a prisoner, but I didn't remember rations being this low.

"Have you ever considered that maybe it wasn't the emperor who ordered my imprisonment?"

I nearly choked on the rebuttal I had already prepared. "Who else would send you to me? Only the emperor knows I exist."

"Of Sipan?"

"Duh, of Sipan." I rolled my eyes, what was she getting at? "Are you okay?"

"Hm." Her hands stopped their motions, indicating to me that she was deep in thought. I took the opportunity to look around, realizing how pretty the forest was, especially as the light filtered through the trees and landed on her light brown skin—

I cut my mind off right there. I did not need to be going down that path. She was a prisoner. Nothing more.

But as much as I repeated that to myself, I could already feel that things between us had changed.

I just hoped it wasn't in a way that would affect my ability to do my job.

Looking back, I'm sure the gods were already laughing at what was to come.

Eleven

AZUCENA

I knew I should have told him that the emperor had died and that I was his daughter, the current empress, but something about this entire situation was still just so suspicious. I had no idea who he was truly working for, and whether or not he was just playing dumb to try and trick me into disclosing information. I knew I needed to figure out his intentions, and whose side he was on, and fast.

Unfortunately, the next sun-cycle, my plan to discover who Rurac was working for, took a turn for the worst when I woke up with a distinct cramping in my gut. Running to the chamber pot in horror as the first rays of Inti peeked over the horizon, I quickly contemplated how to approach this sensitive topic with my less-than enthusiastic non-friend of a jailer.

Lucky for me, I didn't have to spiral too long in my thoughts, because Rurac must've heard me moving about, as I heard his heavy steps lumbering toward the door, I didn't want him to open it to find me like, well, this, so I shouted.

"Don't come in!"

There was a pause before, "Why not?"

"I'm on the pot!" I called back, my breathing heavy as another cramp seized my lower stomach.

He apparently didn't know what to say, as there was silence on the other side of the door. I didn't hear his footsteps moving away though, so I knew he was still standing there, waiting.

Deciding now was as good of a chance I was going to get, I shouted, "I need . . . uh . . . some cloth. For my menses!" I added the second part after realizing he probably wouldn't understand otherwise. That's when I glanced down at my undergarments, which also needed to be replaced. "I need some new clothing as well!"

Whether he thought I was being facetious or not, he didn't say. Instead, I heard the sound of him scuffling away, presumably to get me what I asked for.

It took a while though, as I sat there on the pot battling cramp after cramp. It was somewhere between cramp seven and the great god Inti finally fully rising over the horizon that he returned.

He knocked twice before saying, "I'm covering my eyes, but I'll be opening the door to give you the items." He didn't wait for my agreement before following through.

The whole situation was a new type of awkward. I didn't really know what to say, watching as he did as promised, opening the door with a hand over his eyes, a cloth bundle grasped in the other hand. He set it on the bed before backing out of the room. "I'll get you some water too—for washing." The words tumbled out of his mouth, his hand seeming to shake when he returned with the clay pitcher, set it down, and closed the door behind him.

Using the pitcher of water to clean myself, I grabbed the clothes from the bed, shocked to find a whole new outfit in addition to new undergarments and the cloths I needed. I quickly dressed, piling my other garments to be washed. Although my old tunic wasn't soiled, it was definitely a bit smelly and dirty from having been worn so many sun-cycles on end.

The new tunic he had brought was slightly larger, but had clearly been designed for a feminine frame. The colors were deep and decadent, the type of weaving similar to those of the royal weavers in my employ. As I ran my hand over the wool, I could tell it had been once been dyed a much deeper color, which had faded with the passing of time. While it was not styled like the decadent summer dress I had arrived in—my preferred style— it would work for now.

Not feeling like doing much else, I crawled back into bed, coiling myself into a ball and tucking the blanket around me.

WHEN I WOKE AGAIN, there were shuffling sounds echoing in my room. Peering through slitted eyes, I noticed Rurac, a red halo surrounding his head, leaning over my pile of dirty clothes.

"I'll wash those tomorrow," I mumbled. Or at least I thought that was what I was saying—it came out fairly garbled by the time the words forced their way past my lips.

"Nonsense. You are unwell. I will wash them for you."

I opened my mouth to argue, but a cramp came just then, causing me to moan instead.

Rurac dropped the pile of clothing and moved closer. "Are you ill? Do I need to fetch a healer?" There was concern etched on his features, which confused me, as his aura showed something different.

Swallowing, I shook my head. "This is how—" I gasped. "—normally is for me, though the kitchen staff usually prepare me a special soup to—" Another gasp. "—help with the pain."

"Oh."

I peeked through the sliver between my eyelids again, confused as to why he was still surrounded by a red glow. What could he possibly be lying about as he inquired about my condition?

The silence in the room grew, and I thought for a moment that maybe he had left, but then I heard the rustle of clothes as he shifted his weight.

"You can leave," I whispered, my hand gripping my midsection. "There isn't anything that can be done."

He focused on the way I was lying before he audibly swallowed and headed for the living area. "I'll be back," he sputtered as he closed the door behind him. I rolled over to face the wall before remembering that he had been intending to wash my clothes. Using the last of my energy, I peered over my shoulder to see the stone floor was bare.

He had taken my clothes to wash them.

Something that I had only read about in historic Quipu's snaked through my gut. I suddenly felt a bit of shame for how I had been treating Rurac and my plans for escape. I had been downright nasty to him, yet here he was, taking care of me on one of my worst sun-cycles.

In that same thread of emotion, I felt something akin to acceptance which I quickly pushed away. This could be a trap. After all, there was a red halo over his head, and he truly had no reason to help me . . . did he?

I had never spent much time around males, only calling the ones to my room who were trained to provide sexual services. And my mother had always warned me that they were not to be trusted . . . but now I was wondering: did men who intended to hurt you do your laundry?

Even if they did, the color red hovering over him indicated that he was lying. But what could he possibly be lying about?

I was too tired to pursue any of those thoughts further, so I resolved to close my eyes and tried to keep from crying out.

But the image of Rurac helping me was imprinted on the back of my eyelids.

Twelve

RURAC

It had been a hard morning. Azucena was obviously ill, and when she had asked for clothing, I had done something I hadn't dared to do in my entire life—I had gone into the room my parents had shared before their deaths.

Granted, I had likely been in here as a boy with my father, but I had never dared to poke around in the items he kept in here. Now, as I shifted through several items of clothing and blankets that were likely woven by my mother, I felt a twinge of sadness for the woman I never met. While I knew she didn't need her clothing any longer, it still felt weird to allow someone else to wear the things she had woven for herself.

I currently had three piles, one of clothing and blankets I would save for myself to remember her by, and the second pile for the girl, to use in the coming sun-cycles. The rest were in the final pile, for me to take to market for trade.

When I saw the way she had grabbed her stomach this morning, I had felt my heart come to a stop. I told myself it was just because I didn't want to find out what the emperor would do if I accidentally killed his prisoner, but I knew there was probably another reason too. But I refused to think about that right now. I was just worried about my continued payments from the emperor if she died. They would likely never trust me with another prisoner again.

I was just worried about my job. That was all.

Tucking the bundle under my arm, I checked in on her one final time, only to find her curled in the same ball on her bed, before venturing out the door and down the hill. Though she was sleeping now, the nearest village was quite far and it would be a while before I returned.

The forest was quiet, the birds having already headed to a lower altitude for warmer lodging during the colder portion of the solar-path. Though the bears and pumas were likely still around looking to eat their fill before the cold came, they didn't bother me throughout the trek.

It was near midsun-cycle by the time I arrived in the village, heading for the hut on the edge, which had housed the healer I had come to fetch to try and help my father all those solar-paths before. I didn't really know anyone else in the village other than Kuntur, so hopefully she was home. But when I called out a greeting, none was called back.

"Hello!" I tried a second time, louder.

"If you're looking for Laka, she's not here."

I spun around to face a young man who couldn't have been much older than myself. Though while I was wearing faded, threadbare clothing, he was dressed in items that appeared new.

"Where has she gone?" I asked, already fearing the answer I knew was coming.

"Hana Pacha. Six sun-cycles ago. She was on the bridge when it collapsed."

I felt my shoulders slump. Laka had certainly been old when I had come to seek her advice for my father, but I hadn't realized how old until that moment. But then the last thing he said sunk in. "The bridge collapsed?"

"Yeah, the one connecting us to the main portion of Sipan I'm afraid. The ropes were just too old, they gave out."

My eyes widened. This meant if anyone was coming to collect Azucena it would be ages before they arrived. Though I hadn't been to the bridge recently, I knew what he was talking about. The ropes had long been frayed and the wood rotted through. It had only been a matter of time before it gave up. I put my hand on his shoulder and gave him the sign of my condolences. "I'm sorry for your loss." He nodded his thanks, and I returned to the task at hand. "Is there another healer?"

The man shook his head. "Not in this village. I'm Laka's son, Rocio. I learned a few tricks from my mother, so maybe I can help?"

I couldn't explain it, but something about the idea of having a man take a look at Azucena when she was in this compromised state caused my stomach to roil. I promised myself, again, that it was just because I would lose my job if she died as I shook my head but held up the bundle. "It's all right. I'm also looking to trade for food."

The young man nodded, eyeing the bundle. "Down at the market, they can probably help you out, but be warned, with the pass bridge gone, we haven't gotten goods from the capital in a while."

I frowned. The bridge would likely be repaired during the dry season when it came, but it also meant it would be a hard winter for everyone on this side of the pass. I must have looked more haggard than I thought, though, because then he added, "Are you sure I can't help you in any way? I know my way around the healing spices, at least."

"It's not for me," I corrected Rocio. "It's for my p—wife," I stumbled, realizing I couldn't very well tell this man I had a prisoner for the emperor in my hut.

"Womanly troubles?" he guessed, his head tilting to the side, a knowing gleam in his eye.

I nodded my affirmation and he pushed past me into the hut, returning in a few moments with a bundle of herbs.

"Here. These will help with the pain."

I took them from his outstretched hand, using my chin to gesture to the bundle under my arms. "How much?"

He shook his head. "No need. It's just a few herbs."

I dipped my head in thanks.

He smiled, accepting my thanks, and then pointed down the hill. "You'll want to get going to the market if you're to make it before they pack up."

One glance at the path of the sun told me he was right and I quickly bid him goodbye before making my way further into the village. I passed several groups of people, some greeting me and others glancing at me suspiciously before ducking into their homes. While I hadn't been into town for a while, I was sure I would see at least one familiar face, but apparently that wasn't going to be the case.

I thought about stopping by Kuntur's hut, my only friend in the village, but I knew he would ask me about Azucena and how things were going. I couldn't understand the feeling of unease that came over me at the prospect of discussing her with anyone else, so I just brushed it off and resolved to stop by his place later, after the end of the moon cycle—when Azucena was gone.

Three sneers and four odd looks later, I reached the center of town, where many colorful stalls were set up, with sellers displaying their wares. There had to be at least fifty stands—maybe half of them selling textiles and materials to make Quipu's, the other half selling food. Many of the merchants were late in their solar-paths, their children or grandchildren loitering near their stands to help as needed. Quick to pass by the textile stands, I found the food stands from the scent alone, bartering rapidly for as much as I could carry. Though there were a few merchants that sold cooked foods, which had originally led me to the stands, it was typically much easier to barter for large amounts of raw foods than a small bit of cooked food—something my dad had taught me as a young child.

While the buying power of textiles had definitely shifted since

I last ventured into the market, I was still able to procure a decent amount of potatoes and corn to last us until at least the next moon. I did stop to peruse the spices, but in the end, didn't trade for any, opting to save the last woven blanket I carried in case I needed to return for more food.

The market wasn't too crowded, which was better for me as I tended to avoid crowds—whether that was because I was raised in seclusion or was born to prefer it, I wasn't sure. Though my father had taken me to the market at least once per moon cycle as a child, I tended to avoid the village for as many solar-paths as possible, only venturing to the market when desperate, like now.

Provisions procured, I bid farewell to the last man I had bartered with, a smile on his face as he ran his hand over one of my mother's textiles. He was older, sitting on a worn blanket, his shoulders hunched over his wares. While I hoped he planned to use the blanket for himself come the cold season, I knew it was just as likely that he would trade it away before the end of the sun-cycle. I turned away from him, a bit sad to part with something of my mother's I had only just discovered existed.

Inti now low in the sky, I hurried back home as fast as possible, hoping that Azucena was okay. I hadn't intended to leave her for so long, but the errands had taken much more time than I had anticipated.

As I made my way out of town, I passed a colorful mural, which seemed to gleam in the setting sun. I can't explain why, but I paused for a moment and backed up to take in the full glory of the piece. Starting near the bottom, I worked my way up, noticing quickly that the mural was several beautiful and deep colors delicately painted in an image of a beautiful woman. It wasn't until I got to her face that I started to really notice the similarities. Narrow nose, dark wavy hair, and a small dark mark on her left cheek.

It was Azucena.

The realization washed over me like a bucket of ice cold water, and I immediately began searching the painting for any indication of who this woman was. There was no information whatsoever.

Still aghast, but resolving to ask Azucena about it when she was feeling better, I turned back toward the dirt road that would lead me out of the village and back toward my home, my thoughts swirling.

Why had they painted Azucena? How important was she to the emperor? And if she had done something criminal, as I suspected, why hadn't the mural been painted over in the image of someone else?

Something here wasn't adding up, and Azucena had some explaining to do.

INTI WAS LONG GONE from the sky by the time I pushed through the door and into the small house. It was nearly dark inside, the fire I left in the kitchen burned down to embers.

Although I was positively itching to ask Azucena about the mural, I knew she needed to eat and drink the herbs Rocio had given me. I was going to brew them into a tea to ease her pain.

I peeked through the door to the bedroom quickly, unable to resist the urge, finding her still curled in the same position in which I had left her. I ached to wake her right away, but knew it was probably better if she was asleep if she was in as much pain as she had been this morning.

Working quickly, I cut the potatoes to make a mash, adding what little herbs I had left indoors, before making the same cornmeal I had been making for several sun-cycles now. While I was used to such a bland diet as a peasant, I could tell Azucena wasn't—

And just like that I was back to thinking about the mural.

Desperate for answers, I picked up the pace, brewing the tea while the potato cakes and cornmeal cooked, before tossing everything in two bowls—which I balanced in one hand—a wooden cup with the tea held in the other as I shouldered open the door into the dark room.

Usually, I lit candles later at night, but I didn't have any hands left, so I set everything on the chair before pushing open the curtain so the light of Quilla could filter in. At the sound of my movement, Azucena stirred.

"Rurac?" she whispered.

"It's me." I moved back to the sitting bench, holding the bowl and the mug out to her. "This is an herbal mix that should help your ah . . ."

"Menses." She gratefully took both items from my outstretched hands, her lips taking a delicate sip of the tea before wincing at the temperature.

"Careful, it's hot," I cautioned her.

"I noticed," she replied, but the usual haughty tone was gone from her voice.

My stomach growled as a reminder that I hadn't eaten all sun-cycle, and I tore my eyes away from Azucena, taking a bite, only to look up a beat later to see her stirring her bowl listlessly.

"You're not hungry?"

"I struggle with eating during this time." She took a quick bite before continuing. "But I know I need to keep my energy up so I will eat as much as possible."

We each took another bite, the room filled with a calm silence. Once she had gotten through a grand total of about five bites, I couldn't wait any longer.

"Azucena, when I was leaving town, I saw this mural and—you're going to think I've lost it—but it looked a lot like you."

She didn't even glance up from the tea, though I noticed the way her lip quirked up in the corner in an almost smirk. "It probably was me."

Any words I had been about to mutter vanished from my mind. "Wait—huh?"

She shrugged, as if everyone had their mural on the side of a building in a small town in the hills. "It was commissioned when I was sixteen solar-paths, I think."

"I'm sorry, but that's uh..." I struggled to find the right way to say what I was thinking. My brain was still stuck from the nonchalant way she had just announced that she was on a mural.

"It's normal when you're the empress."

That did it. I choked on the spit in my mouth. "Did you just say you're the empress?"

"Yep."

I narrowed my eyes at her. There was no way she could be. Firstly, the emperor was male, and I worked for him. Second, if she was the empress because she was married to the emperor, she would be held of equal importance to him—meaning she could order people to be sacrificed. What empress would imprison themself?

She was lying. She had to be.

"You're lying."

She took another bite, delicately patting the corner of her mouth. "I'm not."

I ran my eyes up and down her body. She did look like the image depicted on the mural, but there was no way in Mictlan she was the ruler of the Incan empire. "You are." My bafflement quickly sprouted into anger, and I stood from the chair, knocking it over in my haste. "I don't know who you think I am, but I wasn't born yesterday. There is no way you are emperor. Our emperor is a man—"

"Who died several solar-paths ago. I'm his daughter." Her voice was calm and even, but it did nothing to stop the boiling in my blood. "You know as well as I do that the title of emperor in Sipan is passed down by blood. That blood is in my veins."

"NO! . . . No. You are a common criminal. I don't know why your face was painted on the wall, but you are not the emperor, and you will never convince me of such."

Her chin lifted so her gaze could meet mine, and I could see myself in her gaze, burning in my own anger. I was so angry that I couldn't even form words anymore. Without another utterance, I moved to the door, pulling it open, stumbling through, and closing it behind me with a slam.

Not missing a beat, I pulled up the trap door and climbed down the ladder into my living quarters, slamming it shut behind me. I didn't care what that girl said. She wasn't the leader of Sipan. There was no way in Mictlan.

Thirteen

AZUCENA

Rurac's little temper tantrum came to a peak as he slammed the door behind him and stomped off. But as I tilted my ear to the ceiling, I noticed he didn't stomp far, and there was the sound of another door slamming shortly after.

So, there was more to this hut than I was privy to. Now I just needed to wait until Rurac turned his back and I could explore more . . . hopefully without the stone chains weighing me down.

As I reclined back on the bed, however, I knew any sort of exploration wouldn't be happening any time soon. Not only did Rurac not trust me to begin with, but now he was sure I was a liar, when in fact, he was the one who had been lied to for so many solar-paths—believing my father to still be ruling these lands.

With a sigh, I set aside what was left in the bowl. I hadn't been lying to Rurac about being empress, nor had I been lying about being unable to eat during my menses. I just wish he would realize that, because the longer I stayed here, the more I was starting to think that this had been more than a simple sort of mix-up and that something very serious was wrong in the palace.

But that begged another point.

Why was no one looking for me?

I mean, I couldn't be certain, but I had been told by my advisors that I was beloved by the people, so where were they now? Was no one worried for my well-being after not seeing me for several sun-cycles?

The thought that my advisors, despite honest-appearing auras, had lied to me sat heavy in my stomach and I decided that was a mental path to spiral down on a different sun-cycle.

Instead, I reflected over the colors swirling around Rurac's head as we had been talking. Despite his obvious anger, white clouds had conjured in his aura, meaning the lie he was telling was harmless. (Of course, I knew the lie in this case—it was the fact that I wasn't empress, because I promise you, You remember that part of the story, right?)

Anyway, how could his lie be harmless if it resulted in me being imprisoned by him? Was I here for a purpose? Was this my purpose?

I had never been very religious, as empress, I was automatically guaranteed a spot in Hana Pacha when I died, as the ruling class are deities of our own making. But for the first time in my life I was starting to wish I had paid closer attention during my religious studies. My gift was granted by the gods, to help guide me here on Pacha Mama. So why did I feel so lost and confused?

My brain ached and I knew there would be no following that thought further in this moment. Instead, I lay back down, my arm gripping my stomach even though no further cramps came. I would have to ask him what was in that tea, because not even I could deny that it had worked.

THE NEXT SUN-CYCLE, Rurac never appeared with my morning food. I didn't mind, seeing I was still in too much pain to eat. But by the afternoon, the pain was starting to abate, leaving my stomach crying out loudly for food.

I sat quietly in bed for as long as possible, waiting for the tell-tale sign that he was on his way to feed me. But when he didn't come and Inti began to set in the sky, I decided to take drastic action, yanking open my door to discover a cold bowl of mush on the floor on the other side of the door.

So, he had been here.

Likely before I had awoken. While cold corn mush wasn't my favorite, my stomach was too hungry for me to be discriminatory as I wolfed it down in just a few seconds. Once the bowl was empty, I replaced it outside my door, closing it tightly and dragging my chained foot back to the bed.

I wondered how long Rurac was going to be mad at me for. He couldn't be mad too long . . . right?

I leaned back in the cold bed to focus my gaze on the thatched ceiling, and for the first time since my arrival in this stone hut I began to seriously consider what my fate was slated to be.

And whether or not I had the power to change it.

LUCKILY, the question only had to swirl around my mind for one passing of Quilla, because at daybreak the next morning, Rurac was yanking open my door, the chain gripped in his fit as I jolted awake

"Rurac!" I shouted, my voice still garbled from sleep as I sat up in bed.

"Get up. We're going hunting." He sat down in the chair and attached one side of the chain to his leg.

"What?" I asked, not totally processing his words yet.

"You heard me."

When I didn't move, he reached beneath the covers for my leg.

I yanked my leg from his grasp. "What are you doing. I can't leave the house today."

"Why not?" His voice was nearly a growl.

"The . . . menses." I hadn't checked the flow that morning yet, but it was likely too heavy for me to be away from the house long. Not to mention that while the pain was gone now, it was sure to return with a vengeance once the herbal tea wore off.

"I can get more cloths for you." His lips were pressed into a thin line.

"That's not the problem, I uh . . . need to change them frequently."

His eyes narrowed. "We won't be gone long."

"I bleed heavily," I argued, not willing to back down.

He said nothing as the two of us had a stare-off, waiting to see who would break first.

Unfortunately, it was me, much to my own surprise. There was just something about his brown irises . . .

"Fine, let's go hunting. But I can't be out long." I removed my leg from under the blanket, holding it out in his direction for him to put the chain around my ankle.

"I'll make it fast," he replied.

I highly doubted that. "Wait, I need more cloths." I remembered suddenly. "Now, before we leave." I added when he didn't jump into action right away. His face remained stoic as he leaned down and unhooked his leg from his side of the chain.

"I'll go get more. Wait here."

I rubbed my forehead in annoyance as he turned his back and headed out the door. I was currently chained to the ground and had an extra chain around my other leg. Though it wasn't attached to him at the other end, it was highly unlikely that I would be going anywhere.

I stood there, taping my foot until he returned with a stack of cloths and thrust them into my hands. I nodded my thanks and motioned for him to turn around as I used the pot and arranged the cloths around my waist, tying them so they would stay in place.

"I'm ready," I said once I was done. He turned around to retrieve the other end of the chain, attaching it to his leg before releasing me from the chain beneath the bed. I opened my mouth to ask if the chains were really necessary, but snapped it shut. It wasn't an appealing enough argument for me to poke the bear that was Rurac.

In silence, we made our way from the stone house into the chilly, pre-dawn air, with Rurac carrying the chain between us so it didn't drag on the ground. I wrapped my arms around my shoulders, wishing I had a better shawl, but realized I probably wouldn't need it the moment we started hunting.

Rurac didn't glance back as we started into the woods, his shoulders broad and pushed back, like he didn't even feel the chilly air. That's when I noticed the bow slung between his shoulder blades, next to the quiver of arrows.

"Please don't tell me we are going to hunt with a bow and arrows."

"We are," he grumbled. "And be quiet. We don't want to scare the animals."

I huffed but didn't ask any more questions, my eyes instead darted from side to side as we crashed through the underbrush, wondering just what he intended to hunt.

I couldn't restrain myself with the next question bubbled up. "What animal are we hunting exactly?" Plus, I didn't care if we scared off the animals, that would teach him not to take me hunting next time.

"Whatever we can get," he said over his shoulder. "I'm not picky, but I'm tired of cornmeal."

"Hm," I replied, my pacing slowing as a slight cramp hit and I pressed on my midsection with my hand. "Well, I've never been hunting before. Nor did I ever intend to go hunting." I added the last part to ensure my displeasure was obvious.

"It shows." He suddenly stopped, his arm darting out to the side to stop me, his other hand reaching for his bow and arrow. I peered around him to spot a herd of deer in the clearing in front of us, my eyes widening in awe.

I briefly thought about shouting and scaring them off, but something caused me to second guess myself and remain quiet.

While I had seen a dead deer before, mostly when deer were presented as part of the tithe, I had never seen one alive. And the ones in front of us were truly majestic.

They were large, soft-looking, yet somehow regal. The deer were munching on grass, their brown, fuzzy ears flicking every which way, likely searching for signs of hunters like us.

Without a word, Rurac kneeled, resting his elbow on one knee to steady his bow hand while notching back an arrow. I watched in wonder as he stretched the string back, aimed with one eye closed, and fired the arrow. It made a whizzing sound as it passed through the air, so fast I could barely see it, before it landed in the side of the nearest animal.

The deer made a pained sound and fell, while the rest of the deer immediately jumped into action and bounded off into the bushes, leaving the dying animal crying, alone.

I don't know why, but the whole scene brought tears to my eyes. Something so beautiful and peaceful destroyed by a single arrow—his once-comrades immediately abandoning him. But knowing that we likely needed the meat to make it through the winter, I said nothing as we made our way forward and Rurac pulled his long knife from his waistband.

As he knelt next to the deer, I turned away, instead deciding to observe the trees, the early light reflecting off of their slightly damp leaves. I heard sounds behind me and when I turned back again, Rurac had the deer hung over his large shoulders.

"Let's go," he grumbled, his neck pressed forward due to the sheer size and weight of the deer. Though I was still angry at him for not believing that I was the empress, I couldn't help but marvel at his strength. In the palace, all my meals were simply prepared. I had no idea this was the amount of work that went into it.

We didn't speak as we made our way back to the stone hut, but my mind wondered whether or not I should try to explain to

Rurac, once again, that I was the empress. Something in my gut urged me to do so, like a voice whispering on the wind that my time to save myself was running out.

But as the sun crested the trees and the stone hut came back into view, I decided to let it go for now and push away the niggling in my mind. The last thing I wanted was for us to have another argument and miss out on the deer meat. My mouth was already watering just thinking about eating something other than maiz—especially at this point in my womanly cycle.

Rurac dropped the deer in a heap outside before entering the house, and I followed (after all, what other choice did I have with that dumb chain around my ankle?) only to be shocked when he spun around to face me just past the doorstep. I stumbled back.

"Do you have any proof that you are the empress?"

His words, so different from the night before, shocked me into silence. My thoughts twisted, and I tried to think of how I could prove my status since he apparently didn't totally disbelieve me.

"Um." I thought back to the night of the kidnapping, my hand flying to my wrist where a gold bangle usually sat. "What happened to the jewelry I was wearing?"

His gaze followed my movement, watching the way my fingers encircled my wrist. "You weren't wearing any jewelry when you were brought here."

Well, there went that plan. "Who brought me here?"

He shrugged. "My friend Kuntur. He said a guard for the emperor dropped you at his place down the hill with orders to bring you here."

Now it was my turn to raise my eyebrows. "You don't know the name of the person you work for?"

He shrugged. "My father knew his name, and when my father passed on I was too embarrassed to ask for it again."

I let out a huff. "You really aren't making this easy." I tried to think of another way. "I could tell you all about the regulations for the empire?"

"Won't help." He laughed. "I don't know them, so I have no idea how to check if you are telling me correctly or lying."

"Ugh." I crossed the room and sat down on the bench. "Then I guess you need to take me to the palace. I promise, the minute you return me, they'll tell you who I am."

"The palace is at least a fourteen sun-cycle walk from here."

My eyes widened. How did I get so far from the palace without waking? "How was I transported here in one night then?"

He thought for a moment, his finger on his chin. "Well, for one, they brought you over the pass, but the bridge has since collapsed, so we would have to go around. Also, you were brought on a cart which shortens the journey significantly. I don't own a cart to take us back."

I hated to admit it, but his explanation was logical. "Well then you better be ready for a fourteen sun-cycle adventure." I smirked. This was totally going my way—finally.

"Adventure?" He raises his eyebrows. "I never said I would go to the palace with you."

"Well, you can also just release me, and I'll find my own way," I hedged.

"Not a chance," he snapped. "I guess you'll just have to wait until my boss comes to collect you."

"Now wait just a moment." I held up a finger. I was not letting him crush my hopes that fast. "You asked if I can prove it and I told you that I can. Now, you have to allow me to prove it to you by taking me to the palace."

"And what if they come to collect you while we are gone?"

And just like that, he walked right into my trap. "Is there more than one way to the palace?"

"Just the bridge and the path around."

"And will they fix the bridge in fourteen sun-paths?"

"Likely not."

"Very well." I smirked. "Then we will pass anyone on their way here as we make our way to the palace, right?"

He tapped his finger on his chin, looking for a flaw in my suggestion. "I . . . guess," he relented.

"Then it's settled—we begin the journey tomorrow. If we meet anyone on the path who has come to collect me, we can ask them to verify my identity. If we don't pass anyone, then we make it back to the palace and verify my identity there."

"And if we get to the palace and you're lying?"

I shrugged. "The way I see it, you saved them a trip. They can torture me in the palace dungeons or execute me there."

"You're pretty confident for a supposed criminal."

"I am." I laughed. "It's almost like I'm actually the empress or something."

My words hit home, and for the first time since I arrived here, he actually looked like he believed me. "It's settled then," he agreed. "I'll prepare the meat for travel, and we will leave tomorrow."

"Excellent." We were finally getting somewhere, and soon I would be back in my palace with my favorite chicha morada and not a care in the world. Then, he would see what a mistake he had made.

And nothing could possibly go wrong.

Well . . . almost nothing.

Fourteen

AZUCENA

We had decided to leave early the next morning, both in hopes that my menses would be light enough to travel, and so that Rurac had the entire evening to pack food for us to carry. I would have offered to help, but he had quickly learned that my skills in the kitchen were next to none, so it was much more efficient that he packed the food while I . . . basically did nothing—which is what I was good at anyway.

Okay, that didn't sound very nice, but with one leg either chained to the ground or another leg, it was really quite hard to be helpful.

Regardless, I slept fitfully, dreaming of all the ways this plan could go wrong. So, when Rurac pushed open the door as the night stars still twinkled in the sky, I was sitting up in bed, all the unused cloths in a pile next to me on top of the tunic I had arrived here in—freshly washed.

Rurac said nothing, just dipping his chin at me before attaching me to the chain that was attached to him. While I knew the chain brought him security, I hoped he also realized how little I knew about the lands that I ruled over. I had never been in this part before, and I certainly would be no help on a fourteen sun-cycle journey by foot. Not to mention I wouldn't be trying to run off, now that I knew how far of a trip it was. Plus, why would I leave my guide behind? I was the empress, not dumb.

After adjusting the chains, Rurac rose to his full height, something dark gripped in his hands. I realized almost immediately they were sandals—the ones the people of the hills wore to protect their feet as they climbed over rocky terrain. They weren't quite my size, but they were clearly made for a woman, so they weren't Rurac's.

Sensing my unspoken question, he mumbled, "They were my mother's."

I nodded, knowing how tender of a subject the death of a parent was. Once the sandals were tied, I stood, taking a look at the huge leather pack Rurac had strapped to his back.

He held out his hands for the cloths gripped in my fist and I passed them over.

"Are you ready?"

"Sure am." This sun-cycle was certainly going to be a long one, but it was a step in the right direction to prove who I was, and return to the life I knew best. The life where I was an empress with everyone at my beck and call, and Rurac was just some peasant who had become a pawn in some giant mix-up.

We slipped out the front door just as the light of Inti began to wake in the sky, the tendrils of my dark hair blowing lightly in the breeze. I had tried to braid it so none fell loose, but it hadn't worked as well as I had hoped. I usually had my yanakuna to braid it for me.

"We need to move quickly," Rurac directed me as he closed the door to his hut behind me, securing it with a wooden beam so that no animals would accidentally wander inside in his absence.

"Why?"

"A storm is coming."

I wrinkled my nose, looking from one edge of the dawn to the other. There wasn't a single sign of a cloud in sight. "It doesn't look like it."

He leaned his head back, his long hair blowing in the breeze as he tilted his nose to the sky before looking back at me and tapping it. "It doesn't look like it, but I can smell it in the air. I want to get as far as possible before nightfall, as that is when it will hit."

"Hm," I murmured but didn't argue. I knew little, if anything, about the weather, but the colors around his head were red, and my gift never lied.

Rurac wasn't being honest with me about the storm.

I wasn't sure in what way, but I would figure it out.

He began walking toward the brush and I followed, the chain dragging in the dirt between us. As we crossed from the open, grassy field in front of his home and ventured into the woods, the sound of the chain dragging in the dirt was replaced with it dragging in the dead leaves. Remembering how he had carried it while we were hunting, I leaned down to pick it up, but he stopped me with his hand.

"There's no need to be quiet now. In fact, I would prefer if we made a little noise to scare away any pumas."

"Oh." I righted myself and continued following him, the silence stretching between us.

I realized it would be an extremely long day if we didn't speak to each other. Plus, I secretly hoped if I asked him about himself, he would ask me about myself.

I loved talking about myself.

"So, tell me about your parents."

He peered over his shoulder, his eyes narrowing into slits. "Why?"

I rolled my eyes at his disdain and the fact that, apparently, he was taking the "us being enemies" thing quite seriously. I rolled my eyes as I motioned to the trail in front of us. "Because this is going to be an extremely long fourteen sun-cycles if we don't have some sort of conversation."

"Fine," he relented, but I could tell he didn't mean it. "My mother was a weaver, and my father was a Game and Prisoner Manager for the emperor—as you likely assumed."

I rolled my eyes a second time. "Okay, but were they good

parents? Did you enjoy spending time with them? What were their favorite foods?"

He was silent for a moment. "I guess."

"Those weren't all yes or no questions."

"I know." He let out a breath. "My mother died giving birth to me, so I can't answer most of those questions for her. As for my father . . . I did enjoy spending time with him. But he was a quiet man. Just as I am."

I closed my eyes for a moment, trying to imagine a quiet life, but the palace life I grew up in appeared behind my eyelids —music, voices, and all. "Do you ever get tired of the quiet life?"

He tilted his head from side to side, thinking. "I don't know much else."

"And your father's favorite food?" I prodded further.

"I don't really think that was something he had the luxury of." He turned to look at me, the early morning light glinting off his irises. "What about you? Do you know what your parents' favorite foods were?"

I couldn't help it, but the mention of my parents, and the chance to talk about me, brought a smile to my face. "My father used to love potatoes—any type, any way you could make them and he was satisfied." That thought led to the memory of his last meal and the smile instantly fell from my face. "My mother was a bit pickier, but she also enjoyed potatoes. Though, I think she and I shared our love of chicha morada."

"Chicha morada?"

"You've never had it?"

He shook his head, reminding me for a moment of our drastically different upbringings.

"It's a beverage brewed from purple corn. I thought everyone in Sipan made it at some point or another."

Rurac thought for a moment, his lips twisted to the side. "My father may have—maybe my mother made it. But when she died, he found himself suddenly cooking for himself and caring for me as a babe and well . . . a special beverage like that probably didn't take priority."

I frowned.

"But you seemed to love your parents a lot," he added, noticing the expression on my face.

"I did." I sighed. "They were really great parents. Of course, I can't compare them to any other parents, but I really don't think I could have asked for better."

He kept his gaze trained on my face. "What happened to them?"

The question shocked me. It really shouldn't have, since I had learned by now that Rurac's political knowledge of the empire was severely lacking. But for so many solar-paths I hadn't had to explain how my parents had died. Everyone had just known.

"Ehm." The word I was trying to say got caught in my throat and tears brimmed at the edges of my eyes and I reached up to brush them away, apologizing. As empress, I was never allowed to cry in front of subjects—only in private. "Sorry," I sputtered. "Most people just . . . know. It's hard for me to put it into words." When I looked up, Rurac was eyeing me from the corner of his eye, a frown on his lips. Afraid to disappoint him, I quickly explained. "It was a cough of some sort. The same one took both my parents about ten solar-paths apart."

"I'm sorry to hear that."

I shook my head, brushing away a second tear that tried to break free. "Don't be. You lost your parents too. We are alike, you and I." I ended on a whisper, realizing for the first time in the days since I had been placed in Rurac's care that we really were two of a kind, social class aside.

I wasn't sure if Rurac came to the same conclusion, but he didn't ask any more questions, and as the sun rose from below the horizon to above the trees, the only sound between us was the chain rustling the leaves as we made our way through the forest. At some point, my stomach started grumbling, but I didn't want to be the one to slow our pace, so I remained silent until Rurac finally came to a stop in front of a felled tree, letting the pack slide from his back.

"Let's stop for food."

I didn't argue, and within a few minutes he was handing me a bit of deer jerky.

"It didn't dry fully," he explained. "But it will get better as we travel. I also brought some of the potatoes from the market I visited the other day, so we will heat those for dinner."

My heart lifted at the thought of potatoes, and of society. "Will we be able to go into some of the villages on the way?"

Rurac nodded. "Yes, but not the ones near where I live as I am well-known and don't want word to get out that I am disobeying orders. I could lose my food stipend."

For the first time since my kidnapping, I realized that Rurac, though he was stubborn about believing I was the empress, was truly trying to do what he thought was right. As empress, I hadn't known any similar fear of making a mistake. I was given the throne by blood, and my word was law. I never had to worry about doing or saying the wrong thing and losing my access to food. The thought made the small bit of jerky sit like a rock in my stomach. Even though I knew I could pardon Rurac immediately once I figured out what happened and took back my throne, I knew that rumors spread fast, and whoever was giving him orders could hurt him before that. I wasn't sure why that bothered me so much, but it did.

When I was finally able to break free from my mental spiral, I found Rurac's dark eyes trained on my face, questions clouding his pupils. "Is the meat okay?"

I nodded furiously. "Yes, sorry, it's great." I forced a half smile past my lips.

"Good. I'm afraid we will have to ration it carefully. I brought what I could carry, but I don't have as much to trade as I would like."

"You brought items to trade?"

He nodded and pulled a bundle out of his pack. "The last of my mother's weaving."

I reached over and took the top blanket from him delicately, running my hands over the finely woven threads. "These are beautiful."

"My mother was talented," he agreed. "I'd rather not part with any, but as I told you before, it's been a rough growing year, and I don't think I'll have a choice."

I swallowed. What was it about this man that was pulling at my heart and destroying my always-in-place facade? "We will try our best not to. If we must trade them, when we get to the palace, I can give you the spices you need to in order to get them back on your way home."

He raised his eyebrows. "That easy? These will fetch a high trade value."

I nodded and pointed to myself. "Empress, remember?"

"Well for the sake of my mother's weaving, I hope you're not giving me false hope, as it would be nice to keep at least one of these."

I passed the blanket back to him, ensuring his hands were on it before removing my own, the feeling of his hands on mine brought a whisp of something I couldn't name to my chest. "We will save at least one for you, I promise."

Rurac tucked away the weaving in his pack before rising from the ground. "Ready to continue? We've got lots of ground to cover before nightfall."

"Yes." I rose to my feet, brushing off the dress which had seen better days. "The sooner we get me back to the palace the better."

For me.

———

THE AFTERNOON CONTINUED in a very similar manner to the morning as we shared more about our childhood and family. It was so interesting learning about a different walk of life that I had never imagined even existed. Though my childhood had contained challenges, none of them included wondering where my next meal would come from, or how we would weather the winter. But that was something that had ruled Rurac's life, and something I felt I needed to understand better, especially if I were to consider helping him once we arrived in the palace. Which I still wasn't sure about.

As the light faded from the sky and the temperature began to drop, we stopped to set up camp. Rurac built a fire for us to roast potatoes before turning to make a shelter for the night.

I poked the potatoes with a stick from time to time, using the stick to roll them over on the stone by the fire without burning my fingers. I was so focused on my task, it wasn't until the potatoes were soft to the touch and almost fully cooked that I turned around to realize Rurac had set up only a single shelter.

"Only one shelter?" I asked, tilting my head to the side.

Rurac surveyed what he had set up—the one woven blanket cast over a low-hanging tree branch, the ends pinned to the ground with large stones. "Yes, this is all I had to spare. Especially if you want to sleep on the second blanket I brought, as opposed to the cold ground."

My eyes drifted to the pile of blankets still sitting by the fire.

"We need at least one blanket each to cover ourselves, and that's all I have," he added.

I bit my lip. I wanted to argue that I shouldn't have to share a tent with a peasant like him, but then again, he was willing to sell his mother's blankets to get us back to the palace. Not to mention that he had carried the pack and all of our supplies himself. I had no room to argue, though I wanted to.

"Looking forward to sharing the shelter with you, then."

Rurac's mouth dropped open in shock and he immediately rushed over to set his arm against my forehead, which I immediately shoved off. "Don't touch me."

"Sorry, I was just seeing if you were ill. You agreed much more quickly than I expected."

I raised an eyebrow. "So, you knew all along there would only be one shelter for us to share?"

Rurac motioned to the chain—which was still around my leg —and the boulder it was currently attached to. "I planned on it, yes."

And just like that, any pity I had felt for the man over his tragic childhood evaporated. "Hmp."

How could I forget that I was still his prisoner?

Rurac finished setting up the shelter in silence as I munched on my share of the potatoes. I didn't want to admit it, but they were delicious, and I was thankful they weren't corn mush. But I wasn't about to give Rurac the satisfaction of my thankfulness.

Once dinner was finished, came the awkward moment where we both stared at the shelter, neither of us wanting to make the first move to lie down.

"Um." Rurac turned to me, his eyes looking anywhere but mine, and motioned to the bottom blanket. "Do you prefer sleeping on one side or the other?"

"You mean beyond having my own bed, as I am accustomed to?" I crossed my arms over my chest, waiting for the normal annoyance I felt at not getting my way, but to my surprise, it didn't come.

He mimicked my movements, his eyes shifting to mine before narrowing. "Fine then, I choose the left."

I raised one of my eyebrows. "And if I wanted the left?"

He shrugged, and I could have sworn he glanced at my lips as he retorted, "You should have spoken up then instead of complaining."

I huffed as I slid into my side of the tent. Rurac swiftly made the adjustments to my stone tether, reattaching my ankle to his, before taking the other side.

Even lying on our backs, as far apart as our respective edges of the shelter would allow, we were quite close. It was a small shelter.

"Well, goodnight," he murmured.

"Same to you," I replied, determined to stay in my rigid position on my back the entire night, not allowing our skin to graze in the slightest. After all, even being just this close to a peasant was much too close for my comfort.

Within moments, he was asleep, his gentle snores breaking the silence of the forest night. At first, I was annoyed, but soon, his snores became like a lullaby, and I, too, drifted off into the welcoming abyss of sleep.

Fifteen

RURAC

That night, I slept deeper than I had for a long time, as, for some reason, the nightmares about starving during the cold season, which usually plagued my sleep, didn't come. Instead, I felt safe, warm, and secure. As sleep began to fade and I became once again aware of the surroundings, I realized there was something warm and heavy draped over me.

For a moment, I panicked, but then I remembered the events of the night before and I cracked my eyelid to find Azucena lying half on top of me, her arm and head draped over my chest, one of her legs hitched over mine. I couldn't lie, it was extremely comfortable. But it was also too comfortable as my cock started to stir and was all too happy about being half covered by a woman.

Throughout my coming-of-age solar-paths, while most of the young men in the village had been seeking out women and participating in trial marriages, I had been busy trying to keep my father and I afloat. Though I had taken some walks in the woods with a few pretty women, nothing had panned out and I hadn't spent any time this close to a woman in nearly ten solar-paths—something my dick was achingly reminding me of.

Azucena's chest rose and fell with deep breaths, indicating she was still asleep, and I knew I had to disentangle us before she woke, otherwise she would panic at the sight of my appendage attempting to protrude through my pants.

Slowly and gently, I began to shift her off of me. The leg was easy, but then came the time for her arm and head. And, of course, it was as I was attempting to sweep her hair to her own space that she woke.

"—ghths, gah!" She jumped back, yelling, "No touching!"

I hurriedly shifted to a sitting position, bunching the blanket in my lap to make this less awkward.

"What were you doing?!"

I tried to play it cool. "What was I doing? I woke up and you were half on top of me."

"Ha!" she scoffed, brushing her hair out of her face. "Like I believe that."

I rolled my eyes. "Don't you think if I would have wanted to take advantage of you, I would have done so already?"

She narrowed her eyes in that strange way she always did, her pupils searching the area above my head. It was clear she was still half asleep, and I had to admit the look on her face was, well, adorable.

After a moment of searching for an answer, she relented. "I suppose you're right. Though, I'm not apologizing for what I do in my sleep."

"I didn't expect you to," I replied as I stood in the shelter, my hard-on abated enough that I could move to place the chain currently around my ankle under the boulder once more. "I'll be back." She didn't say anything as I moved out of sight, just behind the shelter to relieve myself. While I knew it wasn't fair that I got to move about freely to do my business and she had to do hers with me only a chain length away (though I did turn my back like a gentleman), I still didn't trust her enough to do without the chain.

Returning to the camp, I pulled some jerky from my pouch, handing her a piece before reattaching the chain to my ankle and slipping the key in my pocket. "Eat quickly, so we can get moving. We have a lot of ground to cover this morning."

She nodded, her cheeks already bulging with the chewy jerky. I knew the low rations were harsh on her, evident by her voracious eating at every meal, but if we wanted to make it to the palace, we had to be conservative—unless I could find something to hunt.

As if the gods had been listening, a large, multicolored llama chose that moment to wander into our camp. I observed as it meandered around, looking at our snuffed-out fire and sniffing the blanket that was lying over the trees to form our shelter.

It started stepping even closer, and I began to inch my hand toward the knife I kept in my belt. It would be hard to kill such a large creature with a small knife but—

My motions were interrupted when I felt something touching my hand. I looked down to find Azucena's hand on top of mine, blocking it from connecting with my knife.

"The llama," I hissed, trying not to spook it. Its ears twitched.

"I know," she whispered back. "Let it be."

I let out a low grumble. "We need food, Azucena."

"I know," she replied. "But we are not eating a llama."

Now she was just being ridiculous. "And why the hell not?"

"They're the spiritual guide assigned to me by the gods. If I allow one to be killed, it would be like allowing someone to kill me."

"You can't be serious," I huffed. I was still trying to be quiet, but the llama had been growing increasingly suspicious and began moving quickly away from our camp.

"I am," she snapped and the llama darted into the bushes.

"Ugh," I groaned, beginning to pack up our things. "It's clear you've never been hungry."

"It's clear you've never been empress," she shot back, taking an angry bite of her jerky. "You wouldn't like it if I killed your spirit guide."

"Actually," I corrected, as I angrily rolled the blankets, "I wouldn't care because I don't have one."

"I'll give you one," she suggested. "Then we will see—"

"No. I'm not having a spirit guide." I shoved the blanket in the pack. I couldn't wait to return this empress to where she belonged—if she even was the empress. When she had first proposed this plan of hers, I'll admit, I was hesitant. But when she explained that we would either make it there, or cross paths with the emperor, I figured it was a good enough idea. I just hoped it wouldn't get me in trouble.

"Well, I'll choose one for you and I won't tell you. So there."

I rolled my eyes. I don't think she realized how much I genuinely did not care about her stupid spirit guide. But now that I thought about it, she was basically as stubborn as a llama, so it was a good pick by the gods. Keeping that in mind, I didn't say anything back, content to continue angrily collecting our things. Scratch that, not our things, my things.

Once she finished her breakfast, I took her to the edge of the forest, turning my back while she relieved herself, still refusing to say anything in my anger over the lost llama. As I kneeled down to attach the pack to my back, she eyed me warily.

She swallowed whatever she was about to say, motioning to the underbrush. "Lead the way already."

I felt a bit bad about our argument, and the more I thought about it, the more I realized having a spirit guide wouldn't be too bad. Still, my pride prevented me from saying anything, even though it weighed heavily on me as we walked in silence, something that seemed strange after our lighthearted conversations of the sun-cycle before. The only sounds were the crunching of leaves and grass as our feet (and chain) moved through them, and the occasional sound of birds moving from tree branch to tree branch.

With a sigh, I finally broke the silence between us. "So . . . what does being empress entail anyway?" I glanced over in time just to see her roll her eyes.

"Why do you care?"

"Um." I searched for a plausible reason because telling her I kind of, sort of . . . cared about her definitely wasn't a good plan right now. "I'm just curious how someone who can't cook, hunt, or farm is able to control an empire."

"If you must know, my parents taught me a lot about the spice trade, the gods, and how to talk to people. But above all else, they taught me how to delegate. It's how any good emperor rules. I can't control everything, and I shouldn't try to."

It made sense, honestly, and I told her so. "So, if I get really good at delegating, I can be emperor?" I joked.

She laughed and shook her head. "Not a chance, you need blood that's been touched by the gods, remember?"

"Oh, right." I smiled. "Any idea where I can get some of that?"

She smiled back, letting me know that my joke was indeed lightening the mood as I intended. "I think you have to be born with it." One of her curls fell across her cheek and I fought the urge to brush it away, instead turning forward and focusing on the ground ahead of us.

I guided us from the woods along the edge of the cliff where the bridge that had connected this hill to the main city of Sipan just a few sun-cycles earlier used to be. "The bridge to the city used to be here." I motioned to the edge of the cliff, and Azucena cautiously stepped toward the edge to look down.

"It's a long way down."

"I know," I replied, subtly moving back from the edge so she would be forced to as well. I couldn't explain it, but the thought of her being too close to the edge was causing my stomach to roll for no apparent reason. "It's why the bridge being out is such a big deal. We have to go all the way around now."

"Why haven't they repaired it yet?" she questioned as we continued on our way.

"I'm not sure." And I wasn't lying. "In the past, this bridge was always just . . . here. It was old, and I'm not surprised it fell, but I don't know whose responsibility it was to repair it. Maybe— probably—the emperor's."

I watched her face as the last words left my mouth, but rather than angry, she seemed pensive, maybe almost sad. I couldn't quite read the emotions on her face, and it was driving me a bit crazy. I found myself wanting to ask what she was thinking, what was making her face look like that, but I restrained myself.

We walked all sun-cycle, and I didn't offer anything to eat between the two meals and she didn't ask. But by the time Inti left the sky, my stomach was rumbling, right along with hers. "Why don't we get ready to stop for the night?"

She nodded her agreement, and I quickly found two rocks close enough together that I could wedge my end of the chain between, leaving her to rub her feet, likely aching from the too-big sandals I had lent her, as I headed into the forest for firewood.

I returned to find her leaning against the boulder, her eyes off in the distance. The sun behind her head cast a light over her features. I couldn't explain it, but as the sun glinted off her dark hair and tanned skin, she looked regal, even in borrowed clothes that were too big and worn, and for the first time I could envision her truly as an empress.

My thoughts were cut short, however, when a low rumbling reached my ears.

I searched around for the source, my eyes catching on the ground beneath her feet, which was starting to shift and crumble. "AZUCENA!" I shouted, dropping my firewood as my heart rate spiked before plummeting into my stomach. "GET AWAY FROM THE EDGE!"

It was a nightmare come to life. Everything was moving too fast, except for me. My movements slowed, like I was making them through mud. As I rushed for her, several things happened simultaneously.

First, the ground underneath her feet fell, leaving nothing but empty air.

Then, she did.

I reached her just as the boulder holding her chain began to tilt. Realizing the only way to save her was the chain attached to her ankle, I dove for it, catching the empty, round end in my fists as I landed on my stomach. The weight of Azucena dragged me to the edge, and it was only by digging my elbows into the dirt that I managed not to follow her over.

My gaze connected with hers, which was filled with fear as she realized she was hanging upside down by her one leg, panting heavily.

"Rurac?" she choked, tears streaking her face.

"I got you," I promised. But at that moment, I noticed we had another problem. Azucena was sweating, and the chain was slipping over her ankle and it looked like it could slip over her foot entirely. "Azucena," I gasped, and she turned her fearful irises to her ankle.

"No."

My eyes darted around, frantically looking for a solution. That's when I spotted the rocks. "Azucena, I'm going to need you to start looking for handholds on the cliff face."

"I don't know how to climb." Her voice was quiet, defeated.

"You're going to learn right now. Please, just reach out your hands, find some holds, and pull yourself to the wall." She did as I asked, her eyes avoiding the drop which would likely kill her if she didn't. My heart was beating so fast I thought it would leave my chest. "There you go." I let out a breath as she found some crevices for her hands. "Now, look for more. We want to get you right side up." My biceps strained with shooting pains from the effort of keeping her upright, the sharp stone edges of the chains digging into the soft flesh of my hands.

She found another crevice a bit further up, her body now in a curve. Then she found one even closer—close enough that I could likely reach her with my arm. I did a quick release of pressure, only to realize I needed both arms to hold the chain. Meaning, I didn't have one to use to reach for her.

I groaned, my stomach flipping in fear. "Azucena, I'm going to need you to trust me." My gaze settled on the chain, which was digging into the top of her foot. It wouldn't hold much longer. "Do you have good handholds?"

"Yes." Came her tiny voice.

I tried not to focus on the fear I could hear in her tone. "Okay. I need to let go of your chain in order to reach for you. You need to hold on for a few blinks, but I will grab you, okay? I will not let you fall," I promised her, hoping it wouldn't be in vain.

"Okay." She gasped. "I'm slipping!"

"Hold on!" I yelled, preparing to drop the chain. "Three . . . Two . . . One!" I let go of the chain, my hands immediately searching blindly for her wrists. They found purchase just as I felt her weight shift, putting her entire weight where her hands rested in the crevice.

"I can't believe that worked," I gasped, still hanging over the edge of the cliff. But at least I had her in my hands instead of a stone chain.

"Pull me up already!" she called from below, which caused a rock to sink in my stomach, as I realized I hadn't thought this far in advance. On my stomach, I didn't have the full strength of my upper body, but I wasn't about to admit that to her.

"I need your help. Try to get your feet in some crevices so I have leverage." The sounds of pebbles falling reached my ears as I began to scoot backwards enough to get my knees under me.

"I'm trying! There isn't much—oh Sapa," she cursed.

"Don't look down! Keep trying!" I coached as I got one knee under my body. I just needed to get the other, and then I could get her up. As she struggled to find purchase for her feet, I felt my hold on her growing slick with sweat. I knew it was now or never.

Taking a deep breath, I moved my second knee underneath my body, yanking back at the same time to pull her up, leaning so that we didn't topple over the edge. The result was her landing on my chest, knocking the breath out of both of us, but I didn't care. I wrapped my arms around her body and closed my eyes in exhaustion. I had saved her. She was safe. My heart started doing its own little happy huayno in my chest.

I don't know how long we stayed like that, but I eventually became aware of a small tapping on my shoulder. "Um . . . Rurac?"

"Hmm?" I hummed back, adrenaline still coursing through my veins.

"As glad as I am to be alive, can we please move away from this edge before a second landslide takes us both?"

I opened my eyes and immediately realized what she meant, as we were still only a few steps from the edge. Acting quickly, I pulled us both to our feet and back into the safety of the trees where I had conveniently left our pack. At least I hadn't lost all of our supplies.

Azucena collapsed against a tree stump. "I thought I was going to Hana Pacha today."

"I did too, for a moment," I admitted, leaning against the other side of the tree, wiping more sweat which had accumulated on my brow.

"Rurac?"

"Hm?"

"Thanks for saving me."

"I just did what any kind person would do," I said, turning my neck to take a look at her leaning against the tree, her eyes closed, hands crossed in her lap, bruises blooming on her wrists where I had caught her. My stare trailed the rest of her body, noticing the chain around her ankle was gone.

She must've opened her eyes at some point during my evaluation because she chuckled, "Don't worry, I don't know the way back to the capital—I won't run. Chain or no chain, you're stuck with me."

"I'm just glad you had it," I said, avoiding her insinuation. "I don't know what would have happened otherwise."

Azucena seemed to think the same thing as she frowned once more. "Me too, Rurac. Me too."

Sixteen

AZUCENA

We had both been so tired from the near-death experience the night before, that neither of us made a single comment about our shared sleeping arrangements when we crawled into the shelter, practically half asleep. But the next morning, when I woke to find my head once again resting on Rurac's chest, I elicited a groan.

"Oh, come on." My voice was still low with sleep. "You are definitely lifting me over here in your sleep."

Though his eyelids were closed, I could tell by the colors drifting in his aura that he was awake. "Not true," he mumbled back. "You're the one who apparently wants to be closer to me in your sleep."

His aura flashed white, so if he was lying it was harmless. Regardless, my gaze narrowed as I extracted myself from my position on top of his body. Though I was a bit annoyed to keep waking up this way, my body didn't quite agree. My lady parts protested that I should try running my arms up and down his wide chest.

These were the sun-cycles when I missed the conveniences of the palace, and of being the empress. Whenever I craved a man, I would just send one of my guards into the square to look for men who were eligible for a marriage and bring them back to the palace. Then, I would line them up and choose one to suit my fancy. After some time alone with the one I chose, I sent them back to the village and they never seemed to mind. Well, at least, *I* felt like they didn't mind. But my time with Rurac was opening my mind in more ways than one.

Squashing the thoughts before they could go further, I ducked out of the tent to pee, thankful I no longer had a chain keeping me restricted.

It wasn't until I was making my way back to the camp that I realized how stiff and sore my body was. I groaned as I tried to rub the tension from my back and shoulders.

"You okay over there, empress?" Rurac called out from behind the shelter, likely taking care of his own business.

"Yeah," I replied, my mind momentarily catching on the fact that he had called me empress, but I decided to ignore it for now. "I feel like I, oh, you know, fell off a cliff."

Rurac's face came into view. "Strange how that happens."

I took a quick catalog of my dress, noticing how it was ripped and quite threadbare. Rurac's gaze must've followed my own, because a few moments later, he was holding out a dress to me. "I brought you a spare. It's the one you wore when you weren't feeling well."

I read his unspoken message and nodded as I took the dress he held out to me. It had belonged to his mother—I knew that now. I slipped behind the shelter and changed quickly. The dress didn't fit me as well as one would hope, but the clothes I arrived in had never been made for trekking the forest, much less dangling over a cliff. I tucked the bundle under my arm after I finished changing and came back around the shelter. "I'm not sure I can wear this again."

"I agree." Rurac nodded his chin toward the bundle. "Is there anything that can be salvaged? Either for trade, or as something else?"

I hadn't thought of that. In the palace, I simply tossed out things I no longer wanted and had no idea where they ended up after. But to a peasant, one dress was likely worth a lot, so I turned the bundle over in my hands, my eyes searching. "I think so."

He held out his hand for the bundle. "I'll work on it when we stop tonight—see what I can salvage." He packed it into his pack before dismantling the shelter and rolling it all onto his back. I felt a glimmer of disappointment, mostly in myself, that I wasn't more handy or able to repurpose items as he seemed to be. It was a foreign feeling, one I wasn't used to, but it punched where it hurt.

My parents hadn't prepared me for this.

I turned away from where he packed, my gaze roving the trees.

"Hey." His large, warm hand came to rest on my shoulder, and I peered at it, about to knock it off in my signature no-touching move, when he continued. "We had different upbringings; I'm sure there are things you are knowledgeable about that would surprise me."

I didn't reply, my lips twisting in disagreement.

"Off we go then." He motioned to the edge of the clearing. "We will stay closer to the trees today. There isn't really a path, but there is less of a chance of the Pacha Mama crumbling from beneath our feet."

I snorted at his comment. It was almost funny enough to jolt me out of my mood, but not quite. I held out my hand for him to lead the way, falling in step behind him as we made our way between the trees.

After a few moments, Rurac glanced back, seeming shocked to see me there. "You're so much quieter without the chain. I almost thought you had run off for a moment."

That did it. I was smiling. "Rurac, I think you mean *we*"—I motioned between us—"are much quieter without the chain."

This got him to chuckle as well. "You're right, *we* are much quieter without the chain."

My mind flashed back to a question that had been nagging at me since he had first put the chain around my ankle. "Where did you find a chain like that anyway?"

He shrugged. "I'm not really sure, actually. My grandfather was good with stone—if anyone in my family in recent generations had fashioned it, it would have been him. But my father had it for my entire life, and I never asked."

"Why did he need a chain?"

Rurac regarded me over his shoulder, his dark irises searching my own. "During my lifetime there hadn't really been a use for it, as most prisoners"—his eyes flashed—"didn't try to run, until you. But he would use it for large animals occasionally."

I opened my mouth to argue, but he shook his head and continued. "My father told me of a time when we were employed to wrangle the wild creatures of this mountain. I've never seen anything larger than a puma, but the lore tells tales of the beasts in these woods capable of blowing fire and consuming a man in one bite."

I knew the stories he spoke of—my parents had taught them to me as a child as well. "I've heard them too, but I guess I assumed there was no truth to them."

"So, you don't believe in any of the old lore then?"

His question nearly stopped me in my tracks. I had never thought about it before, as I did believe—scratch that—I *experienced* some of the lore. But I had always just brushed off certain stories, like the stories of large, man-eating creatures in these woods.

"No answer? Not even from the empress?" He joked, his elbow bumping into mine as if we were young children jesting. Without hesitation I shoved him. Of course, it did nothing because he was built like a tree.

"If you must know." I was careful to keep my voice even. "I believe in a lot of the lore. Until now, I guess the only one I truly didn't believe in was the man-eating creatures. But you are correct, if I believe in some, I should believe in them all."

Now it was his turn to be pensive, both of us walking silence as the trees began to thin and gave way to a field, stone huts rising in the distance.

"So, what lore do you believe in then?"

My chest tightened. My mother had always mentioned that if we shared our magical power with others, the gods would snatch it back, but I figured hedging around it would be okay. "Well, it has long been said that the bloodline of the emperor has been gifted with magic—a small gift from the gods to ensure a long rule."

Rurac stopped in his tracks, turning to face me. "Are you saying you have magic?"

I gulped. As someone so fundamentally against deception and lying, I wanted to tell him the truth. But I also didn't want to risk losing my gift either. I formulated my response, only raising my gaze to meet his when I was ready. "It is also believed that if the emperor discloses his gift to someone not of the royal line, he will lose it."

Rurac's eyes searched mine, disbelief evident on his face, but I saw him putting it together in his mind. "I see. Any idea what this gift from the gods would entail?" He spun back forward to resume walking, and I matched his pace despite the aching of my legs.

"I was taught that it varies, but it is always a gift that allows the empress—I mean emperor, to perform his job and to deliver fair judgments and policies."

I faced forward, noticing now that the stone huts we had seen from afar were really a small village. On the outskirts, there was a group of children, all of them holding sticks and chasing each other around. I smiled as I watched their game. Children had always been my soft spot. As we drew closer, I picked up my pace and called out to them, leaving Rurac to his deductions.

"Imaynallan!"

The children stopped their play, turning my way. As soon as their faces saw me, they lit up with recognition and the greetings came back in a chorus. One little boy in particular came right up to me, but was careful that he didn't touch me.

"Imaynallan! We are playing war, Empress. Would you like to join?"

I surveyed his hopeful face, and was surrounded by the hopeful look on the faces of many other children, but once glance at Rurac's wide eyes and tense shoulders told me there wasn't time. I knelt down so my face was level with the little boy's. "I'm afraid not today. My friend and I must pass through quickly and be on our way, but perhaps you know of the best route through your village, and can lead us as guards?"

Of course, there was really little they could do to defend us if anything did happen, but I could see by the wide smiles on their faces that they were excited by the prospect of an adventure with the empress. "Of course, empress! Right this way!" He turned and motioned me on. I looked back at Rurac, who appeared a little shocked. To urge him forward, I slipped my small hand into his, allowing the child to take my other hand and lead us both through the village.

The child prattled all through the journey, many of his friends cutting in when he didn't tell a story quite right. Rurac, still shocked, remained quiet, his gaze darting between me and the children, his eyes constantly wide. I enjoyed the journey myself, fighting not to giggle at the fact that Rurac seemed to finally be catching on that I really was the empress.

The walk through the village ended all too soon, and once we reached the other side, the children waved goodbye, inviting us to come play war with them again. I let them know that if we did pass back through, we would, but I didn't make any promises, mostly because I didn't want to break them.

Rurac waved goodbye too, and then it was just the two of us and the sound of our feet crunching leaves in the underbrush as we walked side by side.

"What will happen to me?" Rurac asked, as he gulped audibly.

"What do you mean?"

When he spoke again, his voice was quivering. "When we get to the palace . . . since they will likely think I kidnapped you?"

So, I was right, he did finally believe that I was the empress. And he had a right to be concerned. When he had first held me prisoner me, I would have given anything to toss him into my torture chambers for his involvement. But after these last few sun-cycles together I had come to realize he was just doing what he thought was right. "Nothing will happen to you. We will find who did actually kidnap me, I'll grant you the grace of the empress, and you'll be free to return home."

"Really? You could have me sacrificed to the gods, you know."

"I know." I acknowledged his comment but didn't tell him how heavy the idea of him being sacrificed made me feel. "But you did help me in the end—escape sacrifice, that is. And you didn't let me fall off that cliff. So, it's the least I could do."

"Well thank you, then, gracious empress." He smiled, but it didn't quite light up his face, and I knew he was still afraid. Or didn't trust me to keep my word.

"You're welcome," I replied, inspecting the ground passing beneath my feet.

I was serious. I would pardon him as soon as we arrived in the palace, but I couldn't help but think of how close I had come to escaping and doing just as he predicted. And how one near-death experience had changed my view of everything. Including him.

Seventeen

RURAC

It was our third night on the road, and by this point, our nighttime routine was pretty much second nature. First, I would find a suitable spot for sleeping and set down my pack. Then, I would go to look for wood for a fire while Azucena unpacked dinner from my bag. Once the fire was up and roaring, I would build our shelter while Azucena cooked the potatoes. We would eat, chat a bit, and ultimately lie down in the shelter side by side.

Something about the way we performed those tasks was so, comforting . . . so domestic that I realized somewhere along the way I had stopped thinking of Azucena as a prisoner, and despite my best efforts, we really were becoming friends . . .

I felt that I would later regret this shift in our relationship, but my heart was so happy right now, I brushed away my concerns. For now, we could be friends.

Tonight was no different than the two before, except, instead of having my head under the shelter, I recommended we lie the other way, as we were in a clearing, and I wanted to see the stars. Azucena didn't argue, taking her spot next to me, her palms supporting her head as she gazed up at the sky.

We lay in silence for several moments until Azucena cleared

her throat. "Rurac?"

"Hm?" I didn't move my gaze from where it rested on the twinkling night lights.

"Do you think the stars are watching over us? Like the legends say?"

I swallowed, my irises caressing the path of the great deer of the sky, who watched over the Incas during the fall harvest. "I'm not sure."

"Me either." Her answer was quiet, barely a squeak. "I mean, I suppose I had always hoped . . . but this whole situation has made me think differently."

My lips twisted. With the revelation that Azucena really was the empress of Sipan, it seemed as if the stars really had abandoned us. Who had taken her away from her palace, and why? And why hadn't the stars helped rescue her as the legends alluded? The questions and fears danced through my mind. "We will figure it out, Azucena, I promise." I moved my hand down from behind my head unthinkingly, reaching out to brush my finger down her arm lightly. She shivered. "Are you cold?"

"It's—It's not that."

I turned my head to look at her. "What is it then?"

She made a funny face, and I could tell what she was about to say to me wasn't the answer to my question before the words even left her lips. "Call me Zu."

"Zu?"

She nodded. "It's the nickname I prefer, although I only let those close to me use it. Azucena is too formal."

I turned both words around in my mind. "I kind of like Azucena." She opened her mouth to argue, but before she could I rolled onto my side, propping myself up on one elbow and said, "But I prefer 'empress' above all else."

She blushed. "You can call me empress."

"Excellent, Empress," I joked. She smiled but was careful to keep her eyes on the sky, even though I was now facing her.

"Who do you think kidnapped you? Since you really are the

empress?"

Azucena frowned, and I could practically see the wheels turning in her mind. "I'm not sure, and that's what scares me about this whole thing. What if we are walking into some sort of trap?"

I leaned back, returning to the position on my back. "That's a good point. I didn't think of that."

"That's why I'm empress, I guess." She nudged me with her elbow, the smile back on her lips. "I think of all the tactical things."

"Well, Empress—Zu," I amended. "I'll protect you if it is a trap. Don't worry."

"Thanks, Rurac," she replied, her eyes now closed. "It means a lot to me."

I felt pressure in my chest, and I moved my hand to my heart, wondering what this feeling was. Once it abated, I turned to deliver my reply only to find Azucena's chest rising and falling with deep and even breaths. She was asleep.

Leaning down to pull the blanket up higher, I tucked it around her, and for some reason I still wasn't quite sure about, I leaned down and kissed her lightly on the nose, whispering, "Goodnight, Empress," before closing my own eyes, and allowing sleep to carry me away.

WHEN I CRACKED open my eyes next, the glare of Inti was shining right through them, and I groaned in response, moving to lift my arm to cover them, only to find my arm plastered to the ground due to something heavy resting on it.

I opened my eyes fully to find Azucena snuggled into my side, her face tucked into my chest.

With a happy sigh I pulled her closer and closed my eyelids, intending to fall back asleep, only to feel small hands pushing at my side.

"Rurac."

"Yes, Empress?"

"You're holding me in your sleep again."

I rolled my eyes before realizing they were closed, and she couldn't see them, so I used my words instead. "That's where you are wrong, Empress. You choose to come cozy up with me in your sleep."

"Nuh uh," she disagreed.

I opened one eye, immediately becoming enthralled by her dark brown ones as she gazed down at me. "Yeah huh, Empress. Look at the evidence." I motioned to how we were lying. "I am still lying on my back—how I fell asleep. You are the one who moved closer in your sleep and chose to lie on my arm."

She shook her head, sitting up and scooting away. "No way. Just admit it, you want to sleep close to me."

I sat up as well, shifting the blankets once again to hide my morning hard-on. "Not until you admit it first."

"Psh," she scoffed. "I could go to the marriage market tomorrow and find a herd of men wanting to marry me. It's you who wants to sleep close to me."

Although she meant it as an insult, I knew her too well by now to take it as one, a small smile infiltrating my lips. "You're thirty solar-paths, why haven't you gone to the marriage market?"

Her face immediately colored a deep red, and she looked away. "Tell me," I urged.

She groaned. "Fine. As empress, they bring the most eligible men of the proper class to me to evaluate regularly . . . I just haven't had much interest, I'm afraid. Not more than for one night anyway."

"Ah." My voice caught a little as I searched for an appropriate reply, embarrassed at my own lack of experience in the marriage market. "Must be nice for the marriage market to come to you."

She shrugged. "I suppose. I feel bad sending them all away though." She stood and began rolling up her blanket while I moved to begin dismantling the shelter. "What about you? You're about thirty solar-paths as well, right?"

It was my turn to be embarrassed. "More or less. I'm not exactly sure, as my father wasn't the best with tracking solar-paths. It was something my mother had always done for him, so when she died he . . . uh . . . lost count. But based on the calculations I made when I was old enough to track the stars, I believe I am about thirty solar-paths as well."

She glanced over at me briefly before returning to her task. "And what about you? Any marriage market visits for you?"

Although she had felt shame when I had asked her the same questions, it didn't affect me in the same way, and I simply shrugged. "Never felt the need to. After my father died . . . I basically turned my focus to surviving and it didn't seem fair to bring someone else into my precarious situation."

"Oh."

I immediately felt bad about my answer and wasn't sure why. "Maybe I will go someday."

"Maybe," she replied as I tucked the last of our things in my pack and handed her a piece of jerky.

"We need to eat and walk, Empress; we are behind schedule." I motioned to Inti, already quite high in the sky, and she nodded and fell into step next to me as we both took small nibbles of our jerky.

"What would you"—she took another bite—"look for at the marriage market?"

"What do you mean?" I asked as I steered us toward the path. We were almost down the hill, which was good as there would be no more landslides, but it also meant the long part of our journey was just beginning as we crossed the sacred valley and then had to climb back up the rocks that blocked access to the other side.

"In a woman, I mean. At the marriage market." Her words were steady but unsure.

I thought for a moment before replying. I had never been asked that, but now that I was thinking about it, I realized three things simultaneously. One, I had never had the urge to go to the marriage market, because the woman currently walking next to me was the only one to catch my attention, well, ever. Two, if I had to describe what I was looking for, there was no way I could stomach lying to her—I would have to describe her. And three, if I described her, and she laughed at me, or told me I was an idiot for feeling that way about her, my heart would never survive. I wouldn't be able to bear the thought of her not feeling the same way.

So, I did the only reasonable thing in this sort of situation and I looked out of the corner of my eye, searching desperately for a distraction. Anything to help me escape answering the incredibly awkward question she had just asked. Luckily, I noticed a small creek on the other side of Azucena and a plan quickly formulated in my mind.

In motions that were certainly exaggerated, I pretended to trip on a rock and fall in Azucena's direction. As any reasonable person would, she raised her hands to attempt to stop my fall, but I was just too large, and I knocked us both into the small creek, and then we were both falling. During the fall, I was careful to put my hands out to the side to catch the bulk of my weight, to prevent it from landing on her, as she elicited perhaps the cutest squeal I had ever heard.

"Ack! Rurac!" She pushed me off her and I quickly rose to a standing position, holding my hand out to help her.

"Sorry about that," I apologized as I helped her back onto the path.

"Ugh," she groaned as she tried to brush herself off. "Now I'm all wet."

I motioned to Inti. "You'll dry on the walk, especially if we stay out of the cover of the trees."

"I suppose you're right." She glanced around, ensuring she hadn't dropped anything during the fall. "Well, I don't want to get further behind, so we better get going."

With that, we resumed our walk, with her just behind me as

we continued our downward trod. After a few steps, I noticed she was shivering.

"Are you cold?" I asked her, immediately wanting to smack myself for asking such a dumb question.

"What do you think?" she snapped, keeping her gaze away from mine.

Dread sliced through me. What if she got sick and died, right here, on the road? Then I would really be in trouble when we arrived at the palace. I absolutely needed her alive.

Without thinking, I grabbed her arm, effectively stopping her gait, before pulling her to my chest and wrapping my arms around her back, rubbing up and down. "I'm sorry," I whispered into her hair.

"It's o-okay," she chattered.

We stayed like that for a while, me just holding her and rubbing her back. Something about it seemed so . . . right, even though I knew it wasn't proper, at all.

"Rurac?" she whispered at last.

I pulled back a bit, so I could look at her face, only to find we were much closer than I intended. Zu was taller than most women, and with the way my head was angled down, our lips were so close they were almost touching.

I couldn't explain it, but it was as if the motion of Hana Pacha stopped at that moment. Even the gods seemed to hold their breaths with our faces in such close proximity.

Without thinking, my eyes darted from her brown irises to her lips. I felt a weird sense of satisfaction when I saw her gaze drift in the same direction. Our breaths were intermingling, but we both were practically statues, unable to make the first move. Then, as if drawn together by the gods themselves because they were tired of waiting for us, our faces drifted together until our lips were touching.

Her lips were soft, and from the moment mine touched hers, I never wanted to pull away. In fact, I gripped her tighter, holding her body to mine as our lips moved in sync.

I don't know how long we kissed for, but all too soon I felt pressure on my chest as she attempted to push me away.

I immediately dropped my hands and took a step back. "I'm . . . sorry, again. I . . . should have asked." The words tumbled out before I could think, my lips still tingling from the contact with hers.

"Don't worry about it." Her breaths were heavy as she caught her breath, and I was glad to see she was affected the same way I had been. "I enjoyed it. But it can't happen again."

"Of course." My heart ached as I agreed. I already wanted to kiss her again. "It won't happen again."

"It was a mistake," she added as she enclosed her bottom lip between her white teeth and kept her eyes trained on the ground. "A momentary lapse of judgement." Her neck and cheeks held a slight pink flush which I wanted to ask about but didn't

I couldn't tell if her rationalizing was for herself, or for the both of us, so I quickly agreed again. "Momentary lapse of judgement." I motioned forward, trying to calm my own racing heart which I was pretty sure she could hear. "If you're warm enough, we should continue."

"Yes, I think I will be fine. Thanks." She avoided my gaze as we began our walk, ensuring that there was at least a hand's-worth of distance between us as we walked. I don't know why, but I wanted to reach out and touch her so badly. No matter what I had once thought, there was definitely something brewing between us. And it was irresistible.

If she felt the same, she gave no indication as we walked along the edge of the trees to allow Azucena's clothes to dry fully—something I still felt bad about. It had been childish to push her into the water to avoid answering a question, even if I wasn't ready for her to know how I felt about her.

We marched for what felt like forever, and didn't see any towns, which was a bit surprising to me given the presence of the creek. But at the same time, I knew we would likely pass through some in the valley, and based on last night's revelations, I wasn't necessarily sure it was a good thing. Especially if people were really out to get Azucena.

At some point during the sun-cycle, once our clothes had dried, I shifted our path so we could be beneath the shade of the trees. The further we descended down the hill, the warmer the air grew, which reminded me of the stories my father had told me as a young boy, about the valleys of eternal summer, where they didn't really have a winter. But when I had commented on how good that sounded, my father had cautioned me, saying something . . . *but what was it?*

I grimaced as I realized for the first time that I was beginning to forget some of the things my father had said.

"What are you thinking about?" Azucena's voice cut through my thoughts and I peered over to find her looking up at me through her dark eyelashes.

"Nothing. Just a Quipu my father had told me as a boy."

"Oooo, what Quipu?"

I struggled to remember how the story had ended, the words evading me. "Something about living in the shadow of the mountain in the valley of eternal summer."

"Ah." She nodded. "I know that one well."

Now it was my turn to be shocked. I turned to her, mouth agape. "You do?"

"Yeah." She smiled. "It was something like this: *In the valley, lies the land of everlasting summer. But be wary, as living in the shadow of the mountain can be a danger too.*"

The words snapped into my memory, making it whole again. "That's it!" I mulled over the words for a moment. "But what do you think it means?"

Azucena didn't even hesitate when she answered. "It means that living in the valleys in Sipan can be a beautiful thing, as it's always warm. But being at the bottom of a mountain brings the chance of death—falling rocks, flash floods. You can't get too caught up in the beauty or you'll ignore the dangers."

Her words hit me right in the center of my chest and I

couldn't help but feel like they applied to our current situation as well. Azucena was definitely the most beautiful woman I had ever come across . . . which meant she had the potential to hurt me if I got too caught up in her. Swallowing the revelation, I tried to change the subject. "Wow. How did you know all that?"

"Part of my education as a young girl—besides the ways of trade—was in the old teachings, and Quipus. In case anyone ever had questions, they were to come and ask me. It was something my parents stressed over and over."

I loved the way her face lit up as she discussed her parents and briefly wondered if mine did the same when I spoke of my father. Azucena gazed up at me from under her eyelashes, waiting for a response, I nodded. "Oh. That's interesting." That brought to the surface another memory, which was suddenly on the tip of my tongue, bursting to be shared. "Do you know the Quipu about the boy and the puma?"

She nodded enthusiastically. "That's a popular one. It's a hidden lesson often told to children as they age."

"Wait." I ran my hand through my hair. I couldn't believe after all these solar-paths I was about to solve my father's unfinished Quipu. "How does it end? Before you tell me the lesson."

She raised her eyebrows but didn't laugh or shame me for not knowing. "How much do you know?"

The image of the Quipu at home came to mind and I ran my mind over the mental knots. "The puma was killed by the villagers, and the boy was sad and went to bed."

"Ah yes. You did make it almost to the end. There isn't much after that."

"What? How? How can it end like that?" I was aghast, and a bit upset I had spent my childhood hoping for something more when that was it.

She shrugged. "That's the lesson. After the boy goes to sleep sad, he wakes the next sun-cycle to find that life doesn't have meaning anymore, so he volunteers to be sacrificed so he can go live in Hana Pacha with the gods."

It was my turn to gasp. Although it was common for tributes to volunteer, I couldn't believe that this was the lesson my father had wanted me to know. "But how is that a lesson?"

Her lips pressed together in an odd pattern, as if she was trying to decide exactly how to word it. "Basically, the boy's purpose in life was to hunt the puma. When he was done, his purpose was done—"

I stopped and turned to her, my eyes wide, but before I could speak, she stopped my lips with one finger which immediately sent a jolt to my lower half. "The lesson is that life is about the journey, not the final destination. If you spend your whole life seeking a destination, you will be very disappointed when you get there. But if you enjoy the journey, just as the boy loved hunting for that puma, then you will be happy and feel alive."

"Oh." I willed my blood to slow as she stepped away. Now wasn't the time for that.

Satisfied, she started walking again. "It's one of the most powerful Quipus out there. And one of the most misunderstood."

"I see why," I said. "What's your plan when we get to the palace anyway?" I know I should have asked sooner, but I was just now realizing that we really were going to make it.

She shrugged. "I kind of thought I would just walk in and be like 'I'm back' and then people would bow and everything would be back to normal."

I burst out laughing, but when she stopped in her tracks to cross her arms and stare me down, I realized she was serious. I fought to control my laughter, while also trying to keep my eyes from her lips—which I couldn't deny I felt drawn to. "Sorry, I thought you were kidding."

"I wasn't," she snapped.

"I see that. Well, shouldn't you have a backup plan in case that's not how things go down?" I suggested as I moved closer to her.

She tapped her finger on her chin. "As much as I hate to admit it, you're probably right. I'll think about a way to sneak in if things go wrong."

I sensed she was unhappy, so I didn't prod any further. We walked in silence for a bit, and as Inti began to sink to the horizon, I shielded my eyes to look for a place to camp for the night.

The creek we had been walking next to had grown to become a wide and shallow, slow-moving river. The water at the edges was far enough away from the current that there were small pools with occasional glimpses of fish. I figured it would be nice to spend the night sleeping next to it, and that maybe I could try to catch a few to restock our rations. Once I chose the spot, next to a particularly refreshing pool, we began our routine.

It wasn't until I returned that I realized something was wrong. Zu was standing by the edge of the water, unmoving.

I quickened my pace. "Empress?" I called.

She didn't move. As I came closer, I could see her eyes were open and trained on the water—her reflection looking at me through the water.

"Rurac?"

"Are you okay—"

"Why did you push me into the creek earlier?"

Her words stopped the blood in my veins. I set the firewood down.

"I tripped."

"That's a lie." Her voice was cold.

"No, really—"

"Try again," she snapped, still not looking directly at me.

I sighed. "Fine, I was avoiding your question."

"I knew it!" she shouted as she spun around to face me. What happened next happened so fast I couldn't have stopped it even if I wanted to. She reached out and grabbed both my arms, pulling back to ultimately pull both of us beneath the reflective surface of the water.

Eighteen

AZUCENA

The look on Rurac's face as I pulled him into the water was something that would be etched in my memory for the rest of my life. It was a mixture of shock, sprinkled with defeat, though his lips quirked up at the ends—telling me that he knew, and that we were now even.

As my head dropped beneath the water, I closed my eyes, relishing the feeling of being enveloped by the water. I felt truly weightless, connected to the Pacha Mama, and free. When I finally lifted my head, there was a wide smile across my lips, and Rurac, though he looked a bit like a drowned dog, his curly hair hanging in straight, wet strands, has a smile plastered on his face too.

Better yet, he was chuckling.

"You got me there," he announced once he had caught his breath. "I pushed you in the water to avoid answering your question about the marriage market."

"Why?" I tilted my head to the side as I asked the question, the memory of our kiss at the front of my mind, though I had already assumed the answer.

He sighed, running his calloused hand through his hair, his face scrunched as he appeared to be internally debating with himself. It was silent for a moment before he sighed again and said, "Because, Azucena, you're the only woman who has ever caught my eye. I would have had to describe you."

"I knew it!" I shouted as I stood up. Of course, leave it to me to unceremoniously slip at the exact same moment, causing me to fall on top of Rurac, my hands catching my weight on his chest. "Uhh . . . er . . ."

Rurac looked just as surprised, his eyes flickering down to my lips.

I found myself at a crossroads. On one hand, I truly had enjoyed our kiss earlier, and it had been a while since I had been able to summon a man to my chambers to care for some of my sexual needs.

But on the other hand, I knew that if I gave in to my urge to kiss him, this could accelerate to something more, and fast. Once I started kissing him, I knew I wouldn't want to stop.

What's the big deal? My subconscious reminded me. *It's just sex. It's not like you're engaging in a trial marriage with him.*

My subconscious had a point. Sex was just, well, sex. It's not like I would be tied to him for the rest of my life after a bit of fun. Besides, it had been a long time, and I could just tell him it would only be a one-time thing.

If Rurac noticed my internal debate, he said nothing, his eyes searching my face for something I couldn't quite place.

Unsure what to say—how to bridge this tension sizzling between us—I did the only thing that came to mind, which of course was thanks to Rurac's glance. I leaned in to press my lips to his. *One more kiss wouldn't hurt*, I promised myself.

For a moment, it was like kissing a statue, his mouth frozen beneath mine, but once he realized what was happening and came alive, his lips began to devour mine as his arms came up to grab my upper arms.

Though we were both well into our adult solar-paths, and both knew that this was probably a bad idea, I couldn't deny the sparks that flew between us and I leaned into him even more, my legs settling on either side of his beneath the surface of the shallow water.

He groaned as I shifted, his hands sliding lower to push me down onto his lap, where I could feel him, hard, at the apex of my thighs.

Were we really going to do this?

The thought drifted through my mind about the same time as it must have drifted through Rurac's, because he pulled back from the kiss, panting. "Is this okay?" His voice was gruff.

Panting as well, it was all I could do to nod my head and gasp. "More than okay."

He needed no more encouragement, quickly reaching for the hem of my dress and pulling it over my head to toss it onto the sandy shore. Once I was mostly bare, other than the white slip I had worn under my dress, I shivered, my body still mostly submerged in the chilly water of the river.

Realizing the problem, Rurac hooked his arms under my bottom before standing and walking back to the blanket he had rolled out, setting me delicately on top. Once I was out of his arms, he made quick work of his own shirt between kisses, leaving me in my slip and him in only his pants.

My eyes roved over his chest, impressed by the amount of muscle there. Though I'd had suitors at the palace—some of which I had engaged in sexual relations with—none had looked quite like this. My gaze drifted lower.

"Don't you think we should let all of our clothes dry?" I asked, pushing away my conscience, which was telling me that we shouldn't do this. I would deal with the fallout later.

He swallowed. "If that's what you think is best . . ."

I nodded in affirmation, watching as he backed up and pulled down his pants, leaving him fully naked.

"Like what you see?" he prodded.

I nodded. "Very much so." My voice was barely above a whisper, and before I could say it a second time, louder, for his benefit, he was relieving me of my slip, his lips kissing down my neck and enclosing over one of my nipples.

I moaned.

"I like what I see too," he murmured before kissing down my abdomen. Once he reached my waistline, he paused and lifted his head, pressing another heated kiss to my already swollen lips.

As our lips interlocked and our tongues danced, I ran my hand down the hard planes of his chest until I reached his member, wrapping my hand around it.

He jolted as I began moving my hand up and down, a noise coming from his lips.

"That's . . . perfect." He moaned, his eyes rolling back in his head slightly before seeming to jolt back into the present, one of his hands moving from where it rested on my hip to the ache between my legs as his lips found mine once more.

He was very gentle, slipping one finger inside me before pausing and lifting an eyebrow at me in an obvious question. I nodded my encouragement, unable to vocalize how much I was enjoying it. It had been too long since my last sexual encounter and the fire between us was undeniable.

I pumped him a bit longer until he pushed my hand away. "Let's get you ready for me." He nearly growled as he kissed down my neck a second time, continuing his trail down my chest and stomach. Then he was licking me, his lips enclosing over my clit in a way that felt positively divine.

It was my turn to moan.

He continued his ministrations, using his calloused hands to hold my hips in place as I began to squirm. Just as I started to draw close to my peak, his mouth stopped, and he crawled back up my body to kiss me again. "You taste so good," he whispered between kisses. "Better than I dreamed."

"You dreamed about me?" I whispered back, my eyes wide.

"Not at first." He smiled sheepishly. "Just these past few sun-cycles. It's been so hard to wake up with you draped over me every morning and not dream of doing this." He kissed me passionately for a moment before pulling back. "Are you ready for me?"

I smiled, giving him a slight nod that was a bit shy, even for me. Transitioning my hands to his shoulders, I dug my nails in as he lined himself up and slid into me. Although I had engaged in sex before, something about Rurac felt so different . . . so magical. This whole thing felt like some sort of dream I was liable to wake from at any moment.

I didn't realize I had an odd look on my face until he was whispering in my ear, "Are you okay?"

"More than okay," I whispered back. He looked a bit skeptical, so to show him, I began to use my leverage on his shoulders to move myself up and down and his cock. On the third motion, he must've believed me, because he began thrusting his hips in time to my motions.

"Empress," he moaned. "You feel so good—better than anything I've ever felt."

The compliment would have made me blush, except all the blood in my body was busy elsewhere, so I could only moan in response as I wrapped my legs around his hips, allowing him to penetrate even deeper.

One of his hands came up to grab my breast, lightly rubbing my nipple with his thumb.

My legs started to shake, indicating that I was once again near my peak.

"That's it," Rurac moaned. "That's my beautiful empress."

The words were enough to send me careening over the edge of my climax, my inner muscles gripping him as I saw stars behind my eyelids. I turned my head to the side, my breaths coming in gasps as I came down from the peak.

So focused on my own orgasm, it wasn't until I'd recovered that I realized Rurac was also shaking and had stopped his thrusts.

Before I could say anything, or give him any direction, he pulled out, thrusting in his hand twice before ejaculating on the ground. Once his orgasm was done, he collapsed next to me on the blanket, panting.

"That was—"

"Unexpected," I finished for him, still feeling a bit shy about what we had just done. Had I really just had sex with the man who had been keeping me prisoner for half a moon cycle? I sucked my lower lip into my mouth, wondering where we went from here. At the palace, everything was so much simpler. Nania would show him the way out of my room, help me clean up, and I wouldn't have to see him again if I didn't want to—and I never did.

But here . . . I couldn't deny that something was different with Rurac. But I couldn't put my finger on what. I shook my head, trying to clear away my indecisive thinking. He was just a peasant. And after this was all over, we would need to go our separate ways.

"I've . . . liked you for a long time, by the way."

His words pulled me from my reverie and I turned my neck so I was looking at his profile as he lay on his back, next to me. "Hmm?" I hummed, confused.

He sighed, running a hand through his still-dripping hair. "Since you bit me, actually. I thought you were the most beautiful, albeit also the most annoying, woman I ever met. And when you asked me to be your friend, I said we had to remain enemies because I was already falling for you, and I didn't want to. Nor did I want to admit it."

The sentence warmed my heart but also made me feel exposed as I didn't really know what to say in response as my own feelings were confusing. Instead of confronting what he said, I took the fools way out and changed the subject. "Where did you . . . uhhh . . ."

"Learn about sex?" He didn't seem surprised, nor embarrassed by the question. "I know usually only nobles are allowed sex teachers, but my dad insisted I learn a thing or two once I was of age . . ." He trailed off, likely thinking back to his early, sexually active solar-paths. Then he turned his head toward me, so that I was staring into his dark eyes. "What about you?"

I blushed. "I had several teachers."

"I figured." He snorted. "No shortage of spices to trade there."

Silence settled between us as we both ran out of things to say. Instead, I searched the depths of his gaze, my thoughts running rampant on how things would go tomorrow. How we would bridge this awkwardness.

I started to rifle through the tangled loom that was my feelings.

I liked Rurac, and I had thoroughly enjoyed being with him. But this was a momentary lapse of judgment, and we needed to stop. There was no way there could ever be a future for us, not even sexually. I pictured myself trying to tell Yezema and even Nania about why there was a brute of a peasant in the palace and . . . it wasn't pretty.

"What are you thinking?" he asked, his voice suddenly serious.

I stared at the space above his head, checking his aura before answering. "We shouldn't have done that." It came out as a whisper, but his response was immediate. He shot up to a sitting position, turning to face me. "I don't regret it," I added quickly. "But that was a bad idea."

"Why do you say that?" His lips settled into a frown.

I sat up as well, so that we were once again at the same level. Not knowing how else to say it I blurted, "Because we can't be together, Rurac."

"And why the Mictlan not?"

My eyes widened at his angry tone, which stroked my ego. "Because...Rurac." I took a deep breath and pinched my nose. I didn't want to say what I was about to, but I knew that I had to. "I'm the empress. I'm not allowed to have relationships—even just sexual ones—out of class. You know that."

After the words slipped out, I knew immediately I had made a mistake, as hurt clouded his features and he ran a shaking hand through his hair. "No, I didn't know that. But you're the empress, can't you just change the rules?"

I shook my head, an odd sensation tugging in my chest, but I couldn't figure out what. "That's not what the gods would want."

Rurac shrugged, his frown deepening. "I think they would want us to be happy."

I crossed my arms over my chest. I knew the gods way better than he did, but that didn't make this any easier. "I don't think so, Rurac."

"No . . . NO!" He stood, crossing his arms over his chest. "If you don't want me that's fine. But don't feed me any bullshit about the appeasing the gods. Fine—we won't do this again. But it's because of you, not the gods. And I refuse to regret what we already did."

Without waiting for me to respond he turned and stalked out into the trees, the darkness, which I hadn't noticed, closing behind his back.

Something about the view of him so angry that he left our camp without putting on clothes, made it feel like there was some sort of chasm in my chest. I tried to brush away the pain, but it didn't want to leave.

Suddenly feeling cold, I pulled the edges of the blanket around my shoulders, feeling like I had made a terrible mistake.

Nineteen

RURAC

My feet crushed leaves as I stomped through the trees. Although it was well past sunset, and too dark for me to be moving at this speed through such oppressive obstacles, I didn't slow my pace.

I wasn't mad at her. I was mad at myself for taking a chance on something that was apparently just in my mind.

I had thought when we engaged in sex, it would be easier to tell her the secret I had been carrying the past few sun-cycles.

It was more than just liking her. I was irrevocably in love with Azucena.

But instead of getting to confess what was weighing heavily on my chest and heart, she suggested that we keep our distance. That this was the end of the road for us.

Great. Just fucking great.

I continued my stomping, not really sure where I was going, but knowing I needed to blow off some of my emotions before returning to the camp, otherwise I'd break down in front of her and tell her everything. Something that, based on her revelation, would make things even more embarrassing for me than they already were.

I was so distracted by my thoughts that it wasn't until my

nose twitched at the scent of smoke and roasting meat that I took a moment to pause and actually take in my surroundings.

In my anger, I had journeyed farther than intended from our camp, and the trees in front of me had begun to thin. Feeling a shiver crawl down my spine, I moved rapidly, pressing myself behind a tree. Not that it would actually obscure me if anyone was searching, but I felt safer evaluating my surroundings at least partially concealed.

Surveying the forest around me, several things stood out all at once. There were marred tree stumps, which looked to have been cut down and marked with tools. A sort of bush that usually bears berries this time of the solar-path was barren. And worst of all, there were deep sandal prints in the mud, meaning a heavy body made them.

Someone, or several people who weren't Azucena and I, were traversing this forest.

Under normal circumstances, I wouldn't worry. But with cart travel gaining popularity, the presence of a lot of footprints scared me. There were too many for it to be a spice merchant or someone going to visit a family member.

Continuing my investigation, I peered out from behind my current tree, only to dart to around another once I was sure the coast was clear. I repeated the pattern several times, moving gradually toward the smell of smoke.

The trees thinned further as I progressed, making it even more of a challenge to keep my broad shoulders hidden. And soon, I saw the tell-tale signs of colorful blankets built into shelters up ahead, the lighter colors visible thanks to the moonlight that was now seeping through the spread trees.

Luckily, it was at least dark enough that I was able to crawl my way closer until I was pressed against a tree just outside of their circle of shelters. A fire roared in the middle with several men seated around it. For a moment, my mind flashed back to Azucena, and I winced as I realized I didn't make her a fire before my tantrum. But before I could follow that thought, further increasing my guilt, words tickled my ears.

"Boss says we need to pick up the pace tomorrow. This is taking longer than she anticipated."

I raised my eyebrows at the word "boss" and began counting the shelters while keeping my ear on their conversation. They were speaking my native tongue, meaning they were certainly from Sipan and not enemy tribesmen.

"Yes, sir."

"We need a sacrifice for Capacocha, and soon. Boss says the gods are unhappy, that's why the bridge collapsed."

A third man entered the circle, stirring the fire. "What I can't figure out is why we have to go so far to get this girl. Didn't the Mama-Kuna have one?"

"Yezema says this girl has been chosen for over twenty solar-paths."

The word "Mama-Kuna" sounded strange on his tongue. Though I had grown up away from the majority of the villages, I recognized the name of the home where women chosen by the gods were taken as young girls. Some of the girls from my village had gone there over the solar-paths, though I had stopped hearing about it once I passed my fifteenth solar-path, as the girls were then considered to be too old to be of worth to the gods. So why were they talking about a woman of twenty sun-paths?

"If she's been chosen for so many sun-paths, why isn't she already at the Mama-Kuna?"

I peered out from behind the tree just in time to see the man with the first voice shrug. "I dunno, I just do what the boss says; I don't ask questions. She was apparently trying to disobey the gods and was taken to a special handler on the hill last moon cycle—to keep her subdued until it was time."

My eyes widened and I quickly began counting how long Azucena has been in my care.

The second man shook his head. "Well, if she was supposed to be sacrificed before the end of harvest, the gods better help us get up this hill, because at this rate we won't make it in time."

The words caused my heart to drop into my stomach, my breath stuttering to a stop. Images flashed through my mind of these men dragging Azucena from our camp, making my vision turn red, anger bubbling in my veins as pain slashed through my chest.

No. I couldn't let them take her. If they hurt her, in any way, I would never forgive myself.

Without stopping to evaluate my runaway thoughts, their words wove together in my mind. Despite the age not lining up, I suddenly knew, without a doubt, who these men are looking for.

Azucena.

As silently as possible, I retraced my steps, going from tree to tree, and using the heel of my foot to smudge my footprints as best as possible. It wasn't a foolproof method, as I couldn't eliminate all of mine without also smudging the men's footprints, and that would give me away just as much as my own footprints.

The further I slithered from the circle of shelters, the more difficult it was to see. While I had left our camp just after Inti left the sky, it was the dead of night now, and the thickening trees obscured Quilla. Despite my difficulties, I finally made it through to our camp, only to see Azucena sitting in the dirt by the abandoned pile of firewood, attempting to rub two sticks together in order to light it.

"Don't!" I hissed, rushing forward to grab the sticks from her hands.

"Why?" she snapped, too loud for comfort. "I'm cold."

I put my hand over her mouth, and in true Azucena fashion, she bit down. But I didn't move my hand and pressed my lips together to quiet my own yell.

"Shh." I pulled her flush to my body, my large arms easily holding her in place as she started to struggle against me, obviously pissed about my man-handling her. But at this point, I didn't care—her safety was more important. "I came across several men in the forest," I whispered in her ear. "I think they are here for you. I'm going to let you go now, but don't scream or make any loud noises."

At my words, she fell still, recognizing the seriousness in my voice. I removed my hand from her mouth and continued as she turned around to face me, her gaze wide. "I'm not fully certain but they were headed in the direction we just came from, talking about a girl of over twenty sun-paths to be sacrificed for Capacocha."

"What did they look like?" she whispered back, her eyes darting around our makeshift camp, any sign of her earlier animosity evaporating.

"I didn't get a good look." I used my foot to quickly disperse the firewood from the nice pile she had made, beginning to roll up the blankets we had used for our earlier rendezvous. "I was hiding behind a tree, but there were more than ten of them, all young, well-dressed, wearing many bright colors. I think they were the emperor's men."

Azucena took my cue and began stooping to gather our other items around the camp. She cringed when she picked up our still-soaked clothing from our dip in the river. I handed her a blanket to roll them in as well as my spare shirt to wear over her shoulders. With her spare outfit out of commission, we had to share mine. I pulled on my spare pants.

She pulled on my shirt, still appearing as regal as ever. "Who were they with? Did they say who their leader was?"

I shook my head. "The only name I heard was Yezema."

She gasped and nearly dropped what she had gathered. "That was my trusted advisor. Are you sure they weren't coming to rescue me?"

Now it was my time to look surprised. "I don't think so. There was no mention of a rescue, just the pending sacrifice and complaints about the length of the journey."

She still seemed apprehensive, but she must've trusted what I was saying because she went back to gathering our things.

"Hopefully they didn't see me and we can get a good head start. I don't know how fast they will be able to make it to my house, but once they see we aren't there, coming back down the hill will go much faster than the way up," I continued.

She bit her lip, watching as I heaved the pack onto my back. Without thinking, I held out my hand.

Azucena peered at it like a snake that might bite.

"It's too dark, we need to move quickly and stay together. We can't do that if we get separated," I explained.

She tilted her head, indecisive for a moment before realizing I was right. She settled her smooth hand in mine, and before I could dwell on how her skin felt against mine, we were off, both of us trying our best to make as little noise as possible while also staying near the river to ensure we were heading in the right direction.

Both of us were tired, however, and our pace was much too slow to truly be comfortable. And, as the night wore on, we grew even slower, often stumbling over various obstacles on the path— rocks, branches, and in one case, a small animal, who was none too happy about having his midnight hunting disturbed.

"I don't know how much longer I can go on," Azucena whispered in my direction when the earliest rays of sun were beginning to peak over the horizon.

"We will stop at daybreak," I promised. "We just need to get as far as possible and hopefully find somewhere safe to camp so we can both sleep." I had originally planned to have us take shifts sleeping, but the way my own eyelids were drooping right along with Azucena's, I knew neither of us would be able to stay awake for long.

As the sky transformed from pink to orange, I finally found a small outcropping of rocks that we could camp in for a while. It was a bit away from the river, and a bit too close to the cliff's edge, but with the men following the same river as we were, it was safer to put a little distance between ourselves and the edge of the water. It wasn't the best place, but with Azucena half asleep on her feet, we didn't have a choice.

"Azucena." I pulled her arm lightly, pointing to the rocks. "Let's camp here."

She nodded, slumping over against one of the smaller rocks. I pulled her back up, leading her into the center of the outcropping before allowing her to sit again as I pulled out the two blankets we usually slept on, laying one on the ground and wrapping the other around my shoulders. Sitting with my back against the rock, I pulled Azucena toward me, tucking her under my arm, her head resting on my chest. She must be tired, because she doesn't even complain about the closeness.

"No shelter?" she mumbled.

I rested my head on her hair. "No, we need to be able to leave fast. A fire is too dangerous, too. Just stay close to me; I'll keep you warm."

"Okay," she replied, even quieter than before.

Some time passed, enough that I was pretty sure she was asleep until—

"Rurac?"

"Hm?" I answered.

"Thanks for not turning me in."

"You're welcome," I replied, not sure how to tell her that the thought hadn't even crossed my mind until that moment.

And, until she said that, I hadn't even stopped to consider how this stunt of not turning her in to whoever was currently in charge of these men would likely end my career. Forever.

Twenty

AZUCENA

leeping was rough—both physically and mentally. As empress, I had never had the experience of trying to sleep upright while leaning against a sharp rock. I had a nice, specially made, straw bed. The best of the best. Of course, I can't speak for Rurac, but he didn't seem any more comfortable than me. Throw in the fact that I was jolting awake at every small noise from the underbrush, and the bright light of Inti fighting against my body's natural urge to sleep, and you can imagine how bad it was.

Not to mention, my thoughts wouldn't leave me alone. I just couldn't believe it. I couldn't believe that Yezema had been the one to betray me—or someone in her employ. When Rurac had first said her name, I thought for sure he was mistaken, but at the same time, it suddenly made sense as to how I was kidnapped and removed from the palace without anyone noticing. While I had always been hesitant to trust Yezema, everyone else in the palace certainly did, and as my second in command, they wouldn't have even questioned her.

I just never thought that she would go to this extent to get what she wanted. While she always had been suspicious, I had never taken her for violent.

My mistake.

All too soon, Inti began to sink from the sky, and Rurac was pulling me to my feet, packing the few things we had unpacked and shoving a handful of food into my hands.

"I know this is bad timing," he whispered, "but we need to go into the next town and get some more provisions."

I nodded solemnly, my eyes seeking out the beautiful blankets sitting on top of his pack that I knew we would be trading. I let that thought sit in my mind for a moment, before shaking it out and reaching up to remove my small but shimmering earrings from my ears, enclosing them in my fist before holding it out toward Rurac. "Here," I whispered.

Rurac placed his hand beneath mine, a gasp escaping his lips as he took in the glinting gold earrings. "But—"

I shook my head. "Just take them. Before I change my mind."

He nodded and tucked them into his pocket, the one that had once held the key to my chains, before peering around the boulder. "Let's move quickly, into the cover of the trees."

Once I agreed, we were off, making our way carefully over branches and rocks as we darted from the boulders into the lengthening shadows of the tree boughs. The moment we were there, I let out a breath, though my shoulders were still practically at my ears.

We walked in silence for a bit, my mind going over the conversation we'd had the night before . . . before everything had gone awry. I cringed at how I had spoken to Rurac. Though I had meant what I said—that there could never be anything between us—I could have said it more tactfully.

Never one to allow problems to worsen, I cleared my throat, intending to say something to address the awkwardness between us, but Rurac stopped me by gripping my arm with his large hand. When my gaze met his, he moved his head from side to side. "Too risky."

He was right. I didn't want to admit it, but now wasn't the

time to discuss what had occurred, as much as it bothered me to let it fester between us.

Just as the sky was transforming into shades of purple and blue, we came across a village—a small spattering of stone huts built directly into the hill. The stone streets were nearly empty, as it was quite late, but we weaved our way through regardless, hopeful that someone was still around to trade.

"I've never been to this village before," Rurac hissed. "I'm going to knock on one of the doors and see if they know of anyone willing to trade this late in the sun-cycle."

I dipped my chin, having no argument about his plan.

No one answered at the first wooden door we came upon, even when Rurac knocked twice, waiting a reasonable amount of time in between. While we waited, I shifted my weight from foot to foot, glancing around the area.

The hut was small, most likely belonging to a couple or a small family. There were small symbols carved into the walls, and while they made me feel like I should remember them, I couldn't quite place where I had seen them before.

"All right, let's try another one." Rurac put his hand behind my shoulders, leading me further down the street. I didn't say anything, relishing in the comforting way his hand rested on my back—even if he hadn't intended for it to be comforting to me. Though I did notice he didn't seem to be in a hurry to lower it either.

The next house we tried was also empty, or at least no one came to the door. Again, Rurac knocked twice and waited patiently as my eyes perused the décor, or the lack of it. Just like the first hut, this one also had delicate swirls and other small drawings surrounding the door. Still struggling to remember where I had seen them before, I scrunched my eyebrows when Rurac pulled me toward a third hut, just a short distance down the street.

This time, after he knocked, we heard shuffling inside. Someone was coming to answer the door.

The woman who pulled open the door was thin, with dark hair, her wrists lined with bracelets—an odd sight for a peasant. She smiled widely at the sight of Rurac, her scrutiny nearly passing me entirely.

"Hello."

"Hello." Rurac returned the greeting. "We're sorry to bother you, but we are just passing through and are looking to trade for some provisions. We know it is late, but we were hoping you would know someone willing."

Her dark eyes scanned Rurac up and down, and an unknown emotion bubbled in my gut, making me feel a bit like I might be sick. I gripped Rurac's arm with one hand, the other going to my stomach as I watched the space above her head. It was green, but the unease in my stomach refused to dissipate.

Rurac's eyes flashed to mine, concern filling their depths, which, as a result, brought the woman's gaze to me as well.

The moment they settled on mine, they widened, and I knew she recognized me.

I dropped my hand from my stomach, standing up straighter as I expected her to offer a greeting fitting of the empress, but she did no such thing. Instead, her face scrunched in an odd manner and she turned back to Rurac.

That was weird. I had always been told my people loved me, and in the last village, the children had been so eager to spend time with me. Why wasn't this woman?

As she gave directions to Rurac for someone, a neighbor, who would possibly want to trade, I tried desperately to figure out what I was missing here. What were the signs adorning each doorway? And why had this woman greeted me like Yeze—

It hit me like a gold brick.

Without waiting for them to finish, I grabbed Rurac's hand in mine, squeezing hard.

"Ow!" he said, turning to look at me, angry at the interruption. "What was—"

"We need to leave, now," I hissed. "I'm sick," I lied, just in case the woman was listening.

Rurac didn't even argue, he just nodded, telling the woman goodbye before she slammed the door in our faces. But I was already running, dragging Rurac by the hand as fast as my feet could carry me.

"What . . . was . . . that?" he asked between pants, struggling to keep up with my pace.

"The symbols around every door," I sputtered between breaths. "I knew where I had seen them before. My advisor, the one who's name you heard yesterday, she wore bracelets with the same symbol." We turned a corner, nearly running over a small boy. I apologized quickly but didn't slow my pace. "That, combined with the fact that she didn't show me any respect when she recognized me, I made some quick deductions—we aren't welcome here."

He didn't say anything, but his pace did seem to increase, the only noise our loud breaths as we weaved our way through the thinning streets.

"We can't go much long without food," Rurac stated as we finally left the center of town, the path weaving through fields as we made our way down the slope of the hill.

"I know," I replied, my eyes scouring the fields on either side. I didn't want to steal, but if it meant stopping Yezema from taking over Saipan, I would do it. "How much is left?"

"Enough for something tonight and maybe something small tomorrow."

"It'll have to do." The fields began to thin until we were once again running through land that wasn't being cultivated. With a glance over his shoulder, Rurac stopped, placing his hands on his knees as he attempted to catch his breath.

"I haven't run that far in a long time."

"Me either." I panted next to him, my chest heaving just as rapidly as his.

Once he had caught his breath, he stood up, looking at the

small huts in the distance behind us. "They're going to tell the soldiers I saw that we were here."

"I know." I used my hand to brush the sweat from my forehead. "Let's keep moving at least, get as much distance as possible."

Rurac nodded, and we were off again, this time at a much more leisurely pace.

I decided it was time to bring up the incident. "I'm sorry, Rurac." His eyes connected with mine over his shoulder, his eyebrows drawing together. "I shouldn't have let things go so far between us," I elaborated. "Since I knew . . . we wouldn't be able to have a marriage under the gods anyway."

Rurac's lips were pursed together, and for a moment, he didn't say anything. Then he said, "What I don't understand is why. It seemed like you wanted me, just as much as I wanted you."

"I did." I wasn't going to lie to him. "I just didn't think about the consequences . . . until after, that is."

"I understand," he replied, though I could see the anguish clearly printed on his face, his aura a swirl of mixed colors. "Though I wish you would give us a chance, maybe we could—"

I cut him off, trying to find the best way to explain to him that I did like him, so much so that I found myself dreaming of a future for the two of us in his hut without my ruling of the empire. And seeing as I was chosen by the gods to rule Sipan, I knew for certain that it could never be—even though it pained me to admit it. I wanted him to be happy, even knowing it had to be without me, so I needed to put a stop to this now.

"No . . . I like you, Rurac. And because I like you, I know I shouldn't let you get your hopes up for something I am reasonably sure cannot be."

There was a pause, and I began to panic. Maybe he didn't feel the same way? Had I ruined everything by telling him my feelings?

But then he said, "I like you too, Azucena—Zu. And I wish you would just try."

I shook my head and sighed, but said nothing more as the colors above his head flickered from white to red.

Twenty-One

RURAC

The sound of rustling, mixed with voices, roused me from sleep. I yawned as I stretched, preparing to head out of the tent to create a diversion when I realized I recognized one of the voices.

"She said she saw them run this way. I'm sure of it."

"Yeah, well, where are their footprints?"

Luckily, or unluckily for us, the gods had sent rain the night before. While it had helped to cover our tracks, it also meant we hadn't made it nearly as far as I had wanted.

Trying to be as quiet as possible, I placed my hand over Zu's mouth. Her eyes immediately shot open, her teeth prepared to bite down on my hand. As soon as her dark eyes connected with mine, I held a finger to my lips and she relaxed enough for me to feel confident removing my hand from her lips.

"I see some broken branches in the underbrush."

At the sound of the voice, Zu let out a small gasp and then we both jumped into action simultaneously, rushing to pack everything and get rid of any signs of us having been here. It was taking too long, though—that much was immediately clear as the voices drew closer. In a panic I pushed her into a bush with our half-packed pack, using the heel of my foot to brush away out tracks as I backed away.

"Stay here," I hissed before running off into the trees, ensuring my footprints were visible. Within moments, their voices tickled my ears again.

"It looks like they camped here."

"And look—footprints!"

I paused, holding my breath, praying to the gods they would take the bait and wouldn't take the time to question why there was only one set and not two.

The gods were on my side today, though, as the sound of crunching underbrush reached my ears. They were on my trail.

Pumping my arms as hard as I could, I broke branches and ensured my footprints were clear as I slammed my feet into the ground. I maneuvered toward the brook where I had filled our waterskins the night before. Wading until my feet were barely covered, I fought to run up stream, the power of the water slowing my pace significantly as the sound of the men drew closer.

When I dared not test the gods favor any longer, I dashed from the creek into a bush on my tiptoes to make tracks that more closely resembled an animal than a human as I took shelter behind the large shrub. I crouched down, putting my hand over my own mouth to try and hide the sound of my labored breathing all while ignoring the incessant prickles from the pointed branches. Why did all the bushes have to be so sharp?

I heard the sound of the footfalls passing, but I remained in my hiding spot long until they had passed my location and the splashing of their boots in the water had faded, ensuring I wouldn't be leading them back to Azucena when I retraced my steps.

Once I was positive it was safe, I picked my way delicately and silently back through the forest to where I had left her. When I arrived at the bush I had pushed her behind, I moved the branches, a smile occupying my face . . .

Only the space behind it was empty.

Panic immediately rose in my chest and I became frantic, my heart beating painfully as sweat perspired on my brow. I opened my mouth to call her name but then realized that wasn't the best idea. Just as I was about to start tearing down the forest, tree by tree, Azucena appeared in front of me.

"Oh Inti," I gasped as I enveloped her in a hug, gripping her to my chest as the pain I felt from the possibility of losing her melted away.

"Rurac?" she asked, sounding a bit confused.

"I thought I lost you," I confessed. "You weren't behind the bush where I left you."

She leaned back in my grip, her brown irises boring into mine as she explained. "I had to move. They came too close. I crawled under the bushes—deeper into the trees."

I let out a breath, my eyes pinching shut on their own accord. "I'm just glad you're safe." I winced as I realized what we needed to do next. "But I'm afraid we can't keep going down the mountain."

She jerked out of my grip, frowning as she took a step back. "And why not?"

I ached with the desire to reach for her, to comfort her, but then remembered her words about how we couldn't be a match and forced my arms to remain at my sides. "They're headed that way now. We can't outrun them, especially with the few supplies we have left."

Her throat bobbed as she opened and closed her mouth silently and I could see her mind moving. "But there's no bridge —how—"

"I'm working on an idea." I reached for the pack which was slung on her back. "I brought some ropes and—"

"No," she interrupted me, shaking her head. "I am not climbing down on a rope."

I raised my eyebrows. "Are you afraid of heights?"

Her neck instantly colored red, telling me she, in fact, was. "No," she lied. "I just don't want to fall to my death, that's all."

"Well, the way I see it," I argued, "it's either risk falling to your death and possibly get to the palace, or risk getting caught and sacrificed to the gods. I'll let you pick."

She mulled over my proposition for a moment, obviously debating until I grabbed her arm and began leading her to the cliff. "Obviously we are going to risk you falling to your death, so come on."

"But . . ."

"Admit I'm right," I urged her as I guided us through the trees, ensuring we took a different path than the one I had baited the guards down earlier.

"Never," she hissed, her face downcast as she focused on stepping over rocks and the stream. We both moved slowly, taking the effort to keep our footfalls as light as possible so they didn't leave tracks in the mud.

"You know, letting someone else be right for once might not feel so bad," I suggested as I helped her over a rather large boulder. We were nearing the creek, and I knew the ledge wasn't far beyond that.

"I'm the empress; I'm never wrong." She tilted her face to the sky, tossing her dark curls over her shoulders. *Inti, she was beautiful.*

Focus, Rurac, I chastised myself. *Get her to the palace in one piece, then you can try to change her mind about being together.*

A smile played on my lips. It was too easy to rile her up. "Whatever you say, Empress."

Our bantering stopped when we reached the river and we both had to wade into water up our waists to make it across. Thanks to the rain the night before, the water was colder than usual, and I had to grit my teeth to stop them from rattling. Zu tried to do the same, but I could still hear a chatter from time to time. As we waded up the other bank I leaned down to whisper in her ear. "I think they are on this side, we should be very quiet and vigilant just in case."

She nodded her agreement, and we made our way through the

forest even more carefully than before, pausing to listen every so often for any signs that we were being followed. We took even more caution with our footprints, ensuring any marks we left were covered.

It was slow going, which was good in a way, as it gave me time to get myself mentally prepared for what was to come. Though I had brushed off Azucena's worries near where we had camped the night before, I was shaking in my own shoes at the thought of making our way down the cliff with the rope. Then, there was the question of how we would climb back out of the valley on the other side. But I knew we didn't have any other options. We needed to throw these men off our trail and fast, otherwise we would be left with no options.

As the edge approached, I mentally practiced what I would say to Azucena as we repelled down, trying to be convincing. All too soon, my time to scheme ran out and we found ourselves peering over the edge of the cliff into the valley below. Although we had spent several sun-cycles hiking down from the highest point, it was still a long way to the bottom.

"Are you sure about this, Rurac?" she asked, her voice quivering.

"I am," I answered, scrunching my nose as I watched her gaze go to the space above my head. "Why do you always look above my head, Empress?"

Her eyes flickered back to mine, a sparkle in their depths. "No reason."

Something about her words didn't ring true to me, but there were too many other things on my mind to press now. Setting the pack down on the cliff's edge I pulled out my ropes and began looking for a tree to tie them to. After a moment of hunting, I found a tree that was just far enough from the cliff edge for me to anchor to and I quickly created a knot I knew I could undo from below with a special yank later.

Azucena watched me work, her teeth nearly biting a hole through her chapped lip. "We will be fine, I promise."

"If you say so," she said, her stare following my every move.

Once one end of the rope was tied to the tree, I turned to her and held up the other end of the rope. "Come here."

She came forward, her lip still at the mercy of her teeth and I leaned down, looping the rope around her ankle.

"What about you?" she asked, her eyes full of worry.

I nearly dropped the rope as I realized that I hadn't thought of myself at all. I had been so worried about keeping her safe I forgot there was no way to tie both of us to the single rope in my possession—there were only two ends. Not knowing what else to do, I scoured the underbrush desperate for anything that could help. Unfortunately for me, there was nothing remotely helpful anywhere. With a sigh, I pulled one of my mother's blankets from the pack. "I'll make a sling for myself out of this."

She raised one dark eyebrow. "Doesn't seem like it will catch you if you fall."

I shrugged. "I don't plan on falling. This is for just in case."

Still doubtful, I wrapped the blanket around my back before tying both ends to the rope above the portion where Azucena was attached. Apprehension clouded her features.

Knowing I had to be the strong one, I hoisted the pack onto my back and led her to the edge, ensuring the rope pulled taut. "Just make sure we go down straight," I told her. "This is a special knot that will disengage if we pull it to the side."

She gulped but nodded, her steps slowing as she came to the edge. I bunched up what was left of the rope into my arm, pointing just below me. "You have to go first."

Azucena peered over the edge, a gasp leaving her lips before she backed up a step. Sweat beaded on her forehead. "I don't think I can do this."

"You can," I promised her, holding up the rope in my hands. "I've got you, I promise."

Her eyes once more flickered to the spot above my head before she sat down on the edge, turning around to go backwards.

"Go slow," I directed her, my own heart prisoner in my chest as her first leg dipped over the edge searching for a foothold. "Take your time; find a good foothold and test it with your weight before settling on to it."

She nodded, her jaw firm in a way that told me she was hiding her fear. For my own sanity, I didn't peer over the edge to watch her foot probing the air for a place to land. She must've found something though as she let out a breath and her body moved slightly lower.

We repeated this process a few times until her body was just below the edge. Wrapping one of my hands in a few loops of the rope I backed toward the brink, ensuring there was slack to move but adjusting my hold as we went.

As I moved my weight over the edge of the cliff, I felt my mother's blanket immediately pull. I had lied to Azucena; this wouldn't hold my weight if I fell.

I didn't tell her that, though. The sounds of her pants below were enough for me to know she was struggling with this task enough without my input. I moved just as slowly as her, picking my footholds and handholds carefully as I backed my way down, just an arm's length from my empress, letting out rope as I went.

I was so focused on my task, and not looking down at the valley below, that it wasn't until Azucena let out a little cheer that I realized I was nearly at the bottom.

Looking down to realize I was only a stretch of cliff about my height from the ground, I released the rope and jumped the rest of the way, landing in a crouch by Azucena.

"We did it!" She grinned, pulling my face toward hers to give me a peck on the lips, which caused me to grin as well.

Realizing her mistake, she hastily stepped back and cleared her throat. "You were right. That wasn't so bad."

"Of course, I was," I replied as I pulled the rope to one side to undo my knot, not wanting to admit that I had lied to her. "Step back."

She moved just as the heavy rope came loose and flew over the edge. I stepped out of the way and allowed it to land on the ground beside me before moving to gather it up. Azucena watched.

Once everything was tucked back into my pack, I began leading us through the long grass at the base of the valley. It was said this was the sacred valley of our ancestors, and I could almost feel their approval as I guided Azucena forward.

"Where did you learn to do that?" she asked at last.

I shrugged. "My father taught me—mostly for when we went hunting, but the skills come in handy now and then."

"I'll say," she agreed with a small shake of her head. "I can't believe I just went down a cliff on a rope."

"I'm just glad you were able to go down straight. Made it easy." Although it was true, the words tasted sour in my mouth. "I'm sorry I had to chain you to me . . . by the way . . . when you first arrived."

Azucena shrugged, not seeming bothered one bit. "I deserved it. I did act like a wild animal, after all."

"That you did." I smirked, though the words struck deeper in my belly in a way where it hurt to swallow.

"Don't worry, I will still grant you a full pardon when we arrive at the palace. You have my word." She smiled.

"Thanks," I replied, only worried for what would happen after we parted.

———

INTI CLIMBED high in the sky as we crossed the bowl of the valley. It wasn't the prettiest valley, mostly filled with long, dying grasses that had begun to fade in color as the summer season came to an end. Any food that had been grown here had long been harvested, leaving large, brown patches of overturned dirt. I still stopped to check a few of the patches though, and luckily there were a few potatoes left behind for us—at least enough to get us through another sun-cycle.

Because it was the time of the solar-path where the sun didn't stay long in the sky, it was already growing dark and we were only about two-thirds of the way through the valley.

"Should we set up for camp soon?" Azucena asked as she glanced back over her shoulder, the dark tendrils of her hair illuminated by the setting sun in a way that assured me she was touched by the gods as she had claimed.

I shook my head. "We can't. Don't you know the legends?"

She scrunched her brow. "I don't remember hearing any about not sleeping in this valley."

"Well," I started, "supposedly, if you spend the night down here, you'll be cursed for several solar-paths."

"Hm . . . are you sure about that?" she asked me, her eyes trained to the sky, focusing on how little light we had left.

"No." I let out a sigh and ran a hand through my hair. "I've never spent the night down here, but I don't think we should risk it. Not only because of the legends, but because of the men pursuing us. We are exposed down here. If one of them looks over the edge, we are done for."

Azucena began to walk faster. "You're right—there aren't any trees or anything for us to seek shelter under."

I picked up my pace, only pausing momentarily to refill waterskins as we crossed a small creek along the base of the valley. For some reason, the lie I had told Azucena before we rappelled down the cliff was weighing heavily on my mind.

As she walked in front of me, I couldn't help but evaluate my feelings for her. How was it that just a few sun-cycles ago, I was content to be alone, and now my heart hurt at the fact that we were drawing close to the end of our journey together?

Unable to hold it in any longer, I cleared my throat. "Zu." She slowed her pace slightly so we were walking side by side. "I'm sorry," I apologized.

She scrunched up her brows. "For what?"

"Earlier, when I promised you we would be fine before our rappel. I had no idea if we would be fine or not."

"Oh," she replied, her face tilted downward, leaving me unable to read her expression.

The silence pulled taut between us. I wasn't sure what else to say, but I found myself suddenly spewing words anyway. "I should have just been honest with you—admitted that it was dangerous. Not promise you everything would be fine when I didn't know for certain."

She didn't answer and a bee buzzing by my ear suddenly seemed way too loud.

"Say something," I said at last, unable to stand the silence anymore.

Azucena didn't stop but she let out a sigh. "I . . . just . . . ." She ran a hand through her dark hair. "I can't tell you everything, but this . . . this just changed my entire perception about my life and upbringing."

Now I was confused. "From my false promise?"

"Yes."

I wanted to prod more, but all too soon, we were facing the dark gray cliff face, an imposing and intimidating sight as only the faintest pinks and purples of sunset remained in the sky.

Azucena came to stand next to me, hand resting on her hips. "How are we going to do this?"

"It's not as easy as the way down," I acknowledged, rapidly running through any possible solutions I could think of. With one rope, a pack, and a few blankets, we didn't really have much.

I raked my eyes up the side of the cliff, looking for something —a solution.

"I think we need to tie one end of the rope to your ankle, and the other to me. We will climb slowly, ensuring only one of us is moving at a time. The other person should remain in place securely, just in case the other slips."

Azucena sucked the corner of her lip into her mouth as she always did when she was unsure of something, glancing to the sky one more time before nodding her head in resolution. "Let's do it. I want to be at the top before dark."

"Me too," I agreed, quickly leaning down to tie one end of the rope to her ankle before looping the other end around my waist. I didn't want to say it, but I would have a better chance at catching her this way, rather than attaching it to my own remaining ankle. I could see Zu's brain working as I did so, but she didn't question me.

Once we were both attached to the rope I turned to the cliff face, feeling for handholds. "I'll go first," I said, not even waiting for her answer before I climbed a bit off the ground, testing each hand and foothold before leaving the last. After I had pulled myself up quite a few feet, I nodded to where Azucena stood on the ground. "Go ahead."

Although I could tell she had never attempted something like this before, she didn't balk or hesitate. She simply grabbed onto the handholds at eye-level and began climbing the same path I had moments before. "Stop there," I directed her as she drew close to my feet. "Are you secure?"

"Yes."

I then moved a bit further up the cliff until I was once again above her and secure before calling back down to her to let her know it was her turn to climb.

We repeated this sequence several times, the cliff face losing what little light it had left reflecting on its dark surface as Inti sunk out of sight entirely. The good news was, I could see the top. "We're almost there!" I called down to her as she found a secure spot.

"Good. I'm secure!" she responded.

I climbed a bit more, the top less than one arm's length away. "I'm secure!" I called down, keeping my gaze on the ridge just above my head.

I must've been so focused on being done that I missed all the signs that Zu was struggling and about to fall until suddenly, there came the sound of the rock breaking in my ear and the rope around my waist pulled taut as it caught her ankle. Reacting on instinct, I reached for a tree root which protruded from the rocks, likely from one of the trees just over the ridge, hanging on for dear life.

"Azucena?!" I shouted, breathless from the rope around my waist and the strain on my muscles holding us against the cliff face.

"I slipped!" was the only reply. I wanted to look down, to ensure the woman that now held my heart in her chest was dangling just below me, but I knew if I did, I would lose the precarious balance I was maintaining.

"Can you get back to the wall?"

The rope swung as she attempted to reach a handhold. "No!" she said, and my stomach dropped.

I looked up at the ridge again. I would need to pull her up; it wasn't that far.

I can do this.

Gathering every shred of energy I could from my overworked body, and I placed one hand over the other, climbing the tree root until there was no more root left to grasp. Still, the ridge was just out of reach.

I paused, trying to think of any other solution, but under the crushing pain of the rope cutting off my air supply, I knew deep down that there was no other option.

"Stay as still as possible!" I called down to Zu as I moved to higher footholds so I could jump. I didn't want to tell her, but we only had one shot at this, or we would both find out the answers to all of our questions about the afterlife.

When I felt the rope pause in its movements, I bent my knees, wincing from the pain in my midsection. "Hold on to the rope; let go of any rocks!"

Without waiting for a reply, I went for it, propelling myself up the cliff face with all the energy I could muster.

It wasn't enough.

My hands cleared the ridge and I immediately sunk my hands into the soft dirt, but my lower half was still over the edge of the cliff, the rope holding Zu growing even tighter than before, making me wonder if I would be cut in half by it. My lungs screamed at the lack of oxygen, and my brain began to protest too, darkness clouding at the corner of my vision.

Out of time and out of answers, I scrambled blindly with my feet until I found a foothold strong enough to propel my whole body over the edge. I immediately collapsed in exhaustion, but I wasn't done yet.

The moment I could breathe again, and the darkness abated just slightly, I began shuffling forward, ensuring all my weight stayed on the rope and on the ground. It was slow going but eventually, I felt the pressure on my midsection release as Azucena topped the ridge.

I wanted to turn and check on her, but my body was beat. I closed my eyes, letting the darkness take over.

Twenty-Two

AZUCENA

I thought for sure that I was going to die there, on that cliff face, dangling upside down thanks to the rope around my ankle. It was my fault really. I was the one who had slipped.

Then, thanks to his own grit and strength, Rurac had saved me, pulling not only his own body weight to the ridge, but mine as well. It had taken a while, but once I reached the tree root jutting out from the dark rocks, I had been able to turn myself upright enough to help him save me.

After cresting the hill, I collapsed, my chest rising and falling as I tried to catch my breath. When at last I could breathe, I reached down to touch my ankle, blood coating my hands as I lifted them back to my face.

"Rurac," I said, not turning from my ankle as I tried to think of what we had to wrap it. But when he didn't respond, I turned, only to find him lying face down in the dirt, unmoving. My heart stopped dead in my chest. "Rurac!" I shouted, my own pain forgotten as I removed the supply sack from his back and struggled to roll him over. He was heavier than he looked, but fear gave me the strength to attempt pulling his shoulder back several times until he flopped lifelessly on his back.

Without waiting, I leaned down to press my ear to his chest, a breath of relief passing through my lips when I heard the steady thud of his heart and felt his chest rise beneath my ear. He was alive.

I searched his face again, only to find it flushed and full of sweat—his eyes closed. Something was very wrong.

Knowing this was going to be awkward, but not willing to wait for him to regain consciousness, I undid the rope around his middle, tossing it aside. Afterward, I checked to ensure he was still unconscious before I undid the buttons on his shirt.

It was dark at this point, but the light of Quilla was enough to reveal the ribbons of dark bruising beneath where the rope had clenched around his midsection when I fell. My breath caught. There was no open wound, but my gut knew this was bad.

I was no doctor, but I remembered how the healer had treated me when I was a child and once fell down the stairs in the palace because I had attempted to slide down them on a clay plate. Pain had exploded in my midsection, and she had gently pressed my sides and stomach looking for damage as my mother looked on. In the end, it was decided I had possibly broken a rib, but I would survive.

I did the same now, pressing my palms to his stomach below the red welt, then above it. When I pressed above the wound, I felt something give and I heard him gasp.

My head jolted up, my eyes connecting with his through the darkness.

"I think something is wrong." He gasped, pain lacing his voice. "That really hurt."

"How long have you been awake?" I asked, my hands still resting on his too-warm skin.

"Just a moment. That press woke me."

I nodded. "I think you have a broken rib. Maybe something even worse below."

He closed his eyes. "I feel feverish."

I moved from his midsection to sit by his head, pressing the back of my hand to his forehead. "This isn't good."

"I know," he hissed.

Honestly, I was a bit out of my element here, and I glanced around aimlessly, wondering what to do. Finally, I decided that unpacking and making Rurac more comfortable until I could fully evaluate his injury in the light of Inti, was the best choice. "I'm going to get out our sleeping blankets."

"I don't think I can move," he admitted.

Something about the words caused my breathing to become shallow, but I didn't let him see my fear as I struggled to pull out the blankets out of his pack before realizing we were still much too close to the cliff's edge to sleep here.

His eyelids had closed in the last few moments, so I gently touched his shoulder as I spoke, "I need to move you back from the edge of the cliff."

"It's okay," he mumbled. "I'll move, just . . . one . . . moment . . ."

He trailed off and I could tell by his breathing he wasn't awake. I would have to do this on my own.

Moving behind his head, I brushed his soaked hair from his brow, before placing one arm under each of his armpits. I pulled back with all my might—but he didn't budge even an inch.

I groaned, but I knew I needed to keep trying. The cliff wasn't even a stone's throw away from him. A landslide could, and probably would, take us in our sleep.

I tried a second and third time before coming to the conclusion that I would need to wake him.

"Rurac." I touched his forehead. His brow scrunched but his eyes didn't open. "Rurac," I tried again. I wanted to avoid shaking him, but he seemed to be in a deep sleep. With a sigh, I did the only thing I could think of to wake him—I leaned down and placed a kiss on his lips.

It was a brief kiss, but it did the trick, and soon, his dark brown eyes drifted open to look at me. A smile made a brief appearance on his lips for a moment until the pain rolled back in and a grimace overtook his features.

Before he could question what had just happened, I moved back into position. "I need to move you. Please, try to push with your heels."

"I—"

"Just try," I insisted. "When I say go . . ." I instructed, taking a deep breath as I braced my aching shoulders. "Go!" When I pulled back this time, I felt some of his muscles tense as he used his hands and feet to try and push against the ground—and it worked. I was able to move him one foot.

There was no time to celebrate though, as we would need to do this at least four or five times until I felt safe enough to let him rest.

"One more time," I lied. "Go!"

The second try was successful too, as was the third.

The fourth one only got us about half a foot, and the fifth one even less, so I knew it was time to call it good. Panting, I released my hold on his shoulders.

"I'm tired. So tired." His voice was quiet, lacking his usual spunk.

"I know. I'll get camp set up," I promised him, forcing my aching and exhausted body to stand and return to the blanket I had abandoned. I began trying to throw it over a tree, only to find it was much harder than Rurac had made it look.

I struggled and struggled, probably looking like an idiot as I made attempt after attempt, but I finally succeeded—though the camp looked nothing like the ones Rurac had been making for us. After I finished, I was sweating profusely, even in the cool evening air.

"I should gather firewood," I said with a sigh.

"It's too dark, you won't be able to find your way back if you leave," Rurac said, his breathing labored. "We will just have to use all the blankets and hope we survive until Inti comes."

I knew he was right, and though I didn't want to admit it, it felt comforting to cuddle up next to him under the blankets—all of which I had piled on top of us after wrapping my ankle with strips from the dress I had given up on earlier in the journey. I could feel my blood soaking through the bandages even as I lay next to him, and for the first time since my mother's death, I prayed to the gods. Mostly for Rurac, but also that my ankle would heal quickly so we wouldn't be leaving a trail of blood the next sun-cycle.

Despite the trying climb we'd just had, I found myself unable to sleep—my thoughts spinning. First, they spiraled through what would happen if Rurac was too injured to continue, but I forced myself away from those thoughts and focused on something I could control instead.

When Rurac had lied to me earlier, I had checked his aura and found green, which I had assumed meant he was telling the truth. But now that he had admitted he was lying . . . I didn't know what to think. If he had been lying, shouldn't there have been red or orange above his head? Was green the color of lies and I had been assuming incorrectly my whole life?

At that thought, several events of the past few sun-cycles snapped into place and everything suddenly made sense.

Yezema, my trusted advisor who had always been surrounded by shades of green. She had been lying to me . . . the entire time. There probably wasn't a single bone in her body that was honest.

The realization caused me to sit up straight, my breath once again coming in gasps, my heart rate elevated. Rurac, though I brushed him with my motions, didn't stir—something that immediately reminded me of our precarious situation.

Forcing myself to lie down again—despite my revelation— and cuddle up gently to Rurac, I slowed my breathing, hoping exhaustion would eventually take over and save me from the whirlpool of my thoughts.

I MUST'VE EVENTUALLY FALLEN asleep, because the next thing I knew, the bright rays of Inti were peering at me through the tree branches. With a groan, I stretched and rose to a sitting position, glancing at Rurac lying still beside me.

His chest rose and fell, reassuring me that he was still alive, but I could also see the dark bruising beneath the blanket—so dark it was now black. What was more concerning was that he was very sweaty, but also shivering—evidence he was battling with a bad fever—and his eyes scrunched were closed in a sleep that was anything but restful.

There was no way we would be able to move today.

But at least I could fix the camp I had haphazardly thrown together the night before and see about getting some food. My stomach growled loudly, agreeing with the plan.

The woods on this side of the valley were sparse, and it took much longer than anticipated to find and gather what we needed for a fire. When I returned to the camp, Rurac was still lying where I had left him, but his eyes were open.

I didn't say anything as I set down the firewood before moving to the pack to dig out the last few pieces of jerky and few potatoes we had collected yesterday. We still had a few sun-cycles left of travel, which meant I would have to see if I could find some berries, or hunt for meat, after this was gone. And I had forgotten that though I could collect firewood, I still didn't know how to start a fire on my own.

Wordlessly, I sank down beside Rurac, dividing the jerky and handing him half.

"I don't think I can eat." He gasped.

"You need to," I insisted. "Your body needs to fight off this fever."

He took a few bites, clearly struggling to swallow each one down. Once his jerky was half gone, he pushed the other half back to me. "I can't eat any more. You eat this."

I didn't argue, rather I just tucked the jerky back in the pouch, not sure how to tell Rurac that this was the last of our food. Finally, I decided being honest was better.

"I need to go find us some food. We have a few potatoes for dinner and that's it."

Rurac frowned. "See if there's anything nearby. But if there isn't, I want you to move on toward the palace . . . without me."

"I'm not leaving you," I sputtered between bites, the jerky feeling heavy in my gut. "We're a team."

He shifted, clearly trying to find a more comfortable position, his lips turning into a grimace. "I'm not going to heal anytime soon. They'll catch us before I'm able to move again."

"But if I leave you, you'll be left without food and water."

"I'll—"

I cut him off. "No arguing. I'm staying."

He whimpered, and my mind flashed back to when I had once had a strong fever as a child. I suddenly wished I had spent some time with the empire's healers, just so I would know more of what to do in this situation.

As it was, there was little I could do but wet scraps of cloth and place them on his forehead. I did leave the camp to try to find food, but whenever I ventured away, I was afraid to go too far as I didn't know these woods like Rurac did. In the end, I spent most of the day sitting by his side and worrying, wondering just how we were going to get ourselves out of this . . .

Twenty-Three

RURAC

I didn't sleep that night. Well, not really. I slept some, likely due to the fire festering behind my brow, but whenever I was able to close my eyes for a moment or two, the images passing behind my eyelids were too vivid, too scary, for me to keep them closed.

First, I watched as the men pursuing us, attacked, carrying Azucena off while I just sat there. Once I realized that wasn't the case, the next image behind my eyes was of the gods laughing at me as I was thrown in the torture chambers at the palace. They cackled and taunted me, saying I was a fool for believing Azucena would use her position to save me as I watched my torturer sharpen a knife.

I would jolt awake in panic, only for my eyes to drift closed once more.

In between these terrible renditions of events which were likely not too far from the truth, I would wake to Azucena fussing over me. First, she was trying to make me more comfortable, then she was pressing a damp cloth to my forehead.

"How did you learn all this?" I murmured, my words coming out more jumbled than they had sounded in my head.

"My mom was sick once," she said back, her voice low and heavy with emotion.

"Did she get better?" I asked, my eyelids starting to close of their own accord.

She didn't ever reply. But I knew the answer. Injuries like this often weren't survivable.

The next dream was of the puma, back on the hill near my home, attacking Azucena. This time I wasn't quick enough to stop it, and it ate her. I started screaming and cursing the gods.

My eyes flew open to find Azucena leaning over me, a shushing noise passing through her lips. The look on my face must have been enough for her to understand because she said, "You were yelling."

I nodded, my head turning to the side to take in the pink rays of Inti rising over the far-off horizon. "It's nearly daylight." I turned my head back to our campsite, which was still in a state of disarray. Azucena just wasn't as good as I was at setting up—something that made me chuckle. Or attempt to; the movement hurt too much to continue. "We need to pack up."

Azucena didn't move, her dark gaze scouring my face for something.

"What are you waiting for?"

She just shook her head, her lips drawn into a frown. "You're too injured to move. We have to stay here until you heal."

I knew I was hurt, I felt it in every corner of every limb, but something about the way she said the words made everything seem to sink in deeper. This could be the end of my god-woven tapestry right here.

And Azucena was going to sacrifice her own safety to be with me until the end.

"You have to go . . . on, without me," I begged her, my own voice sounding pathetic and weak.

She shook her head. "Rurac . . . I can't just leave you here." She breathed, lowering her body so that she lay next to me, her head resting on my shoulder. "What kind of person would I be if I did that?"

"You are the best woman I know, Azucena, and you have a life without me . . . waiting for you," I pointed out. "You can't throw away the future of the empire for me."

"I'm the only woman you know." She snorted, despite the serious topic we were discussing.

"That's beside the point." I wanted to roll my eyes, but my head hurt too much for that.

She was silent for a long moment, and I thought maybe I had won, but she didn't move.

"I lied earlier, Rurac. I want to be with you. I know I said it wasn't possible, but I was just scared. You're unlike any man I've ever met. I want us to figure out a way to be together."

Although it hurt to lift my arm, I did, resting my palm on the small of her back. We lay like that for a moment, the sounds of the forest waking up serving as the background music to what was about to be our greatest tragedy.

I grimaced as my resolve settled and I realized what I would have to do to get Azucena to think of herself before me. What I would need to say to ensure she left and continued to live her life. Because, although we had had a rough start, and she had a lot to learn, I could see now that she was a great ruler—would continue to be a great ruler. She needed to go on and she would never make it through this forest with me as deadweight.

"Follow the path of Inti, but head in reverse, to where he rises. Now that we are on the other side of the great, sacred valley, the place where it rises is where your city, specifically your palace, sits —just below Inti's temple."

"I'm not leaving you, Rurac."

I let out a deep breath, mentally preparing for the next words to pass my lips—the way they would stab my heart clean through.

"You have to. I don't want you here, Azucena. I want you to leave."

"I know you think that, Ru—"

I cut her off. "It's not a thought, it's the truth. I lied before. I don't like you—not like that. You annoy me. Now, leave."

She pulled back from me, her mouth open in shock. I immediately dropped the hand that had been resting on her back, hoping she didn't notice how it had still been rubbing her back even as the lies passed my lips.

"You . . . you don't mean that," she sputtered.

I gritted my teeth. "I do." I pressed my lips together, forcing the lump in my throat down. "I don't ever want to see you again. You're just a selfish empress."

That did it. Seeming to forget I was injured, she pushed herself away from me, her eyes coming to rest above my head before her frown deepened once more.

But my words were apparently enough, as she began silently collecting a few things from where they were around the campsite, though I noticed she neglected to take the food pouch and waterskin that rested on the ground near my head.

"Take everything," I huffed. "It all reminds me of you."

She moved her head to the side, enough that I could see the water trailing down her cheeks. The sight was an immediate punch in the gut, especially because I couldn't move to comfort her as I so desperately ached to. But then I remembered that was my goal here, and I forced myself to look away—anywhere but her beautiful face.

My words didn't work, though, as she didn't move any closer to retrieve the items she left behind. In fact, several moments later, when I turned back to see the air that once held her form empty, I noticed she had left almost everything . . . and moved it closer to me so I wouldn't have to move to reach it.

That realization alone was almost enough to end me, right then and there. The once selfish empress had taken nothing for herself.

Resigning myself to what was likely my last sun-cycle, I closed my eyelids and tilted my chin toward Inti, allowing him to warm my face with his rays. I must've slept more, because the next thing I knew, a shadow was blocking his light.

Thinking it was nighttime, I sighed and began to struggle to rearrange myself into a more comfortable position. I had never realized that dying would be so uncomfortable.

"Ehm."

My eyes shot open to realize I was surrounded by several guards who were dressed in clothes that matched the colors of the trees. They were staring down at me, their frowns blended in with their disguised faces.

"Where's the girl," one growled, his eyes narrow.

"What girl?" I asked, careful to keep any recognition out of my voice. I shifted, forcing myself to swallow the cry of pain that bubbled up. "I was hunting when I fell and injured myself."

"Lies." A female voice cut through the rest, and I watched as the men parted to let her through, a single, torn, garment clutched in her fist. "Whose dress is this then? Yours?"

I appraised the woman who appeared to be several solar-paths older than the oldest woman in the village near my home. This had to be the advisor Zu spoke of. Keeping that in mind, the lie came to me like a gift from the gods themselves, placed directly in my mind in front of my abhorrent pain. "Yes, my mother's. Her blankets are in the bag too."

She arched one of her thin eyebrows. "And why are you traveling with them?"

"To sell them to fund my travels."

She tapped a long fingernail on her chin, my gaze drawn to their pointed tips. "All of this for a simple hunting trip? Who did you say you were again?"

"I didn't." I let out a gasp as one of the men nudged my side with his foot.

"I thought so," she snapped, her black eyes roving up and down my body. "He's the one we want. Take him and all the stuff. He will lead us to the girl."

"Wait, there is no girl—" I tried to argue but I was cut off when four of the men hoisted me over their shoulders, each one taking a limb. It was painful, but also less painful than being dragged on the ground. I also had a bird's-eye view as the men ransacked what remained of our meager camp, shoving everything in my sack which was tossed over a fifth man's shoulder.

I didn't have much time, but I knew I needed to think of something to get them off of Azucena's trail, and fast.

"I saw the woman I think you are looking for though, and she was headed into the valley," I suggested.

One of the men carrying me squinted at me over my leg, which rested on his shoulder, but he seemed unperturbed, obviously waiting for the woman to shout directions.

"I know Azucena." Her voice came from behind my head and raked down my spine like a knife. "And she is in a rush to get back to her palace, I just know it. She would think of nothing else. Continue on, men."

I wanted to argue. I wanted to tell this relic of a woman how Azucena had changed over the last few sun-cycles and that, in fact, she hadn't wanted to leave my side until I had forced her to. But despite my urge to gloat, I knew I would need to save it until we were both out of this situation.

I felt the hope in my chest deflate and I felt my body grow heavier as the men lugged me over rocks and around various trees.

Although Azucena didn't trust the gods, I sent up a quick request, hoping that they had seen our plight and taken our side.

Otherwise, Azucena's life tapestry would end just as mine was about to.

Twenty-Four

AZUCENA

"**G**ah!" I grumbled as I plodded through the sharp underbrush. The dead bushes tore at my skin, causing rivulets of blood to stain my clothes, but I no longer cared enough to adjust my path to go around them.

How dare he?

HOW DARE HE?

He just led me on like...like...*GAH!* All this time, he acted like he was starting to like me, and the moment things grew serious, and I told him the truth about how I felt about him, he ripped everything out from under me. And what's worse is that his aura told the truth. I could have assumed that he was lying to protect me, but his aura had been a fierce shade of red.

He really didn't want me around.

I glanced up at the sky to ensure I was still on the right path— at least I assumed it was the right path. His aura had been blue as he had given the directions, meaning they had to be true.

Even though I was mad at Rurac, and the anger simmered deeper the longer I walked, I had to admit, it was quite lonely without him. I kept wanting to point something out, or turn and say something to him, only to find he wasn't there. Something which caused my shoulders to slump lower as the sun-cycle wore on.

I had never been lonely before. I had simply liked being alone. People were a nuisance I dealt with during the sun-cycle as empress, before attaining peace in my room with my llamas at night.

But now, in the semi-silence of the forest, I actually craved the presence of the man who had once been my jailer. The same one who had turned around and told me he had been lying the whole time . . .

Suddenly, it hit me like the spit of a pissed-off llama. Before we had started the descent into the valley—which had changed the whole trajectory of this journey—Rurac had told me it would be easy and that we would be fine. Which, obviously, had been a lie, as he confessed later.

But when he had told me that, green had floated around his head—a color I had usually associated with partial truths.

A color which had often occupied the area around Yzema's head in the palace.

I had forgotten about my earlier revelation, due to Rurac's life-altering injury, but now that I seemed to have endless time of marching through the forest to Sipan, I started digging through my memories, analyzing from the moment I had first discovered my gift until now. I saw a wide range of colors, but seeing red—a complete lie—was so rare . . . what if it didn't mean what I thought it meant? Although my mother had coached me a bit in my gift before her untimely death, she only had her limited knowledge to go off of . . . meaning . . .

We could both be wrong.

The realization hit me so hard, I had to stop walking and crouch by a tree as I tried to sort through what I thought I knew about auras. What if my mother had been wrong and the colors weren't simply a truth versus a lie but rather a full and complex range of emotions?

What if orange was the color of feeling sly, rather than a lie, and white was the color of caring—often indicating that someone was telling a kind lie because they cared about you? Maybe green wasn't a range of the truth, but rather a signal of envy, of someone wanting everything you held dear? Purple and blue—those often appeared over the heads of villagers as I listened to their plights. Maybe those were actually something akin to hope and happiness.

So, what was red then? Before Rurac, when had I seen that color?

The only time I could think of was above my mother's head as she rested on her deathbed. She had told me she was feeling better, which I had assumed was a lie . . . but what if she just loved me and that was all my gift had been trying to convey?

After all, I hadn't seen red anywhere else until above Rurac's head during the journey.

The world spun, and I felt dizzy knowing I had been following my gift the wrong way for so many solar-paths of my life.

And I was sick over the fact that Rurac had lied to me. He loved me and because he loved me, he had lied to me to get me to leave.

Because he loved me.

I felt lightheaded and had to put my head between my knees to take in some deep breaths of the cool evening air. The pressure of all my mistakes, my rash decisions, my inability to stop and listen and learn . . . it had led me here.

It had led me to Rurac.

I knew then that I only had one choice, and that was to make my way back to the camp. I didn't care anymore if I continued to be empress or not—Yezema could have the job. I just wanted to spend time with the man who had taught me more in one moon cycle than my parents had in their entire lifetimes. Even if he was gravely injured, I just wanted to hear his voice and feel his warmth near mine.

Rising from my crouched position, I looked to the sky, trying to estimate how far I had come. Deciding that following Inti would eventually get me back to at least the cliff's edge (and I was reasonably sure I could find our camp from there) I set out, walking much more carefully than I had during the first portion of the sun-cycle.

It was as I was picking my way around a particularly pokey bush, that I heard the sound of leaves crunching underfoot. And not just one foot, but several.

Taking the lessons learned from Rurac in stride, I rushed to crawl under a nearby bush, ensuring the branches hid me entirely. It wasn't comfortable at all, and I was sure to have even more scrapes, but Rurac needed me.

"Do you see any sign of her," one voice called to another. I held my breath.

"No, she must be faster than we thought."

I observed as several sets of feet in palace-issued sandals, stomped past the bush. I suddenly realized that I hadn't taken any time to observe the density of the bush, and I hoped it was dark enough to obscure the colors of my clothes.

My hand was pressed to my mouth, and my lungs burned without air. But still, I held my breath as another few sets of feet passed me by. Yezema had brought what had to be half of the palace guards to find me.

When the last set of feet passed my hiding spot, and the sounds of the shoes crunching faded into the distance, I allowed myself to breathe again, but I dared not move until there were no sounds of their footfalls left—because if I could hear them, they would be able to hear me.

Once the silence of the forest had returned, I emerged from my hiding spot, covered in dried blood, with small sticks stuck in my hair. But there was no time to preen—without thinking I bolted off in the direction they had come from, desperate to get back to Rurac and hoping he had made it through the sun-cycle without being found by the guards.

Apparently, I hadn't moved far in my anger, because before Inti left the sky, I came to the edge of the cliff where everything had changed—drag marks marred the ground where I had struggled, and mostly failed, to move him out of danger. Although the sight of them caused me to worry, they made an easy path to follow into the thicket, where signs of our camp were still visible.

But even though there were signs that we had stayed here for the night, my stomach clenched as I realized the obvious—

Rurac, and all our supplies, were gone.

Taken by the woman who had stolen my empire.

Twenty-Five

AZUCENA

I'm not going to lie, the devastation of finding our camp empty took me a moment to overcome. Remember, before this little adventure I had rarely left the palace, so this was all still sort of new to me. Even before, when I had left Rurac, at least I had known he was there if I needed to go back. Now I was well and truly on my own.

Once I did finally find my bearings, I ran into another issue—it was dark, and Rurac had only given me directions for daylight travel.

Too antsy to stay still, however, I meandered my way back to the cliff, sitting in one of the drag marks as I watched the moon rise high in the sky.

I didn't want to be a sitting duck all night, but I wasn't really sure what else to do, walking directly away from the cliff would work for a while, but I also knew that navigation was nearly impossible in the dark for humans.

I had my second major realization of the sun-cycle while staring at the trees as the moon rose in the sky.

The stars could lead to me the palace.

Every emperor throughout Sipan history was taught how to read the stars before anything else. Not only were they proof that our gods existed, but they were how we tracked the seasons—knowing when to plant and when to harvest. They were also our guides, and the reason I had come to know the llama as my spirit guide. Every night, I had stared up at the stars from the balcony outside my room, and I knew exactly which stars I spent my time looking at during each season. Meaning, if I could find those same stars and walk until I had that same view, I would find the palace. . . or at least I would be on the right track and Inti could help me once the night had passed.

Excited at the prospect of my plan and the surprising nature of my own unknown wisdom, I stood quickly and brushed myself off, ensuring I stepped back from the cliff edge before turning my nose to the sky.

There were so many bright flecks occupying the dark abyss, it took me several moments to orient myself to find the great Atoq —the fox of the sky—which usually frolicked right outside my bedroom during the winter moon cycles. As soon as I spotted him rising over the horizon, I felt a sense of comfort, knowing he would guide me back to my life, and hopefully, back to Rurac.

I WALKED all through the night, until the rays of Inti began to sneak over the horizon and crawl over the rolling hills, which had become the prominent landscape feature after I finally left the woods some time ago. Although these particular hills didn't look familiar, I knew for a fact that there wouldn't be any more trees, and that the Sipan metropolis, the city that had been my home for over thirty solar-paths, would eventually appear over one of these peaks.

With my determination also came a large rush of fear. I knew it was unlikely, but the thought that I could be moving faster than Yezema's men was at the forefront of my mind, causing me to duck in fear with every hill that I crested, afraid that I would see their colorful palace-issued tunics on the next ridge. All it would take was one glance back and my cover would be blown.

Which made me realize that if we ever were to go to war with the neighboring tribes, I would need to change the guard's uniforms—they were too prominent for this landscape. That is, if I was still empress when this was all over.

Despite my mounting anxiety, that never actually happened, and as Inti completed its movement through the skies, the edge of the sprawling metropolis of Sipan came into view.

The hardest part of this journey was behind me.

I became very aware of my exhaustion and hunger, both of which were coming to a peak after walking all through the sun-cycle without any provisions. Any adrenaline that had fueled the first part of my journey had worn off, and every step seemed heavier and heavier until I finally slumped next to a shed on the outskirts of the peasant lands which surrounded Sipan.

I was too tired to truly consider the consequences of napping right where I fell, and my eyes drifted shut before I could make a better decision.

"Miss."

"Miss."

My eyes shot open to connect with the boy who leaned over me. Out of habit, I tried to jump up and back away, only to find I was indeed still against the wall where I had fallen asleep, and any movement I made was impeded by the grey stones, causing me to stumble, fall, and hit myself against the wall on the way down. It was anything but graceful.

"I'm sorry," I managed to gasp out as I tried to collect my bearings. "I must've fallen asleep against your wall here. I'll just be on my way now."

The boy who had awoken me appraised me with an arched eyebrow. Although he couldn't be more than maybe twelve solar-paths at most, his gaze was filled with maturity beyond his age. "You need food and water. Come, my mother will prepare something."

My stomach rumbled at the prospect of food, even if it was corn mush. At this point, I would take anything to quiet it. But as much as I wanted food, I desperately needed to stay hidden and get to Rurac as quickly as possible.

The boy's head tilted to the side. "I know who you are. The town has been told you're missing—kidnapped. My mom can help you get back to the palace. After you eat."

His words were short and succinct, filled with authority that made me think he was touched by one of the gods, even though there was no golden halo around his head. His aura was white though, indicating he cared—as I just recently had come to learn.

"Oh, all right, but we must be careful, some bad men are after me. I will explain more to your mother." Rising unceremoniously and trying to brush the dirt off my skirt to no avail, I followed the boy around the house and to a second, slightly larger one just a few paces off. He motioned for me to pass through the door in front of him, which I did.

The inside of the hut was designed much like Rurac's, with a stone oven integrated into the sitting area, both for cooking and warmth. But where Rurac's home had only held the basics, this room was filled with small wooden trinkets which looked to be made either by delicate or young hands. My gaze was immediately drawn to a small clay llama over the hearth, and I stepped closer to get a better look.

"It's you."

I spun toward the words, which came from the mouth of a woman who couldn't be much older than myself, yet she appeared much more tired. "When Eztil told me the empress herself lounged on the side of our wall, I was certain he was weaving stories again." Her hand rested on her chest, which rose and fell as she explained. "I never imagined . . ." As if suddenly remembering who she was speaking to, she suddenly dropped into a deep bow. "Sapa Inca."

"There's no need for that." I gestured for her to stand. "Not when I look like this."

"Oh!" Her gaze roved my body, though it didn't look like she was judging the threads that had seen better sun-cycles. "Would you like to have something of mine? We look to be about the same size?"

I was aghast at her overly kind offering, but I again shook my head. "There's no need; I have a chest full of clothing at the palace. This will suffice until I get back there."

Her throat bobbed, and her eyes settled on her son, who was still standing in the doorway. "It's just me and the boy . . . If you need an escort—"

I held up my hand. "No need. I don't know how much you have been told, but I was kidnapped—" I paused, debating how much to tell this complete stranger, but at this point, I was running out of hope, and I just needed someone to be on my side. "And I recently found out it was someone I trusted who did it. I need to get back into the palace in secret, because the person who betrayed me is there."

The woman nodded mutely, before snapping into action. "Sit down here." She motioned to a stump that faced a table. "I'll get you some corn and potatoes. I'm afraid we can't spare much."

"Whatever you have will do. I shouldn't overeat anyway."

She turned her back and began pulling items from pots on the counter.

"I can help you sneak into the palace."

I spun to face Eztil, the shock I was feeling likely evident on my face as I appraised the young boy, his gaze still glinting in a way I had never seen from a human so small. "You can?"

"The gods gifted him with the ability to move very silently," his mother mentioned over her shoulder. "It's likely how he was able to walk near you without waking you."

Eztil nodded furiously in agreement.

"But you're so young."

"Eleven solar-paths this year, ma'am. I'm practically a man," he corrected, puffing out his chest in a way that was adorable but made him look pretty young.

"Let me think about it," I acquiesced. "It might be more complicated than even I expect."

"Maybe you can sneak in through the dungeons? I know there is a door there—"

"EZTIL!" his mother shrieked, dropping whatever she was preparing for me to run over and press her hand over her son's mouth. "Sapa Inca, if there is a door there"—she glanced pointedly at her son—"which we have only heard rumors of, know that we have never encouraged any dealings which would go against your kind rulings—"

I stopped her again. "Don't fret. I promise you that I am not the same ruler I used to be. I will prove it to you. I just need to get back into the palace right now. And then, once I do, I can address any portions of my security that may have failed in the past, without causing anyone harm—especially not Eztil. You have my word."

The woman's entire body visibly relaxed at my words, and she dropped her arms to return to the kitchen and continue preparing the food. I watched her movements like a ravenous puma, and when she finally placed the clay plate in front of me, I couldn't resist diving in immediately, taking large bites of the corn on the cob between even larger bites of the spiced potatoes she had prepared. Both mother and son watched me apprehensively, like the nervous deer I had seen Rurac hunt.

Once I was no longer starving, I was able to remember my manners better. "I'm sorry, I didn't catch what you were called." I motioned to the mother.

She blushed. "I am Zoila. My husband was Ocotlan before he left to be with the gods."

I dipped my chin in understanding. "I'm sure my parents were there in companionship if he left sometime in the last ten solar-paths."

"You're too kind," she whispered, her eyes catching on my empty plate. "Do you need more?"

I shook my head. "No, I really must start on my journey to the palace." I regarded her small home. "Do you perhaps have a cloak I could borrow? I am afraid my enemy will have many supporters, and I must venture through the village unseen before I reach the palace."

"Certainly," she replied, rising from one of the other stumps at the table. "I will fetch it."

She passed through a doorway into what I suspected was their only bedroom, but Eztil remained, his large dark gaze fixed on my profile.

"Were you serious about helping me?" I asked him in a whisper.

"Yes!" he nearly shouted before lowering his voice so his mother wouldn't overhear. "I want to be a guard so badly, but Mama says we are peasants and that I will be a farmer like my father in a few solar-paths."

My heart broke at his words. I had never considered how rigorous our society class system was before, but now I realized that Eztil was right—he would likely never have a chance to be something else . . . unless I intervened.

"Let's consider this a trial mission," I suggested. "If you are able to help me successfully then we can see if a guard position would possible be available for you when you are older."

His lips expanded into a grin, and he was practically jumping off his stool at the prospect. "I will be the best guard you've ever had! I'll prove it!"

Before I could say anything else, or ask any more questions, he bound out of the room, nearly knocking his mother off of her feet, her arms laden with a colorful cloth.

She gave a quick glance at her son before turning her attention to me. "Hopefully, this will fit." She shook out the cloth, the sun woven into the back glinting in the sunlight.

"That's . . . very nice," I commented. I had been hoping for something a little less obvious, but I knew better than to spurn her generosity.

Zoila draped the cloak over my shoulders, fastening it under my chin before brushing her hands down it in a reverent manner.

"It's lovely. Did you make it?"

She nodded enthusiastically, pulling the hood up over my head. "It suits you well." Tears shone in her eyes.

"I'll return it to you, I promise."

"There's no need for that, Sapa Inca," she corrected. "I am just happy to serve my empress."

I didn't say anything more, but I knew I would be returning it regardless. I had a chest full of clothing—I didn't need to steal from villagers who likely had nothing else.

Eztil dashed back into the room, a darker cloak tucked around his shoulders and a small spear in his hand. "I'm ready for battle."

Zoila and I both fought the laughter that bubbled in our throats as I patted him on the shoulder. "We aren't going to battle just yet, Eztil—maybe someday. For now, I thought you could just help me get to the hidden entrance to the palace. The one you have heard rumors of, that is."

"Can I still bring the spear?"

I took one look at his face, which was so full of hope, and in the end, I ended up nodding. "But keep it under your cloak, okay? We don't want to draw any attention to us."

"Yes, Empress."

As we prepared to leave, I couldn't help the chill that ran down my spine. I had thought the god were on our side. After all, Zoila and Eztil had appeared right when I was in need, but something told me that everything was about to go terribly wrong.

Twenty-Six

RURAC

"I'll ask you one more time: Where. Is. The. Girl." The tall guard peered down at where I was lying on the bed, my hand holding my stomach. I felt like if I let it go, I would lose it entirely. A healer had been here, but had left a few moments ago only for this brute of a guard to come question me.

"I don't know any girl," I lied for what felt like the hundredth time. "As I told you, I was hunting and injured myself. I brought along some of my mother's things to sell. My mother went to Hana Pacha over thirty solar-paths ago."

"Lies. All lies," the guard accused, lifting a finger as if he was going to poke my injured rib, but lucky for me, the healer chose that moment to return, a bunch of herbs gripped in their fist.

"I'm a loyal citizen of Sipan, and the Game and Prisoner Manager. I have no reason to lie." Each word was almost painful, but after lying to Azucena, nothing could top the pain of watching her face collapse at my words. I grimaced. My fever had broken that morning, hence the interrogation, but I was still in quite a bit of physical pain.

"All peasants lie," he seethed.

"But I'm not just any peasant. As I mentioned, I work for the empress." I was suddenly glad that Azucena had told me the truth, otherwise I might have revealed my lack of information by referring to the emperor as a he.

"We will just see how long that stays true. If you won't tell us where the girl is, we will have to strip you of your duties," he threatened, his eyes narrowing on my face.

Once upon a time, those words would have been the end of me, and I would have caved. But the allocations I received for my work had dwindled so much over the past few solar-paths, that at this point I didn't mind losing them. Especially if it meant Azucena was safe. Despite how haughty she had once appeared to be, I knew she was ten times the empress that her advisor would be. Plus, there was no guarantee that even if I gave her up, I wouldn't still be fired anyway. After all, it didn't seem that Azucena's advisor played by the rules of honesty.

"Then fire me. Because I haven't seen any girl," I huffed just as the healer pressed on my injury, taking some of the bite from my words as I gasped through the sharp stabbing in my side.

"I still don't believe you," the guard spat. "We will allow you to heal, but then you will face the empress for your crimes against the empire. She will make the final decision on your job." Without waiting for me to reply, he spun and left the room, leaving me alone with the healer.

Previously, I had only been familiar with the village healers, which were often just individuals who had an affinity for plants. But this palace healer was something else. They hadn't given a name, and their head was shaved of hair—likely to keep them from having to brush it out of their face constantly. While they had provided me with several herbal remedies, they had also rubbed a variety of pastes over my injury and, at times, just sat there with their hands touching my stomach or my wrist. Then they would close their eyes, as if in a trance. It was all very odd. But it seemed to be helping, so I let them continue their strange process.

Like now, as they sat on the floor near the low bed with their hands on my wrist and eyes closed.

I took the opportunity to glance about the room, taking in the fact that it was much larger than the bedroom I had kept Zu locked in. My stare was immediately drawn to the colorful curtains that fluttered in front of the window.

Sleep had plagued me off and on, and some of it was definitely due to whatever potions they were feeding me. As such, I had no idea how much time had passed since I had arrived, so I decided now was as good of time as any to ask.

"How long have I been here?"

The healer's eyes snapped open, revealing that they were a light color I had never seen belonging to an Incan before.

"Long enough."

Well. That wasn't an answer.

I opened my mouth to ask a different question, but their glare told me that they wouldn't be answering any questions that weren't about my condition.

"How long until I heal?" I tried anyway.

"A while."

Inti, they were impossible. "Anything I can do to speed up the process?"

They shook their head. "Just rest."

I let out a huff. Resting wasn't going to save Azucena from being sacrificed to the gods, and because I had no idea how long I had been here, I had no idea how long I had until harvest—when the sacrifice would take place.

"How did you sustain this injury?" the healer questioned, their fingers brushing lightly over the dark splotch occupying my ribs.

"Hunting," I replied, not willing to give them any details that could be used to trap me.

"Hunting how?"

Oh, now they wanted to talk. "I don't want to talk about it." I shut my eyes, so they would know that the conversation was over, and before I intended to, my mind began to drift toward sleep. Whether it was because of another dose of whatever I had been given to break my fever, or the comfortable bed—which was much nicer than my straw one at home—I couldn't be sure.

Regardless, I fought sleep, trying to figure out if there was a way for me to help Azucena. Just as a plan was beginning to formulate in my mind, the healer pressed down lightly, causing me to gasp in pain.

"It would be easier to treat you if I knew what happened."

I didn't deign an answer. Obviously, they knew I wasn't asleep, but I refused to betray Azucena.

Even if it killed me.

Twenty–Seven

AZUCENA

We passed through town without issue, though as we drew into the more densely populated area right at the base of the hill where my palace stood, I could swear people were growing more uneasy. They didn't seem to glance at us too long, and I wasn't afraid we had been discovered . .. they were just uneasy, and I couldn't put my finger on why.

Eztil traveled close to my side, often peering around corners before he would let me cross an open street. Although I knew he was young and wouldn't truly be much help if a conflict did arise, the joy on his face was worth having him keep me company.

Our journey took the rest of the daylight, and all too soon we were approaching the waters which surrounded the bottom of the hill my palace was built on. You couldn't tell from the outside, but the canals continued beneath the palace, the crocodiles that lived there providing natural protection. My parents had gone to great lengths to transport the crocodiles from the great river up north by stealing eggs, which later hatched into juveniles, that were now full-grown adults.

The water was unnaturally still as Eztil and I stood by the edge, observing the steep hillside on the other side.

"What now, Sapa Inca?" he asked in a quiet but fearless voice.

"You are to return home, okay? I will come find you soon if I'm successful."

He bit his lip, eyeing the surface of the water. "Are you sure you don't need me."

I turned my neck to smile at the boy. "I'm sure. Thank you for getting me through town, but now I must carry on alone."

"I'll wait until you are out of sight."

I bit my lip. I didn't know how to tell him this, but I was about to dive into the crocodile-infested waters to reach the hidden entrance beneath the surface. My parents had developed an escape plan, if we ever needed it, but unfortunately, that plan only worked when you were on the inside on your way out. Going in, as I was about to do, meant I was on my own and could be eaten—something I didn't want young Eztil to see.

"Thank you, Eztil, but I cannot reveal the secret entrance until you are officially a guard, so I need you to leave before I proceed—understand?"

He gazed up at me, eyes wide and full of questions, but he nodded nonetheless, giving me a brief hug before darting back the way he came.

I waited several moments, sending a quick prayer to the gods that the crocodiles weren't hungry before taking a deep breath and diving into the dark waters.

It wasn't until my head was beneath the surface and the cloak filled with heavy water that I realized I had made a few mistakes.

One, it was nighttime and too dark for me to see the secret entrance. While Eztil had navigated us to where he thought it was, I had to hope now that the rumors were precise because I couldn't see anything beneath the water.

And two, I should have removed the brightly-colored cloak.

It was too late for both of those things however, and my only choice was to swim forward before the air I held in my lungs expired.

The water became deeper and then grew more shallow again.

It wasn't until my head was once again above water that I realized I had missed it.

Cursing myself mentally, I took another gulp of air, my gaze darting around above the surface of the water to see where I had gone wrong.

The position appeared correct, from the times I had practiced taking the escape tunnel with my parents, which meant I was likely just slightly off. So close, yet so far.

Taking another deep breath, I headed beneath the water, returning to the deepest part of the water to search for the opening.

Feeling around in the inky darkness, my hands encountered mud, mud, and more mud, but no smooth stone indicating the secret entrance. Dejected, I moved back to the shallow part of the water, giving myself a moment to breathe before swimming in the other direction.

As I allowed the crisp night air into my screaming lungs, there was movement from the corner of my vision, the direction I had just searched.

My heart pounded in my chest—it was now or never. The crocodiles were coming.

Although my lungs hadn't recovered from the previous dive, I forced them to hang on to the little air I had sucked in as I dove and rapidly ran my hands in every direction, searching for the stone. Just as I was about to give up, I finally felt the rough river bottom give way to something smooth.

I briefly debated going back to the surface for an extra breath of air, but a glint of light, much too close for comfort, told me there wasn't time.

Darkness was creeping into my vision as my brain screamed for oxygen, and I paddled to the opening. Releasing the last few bubbles from my lungs, I dove, feeling along the stone as it curved up.

Just as I was sure I wouldn't be making it, my head broke the surface, the stone cell lit up by torches which lined the wall from the outside.

I pulled myself from the water, lying panting at the water's edge. My father had always said that the crocodiles weren't smart enough to dive deeper, but not willing to risk it, I rolled back from the water's edge as soon as I caught my breath.

Exhausted, I debated lying there, with my eyes closed, for a bit longer, but I knew the cell where this exit was located was right in the dungeon's center. I needed to move during their shift change or risk being sighted—which meant I needed to start observing now.

Trying to hype myself up, I rolled to a sitting position, pulling off the heavy cloak and tucking it under my arm.

Approaching the edge of the stone cell, I used the lowest foothold to peer into the hall and take note of how many guards were in the dungeon this evening.

Incan prison cells were small and dark, due to the fact that they were only open in two small holes toward the top. It was impossible to see out of them, and they remained very dark almost all sun-cycle long. When it was time to release a prisoner, a rope was lowered so they could be pulled out of one of the holes. But that was rare, as the cells themselves were quite cruel—although nothing like being chained to a bed in a hut with Rurac—and most prisoners didn't last long.

This cell that I was trapped in was different, however, as a few stones protruded from the smooth surface of the wall, creating a ladder that could be used to enter the cell when needed. Unfortunately for me, a step stool was used to enter the cell from the outside, and it was likely still tucked in my quarters for safekeeping, meaning I would have to drop directly to the floor once it was safe to move.

I maintained my vigil, the cloak hanging on the highest rung so the water could drip out of it while I tried to figure out when it would be safe to execute my plan.

My vigil was suddenly interrupted by the sound of splashing behind me.

Sure that the crocodiles had found a way to follow me, I pulled myself onto the top rung of the stone ladder, balancing myself precariously and hoping the crocodiles wouldn't be able to climb as they could in stories.

In my panic and exhaustion, it took a moment for me to gain the strength to turn around, but when I did, I was shocked to see none other than a tired Eztil pulling himself from the water.

"Eztil!" I hissed, rushing to pull him the rest of the way from the water.

He coughed a few times, despite my attempts to shush him. Hopefully the guards would just think it was one of the prisoners.

"Sapa Inca," he said quietly, his head nearly lolling to the side.

"Eztil, I told you to go home."

"I know," he admitted, his voice wavering. "But then I saw what you were trying to do, and I knew you would need me."

I emitted a sigh, I couldn't believe he had found the entrance after me, though I hadn't been the most graceful in my search. "Eztil you could have been killed."

"I know—I saw the crocodiles," he admitted. "But I had to make sure you made it."

I couldn't help the way my heart warmed at his words. Eztil really would make an excellent guard someday.

He panted for a few more moments, the sound of his heavy breathing filling the cell. Once it was back under control, he turned to me. "Now what?"

"I'm thinking." And I was. My plan had only included me, and now with a young boy tagging along it wouldn't work as well—

A spark ignited in my mind. Maybe it was actually good that he had followed me. A boy would be much less noticeable than I would be prowling about the palace halls. We had many yanakuna who started their palace service at his age.

"I've got an idea, but you need to listen very carefully—"

Twenty-Eight

AZUCENA

Eztil nodded enthusiastically as I laid out exactly where he was to go and the layout of the palace. Although I had only been missing for almost one moon cycle, it seemed a bit strange to be back here. Especially knowing that no one had truly been missing me.

Once I finished, we wasted no time, and I helped Eztil climb up the wall and drop down to the other side. Although it was a precarious drop, he managed it easily, bending his knees as I directed to soften his landing.

He glanced up to indicate that all was well with a hand signal we had formulated before slinking into the shadows. We hadn't waited for the changing of the guard in the end, mostly because I was certain Eztil would be overlooked. But that didn't prevent me now from sinking back against the wall and sending up a quick plea to the gods, my teeth chattering in fear the entire time.

I had directed Eztil to where he could find Nania, my yanakuna who hopefully was still employed. I knew she would be the only ally in the palace I could count on, as we had practically grown up together—though there were likely others who detested Yezema's harsh way of ruling. Regardless, he was to find her first and then she could point him toward the right people to help us. If there were any.

This is where you originally joined this tale. Finding me here, in my own dungeon, trying to avoid my own sacrifice to the gods. Of course, I'm sure you know who the villain is by now, but this isn't the end quite yet, a lot has happened while you were busy getting caught up, so keep reading.

AGAIN, I found myself drifting off from the exhaustion of the past few sun-cycles, and it wasn't until I heard the thump of a ladder and a quiet "Empress" that I even realized I had been asleep for the entirety of Eztil executing his assigned portion the plan.

I peered through the crack in my eyelids, trying desperately to rub the sleep from my eyes as my body flushed in embarrassment. A male guard with a white aura was leaning over me, and my clothes, still wet from my dip in the river, were plastered to my skin.

"Empress," he tried again. "Are you all right?"

I nodded as he helped me into a standing position, my voice escaping me.

"We apologize, Sapa Inca. We knew Yezema's story about you running away didn't sound right, but when no word came of you after so many sun-cycles we assumed—"

I waved him off as I began to climb up the stones to pass over the wall. "It's all right. She's much craftier than I think any of us realized."

As I reached the top of the wall, I found another guard waiting there, with Eztil standing next to him in clothes that fit him well enough for most certainly being borrowed. He waved at me as I tried to calculate how I would get down.

"I'm Atiy, Sapa Inca. I'll catch you," the guard on the ground said, holding his arms wide. "We couldn't find the step stool."

It was a good thing he was ready, because at that moment my

hands began to shake—either from exhaustion or the penetrating cold I couldn't be sure, but I slid less than gracefully from where I sat on the top of the wall into Atiy's arms. As soon as my feet touched the ground, I pushed back from him. It would be quite improper for anyone to see us so close—much less touching.

That thought pierced through my brain like a spear, and I cringed, remembering I still didn't know what happened to Rurac.

I surveyed the guard who had caught me as the one who had awoken me slid down the wall with cat-like grace behind me. "Did Yezema—"

He nodded. "She's already here. She's taken over your rooms, but Nania has instructed us to bring her to your room in the yanakuna quarters until we have enough numbers, or a better plan, to overthrow her."

His mouth was set in a grim line and though I knew I didn't likely want the answer, I asked anyway. "How many do we have?"

Atiy motioned for me to walk down hall toward where I knew the door from the cold dungeons to the palace would be. "Only five, Sapa Inca. I'm sorry, but it appears Yezema had more support than we thought."

I let out a breath and rubbed my forehead. I still didn't know how this had happened.

The guard behind me, as if reading my thoughts, spoke up. "She was bribing them, Sapa Inca. I only found out recently, but that was why she was throwing so many people down here. She was taking extra tithes, which many could not pay, to win the opinion of many members in your court. Then she was taking that extra tithe, pocketing it, and using it to bribe middle class citizens across the empire."

My breath caught and I knew I needed to ask the next question as much as the answer would pain me. "Our enemy tribes—"

He shook his head. "We have no record that this has extended beyond Sipan's borders. So, there's that positive."

My shoulders fell. That was good at least. I should have

known, though, about Yezema. As the only remaining advisor, Yezema had much more control than she should have. I had been so desperate for a break from my duties each sun-cycle that I had let her sit on my throne regularly. Then I had been dumb enough to mention her pending retirement. The news probably made her more desperate, knowing I was to relieve her of her duties soon, and I had likely put her plan into motion.

"I'm sorry I didn't pay more attention," I spoke into the silence at last, not sure how to swallow the bitter taste of the reality I was currently facing.

The two guards nodded to the other two who were guarding the dungeon door, and I realized they must be part of the measly five who supported my rule. A dejecting thought.

Eztil trailed behind us, his exhaustion evident in the way he couldn't lift his feet entirely from the floor, creating a brushing noise with every step.

"This way, Sapa Inca." Atiy motioned to a slim door hidden partially out of view and I ducked into the small dark hallway. My eyes had been spoiled by the torches, and it took a moment for them to adjust. When they did, I noticed the hall we were in was so small, with a low ceiling that made it feel cramped, the guards' heads almost brushing it. "Yanakuna quarters," he explained.

I was glad they had thought of all this, but the fact that I hadn't heard of Rurac's fate still weighed heavy on my heart. "Did Yezema have an injured man with her when she returned?"

Atiy shook his head as he motioned me into a tiny room holding two small straw beds. The beds were pushed up against opposing walls, but there was barely room to pass between them. "I'm sorry. I don't know much about the situation, but I think everyone who returned with the advisor was in good health."

The little flicker of hope that was left in my chest snuffed out.

There wasn't time to wallow in my emotions however, as the guard closest to me began to dive into their plan as soon as the door was closed behind them. If I had thought the room was cramped before, it was now almost impossible to move with the three adults and one child. Eztil, without direction, moved to one bed, sinking down into it and promptly falling asleep. I moved to sit in the other one—just so I could make more space in the room.

"Here's the problem." The other guard glanced at Atiy next to him before continuing. "We are so severely outnumbered we can't simply attack. Rather, we need to devise a plan that would trick Yezema into our hands."

I released a whoosh of breath from my lungs and leaned back on the bed. Despite my nap in the dungeon, exhaustion weighed heavily on my shoulders. Regardless, the wheels in my mind turned. "What if we could lure Yezema into the dungeon and lock her up? With five of us, we should be able to man the dungeon."

The guard nodded. "That's a good idea. How will we lure her though?"

Both of them quieted, eyes resting on me. It made sense, considering I knew her best, yet my mind still couldn't seem to come up with a reason for Yezema to be in the dungeons. She was always the first to delegate a task to someone else, something I used to do regularly too, and it appeared I didn't know her as well as I thought I had. "Hm."

Silence stretched between us, as they continued to watch me, but no ideas came. Finally, I shivered, the cold from my wet clothing like spears dragging across my skin.

The men took notice. "Forgive us, Sapa Inca. We will fetch Nania—she was to acquire clothing for you. We will revisit this plan later."

Without waiting for my approval, they both ducked out of the room, the door closing behind them with a whoosh. Not that I would have stopped them. Despite the precarious situation I found myself in, I honestly couldn't wait to see Nania again. She had been my one friend in the palace—even if she hadn't seen things that way.

It didn't take long before she was slipping through the door, a bundle of clothes clutched in her arms.

"Sapa Inca," she whispered, taking note of the sleeping form of Eztil on the other bed.

"Nania, you know you can call me Zu."

She blushed but avoided my question. "I have brought you clothes." She held them up, and my brow creased in confusion. "This is a yanakuna dress. Putting you in your old clothes would be too obvious."

She was right. Turning away I slipped off everything, including my wet undergarments—the air of the yanakuna quarters warm against my bumpy skin. Within a breath, Nania slipped the dress over my head and was tying the sash behind my waist. I fought the urge to look for a reflecting stone, like the one found in my chambers—I doubted the yanakuna quarters had one. Not to mention, I had gone this long without one . . . meaning I could go a bit longer.

"You're too skinny," Nania commented as she draped a blanket over my shoulders.

"I was held against my will." It was obvious, but I didn't know any other way to address her observation.

Her mouth turned down at the corners. "I'm so sorry, Sapa Inca. I should have been looking for you."

I held up my hand. "You are my yanakuna. The type of help I needed following my kidnapping would be so far outside of your line of work I never expected you to help."

She hung her head. "Still, I feel shame about it. You are my Sapa Inca—one of the gods' chosen."

I placed my raised hand on her shoulder and pulled her into an embrace, something I never would have done before.

"Sapa Inca?" she whispered by my ear. "Are you all right?"

"I missed you is all." I pulled back, the weight on my shoulders refusing to abate. "We need to think of a way to trick Yezema. Do you have any ideas?"

She tilted her head to the side. "Trick her how?"

"Into the dungeons."

"Hm." She pondered for a moment, looking about the small room.

An idea suddenly slithered into my mind. "Is there anyone she's close to? Maybe that she would go looking for?"

Nania shook her head. "I am unsure. I was always assigned to you and even when you were missing I was tasked with being ready to assist you in the case of your unexpected return."

"I understand," I clarified. "But, Yezema must have appointed a yanakuna of her own, no?"

I watched as her face brightened. "Of course, Empress. I have seen her with a male yanakuna often on her heels."

This caused me to raise my eyebrows. It was odd to have a preferred yanakuna of a different gender unless . . . either way it didn't matter. "Excellent. Maybe the guards can lure him to the dungeon."

"Excellent idea, Empress. I will fetch them now seeing as you are dressed."

Twenty-Nine

AZUCENA

After relaying our plan to two of the guards that rescued me, Nania excused herself for what remained of the night, letting me know she would fetch me as soon as the plan was complete. Even in yanakuna clothing, I was too recognizable around the palace, and I would only appear once we had trapped Yezema.

The guards were apparently ensuring they were assigned to the dungeons the next sun-cycle, so that when Yezema was lured there she could be trapped. I didn't know the name of her personal yanakuna, but I had been quite unbothered by matters about the palace that I felt below me prior to my kidnapping, something which I now deeply regretted. While I was uncertain whether I would have been able to avoid said kidnapping if I had paid attention in advance, I knew the way I had been ruling before was akin to blindness, and I needed to do better going forward.

I had fallen asleep with those thoughts floating around my mind, only to wake when Eztil roused and his stomach began growling so loudly I couldn't sleep through it.

"I'm sorry, Empress," he apologized, rubbing his stomach. "I was too excited to eat last night with my mother, and I regret it now."

"It's okay," I assured him, sitting up in my bed and stretching my muscles which had become stiff. The truth was, we hadn't arranged how, or when, we would be fed. Something I now added to my growing mental list of regrets.

"Do you think I can go get food for us?"

I thought for a moment. "No one noticed you yesterday?"

"No, Empress. I think they just assumed I was another yanakuna in training."

He had a point. He was young enough that he could probably convince the cooks to give him something to eat. "I can try and direct you to the kitchens. But I don't know the yanakuna passages, so you'll need to go back to the hall we were in before we entered this door. Then if you go away from the dungeons, you'll eventually be able to smell the food, and can follow your nose until you find the kitchens." I smiled at my own memory of following my nose for snacks during the middle of each sun-cycle when I was young.

"Okay," he agreed, enthusiastic and already heading for the door. "I will bring you something too, Empress."

"Thank you, Eztil." I watched as he slid out the door, closing it behind him. Hopefully he would be all right, as I also was quite hungry.

It didn't take long for the knob to turn and him to return with a tray of food. One look at it told me that it was for one of the higher-ups in the palace—such a Yezema herself—and that it would likely be missed. Hopefully no one saw him take it.

"I could only take one tray. Too many would seem suspicious." He sank down on the bed across from me, setting the food between us. Without waiting, he dove in, consuming some of the plate of fruits—leaving me to start with the potatoes and the dark meat which was likely alpaca.

"Regardless." I delicately spoke around the food in my mouth, unable to pause my eating once I began thanks to the angry pit in my stomach. "They will miss this. If anyone saw you take this, we likely can't have you sneak out again."

He nodded, cheeks full. After swallowing he asked, "How do you know?"

I held up the juicy slab of meat from the plate in the middle, the scent of the rich spices nearly causing me to shiver. "The meat in the palace is only reserved for the higher ranks. The rest only eat fruit and potatoes for breakfast."

He reached for his own slice of meat, moaning as he took a bite. "I never get anything like this at home. Maybe quwi if I catch one, but nothing like this."

My mouth was too full to answer, but I knew he spoke the truth. Most of those living outside of the palace could only afford meat on special occasions. It was a luxury I had grown up with, not realizing it was a luxury.

As I reached for a potato, my heart constricted as I remembered the jerky I had eaten with Rurac. That was something else I needed to address, and soon. He had to still be alive. If he had gone to Hana Pacha before I had the chance to tell him I loved him, I would never forgive myself.

It didn't take long for the two of us to clear the tray, eating every bit. Apparently, swimming had stolen the energy from us both.

Unfortunately, after we finished eating, there wasn't much else to do but sit and wait for Nania to come let us know that the plan had been successful. Eztil, having slept what was likely a full night, prattled on about all the adventures he had been on around his family farm. At first, I listened, giving my input from time to time, but eventually I found myself drifting off to sleep, still not having recovered from the nights of no sleep while traveling on the road.

I AWOKE to the sound of the door opening, Nania rushing inside.

"Sapa Inca, Atiy reports that they have lured your advisor in the dungeon. Come."

Without a word I stood. Eztil did too, but I shook my head. "This is too dangerous, Eztil. Stay here until I send Nania back for you."

"But—"

"No, Eztil, that is an order from your Sapa Inca." I didn't mean for my voice to sound as harsh as it did, causing Eztil's mouth to fall into a frown, but I absolutely needed him to stay here. "Do not follow me this time." I turned to Nania. "Stay with him. I will send one of the guards for you both when it is safe."

Without waiting for them to attempt to argue more, I made my way from the small room and down the dark hall where I remembered entering the yanakuna quarters.

I didn't hesitate when pushing open the wooden door—something I would come to regret later.

With confidence, I pushed my shoulders back and turned down the main hall toward the dungeons, ready to make Yezema pay for kidnapping and imprisoning me with Rurac. Something that had ended up being good—but I wasn't about to tell her that.

A smirk played on my lips as I rounded the corner, only to run into a guard I hadn't seen before. I immediately assumed he was the fifth guard that I hadn't met the night before.

I opened my mouth to ask where I needed to go, but he cut me off.

"What are you doing here? You're supposed to be dead."

Then there was a sharp pain at the back of my head, and everything went black.

Thirty

RURAC

The light filtering through the open window roused me once more. I attempted to stretch, only for the pain in my side to stab me and remind me that I hadn't yet healed from my gruesome climbing injury. I returned my arms to my side with a grimace.

My stomach growled in protest. The trays I was brought had been filled with some of the most decadent food I had ever tasted. It would be so hard to go back to my normal diet after this, but I was savoring what I could while it lasted. I wouldn't be growing thin this winter, that was for sure.

I'd lost track of how long it'd been since my most recent discussion with the healer as I found myself sleeping a lot more than normal—something I was starting to think they were doing on purpose so they could break me.

I had considered trying to talk to the healer again, as I was reasonably sure they didn't like the way the guards had been treating me, but at the same time, it didn't really seem like they were on my side either.

So, if I wanted to help Azucena, I would have to do it on my own.

Struggling to sit up, I rose from the bed and crossed the room to lean out the window enough to spot Inti as he crossed the sky.

He was much higher than he usually was when breakfast was served.

Had I missed breakfast?

I didn't think I had been sleeping that deeply, and usually the yanakuna who brought it would wake me up to eat. Odd.

I didn't get to dwell on that thought too long as the door opened and my healer swept into the room, their eyebrows rising as they noticed me away from my bed.

"You should be resting," they admonished.

Something about the way the words were said caused my chin to dip, as if I could hear my father himself in their words. In shame, I crossed the room and sunk back into bed. "I was just looking at the portion of the sun-cycle we were in."

"We are about halfway between meals," they replied as they sank into the stool by my bedside, specifically for their comfort as they attended to me for large portions of the sun-cycle.

So, I had missed breakfast. I wanted to ask for it, knowing the second and last meal of the sun-cycle was a long way off, but I chose to stay quiet instead. I had been faring okay, only because I hadn't been drawing any attention to myself. If I started now, I may not be able to make it out of here alive. Nor would I be able to rescue Zu.

My heart clenched as her name passed through my mind. I had no idea where she was, but I hoped and prayed to the gods that she was near—that she would be able to reclaim her throne before her advisor could discover her presence. That I was at least buying her some time.

"You are healing nicely." Their words snapped me back into my body.

"Will I be able to go home soon?" I asked.

Their lips pursed, and they said nothing. I had a feeling that although I was allowed certain freedoms in this room, I was still a prisoner, something which their reaction had just confirmed.

Their eyes remained on my ribs, where they were evaluating the dark bruising that had finally faded from black to purple. "Perhaps after the sacrifice."

My eyebrows shot up. I decided that playing dumb would get me the most information. "There's a sacrifice soon?"

They looked at me like I was some sort of idiot. "Yes, tonight, when Quilla in her full glory and crosses the sky."

My mouth felt like it was filled with dirt, and there was a sharp pain in my chest. I wanted to ask who the sacrifice was, but I couldn't risk it. "Oh." I scoured my mind for something to say that would seem plausible, given my feigned disinterested position. "Will I be able to attend?"

"Perhaps," they replied, rising from the stool and heading for the door. Although this individual had been my healer for several sun-cycles, they weren't what I would call friendly, and they didn't say anything more as they slipped out the door.

The moment I was alone, my mind dove into the panic which had been mounting. If there was still a sacrifice, that meant that Azucena had likely been captured. As my thoughts began to spiral and my breath sped up, I stopped myself, reminding my heart that there were other women prepared for sacrifice on a regular basis. After all, Quilla journeyed across the night sky every twenty-eight sun-cycles.

It was to no avail, though. All my mind could think about was Zu—my empress—being prepared for sacrifice. Her going to Hana Pacha thinking that I had hated her enough to beg her to leave me in the wilderness.

That wasn't going to be okay with me. Without considering the consequences, I rose from the bed, winced, and prepared to leave my room. The preparations were simple, considering all of the items I had brought with me to the palace had been taken from me, leaving me with just the pants I was wearing and a light cotton shirt that the healer often removed to inspect my injuries. I worried for a moment about my mother's weavings, but I knew now that I didn't need those to remember her by. I needed Azucena more.

I was committed to finding Azucena to free her if it was the last thing I ever did.

Resolve in place, and looking as put together as I could for having just spent the past several sun-cycles in bed, I turned toward the wooden door.

To my surprise, the door wasn't secure in any way, though it did hurt my side to exert the force needed to push it open. And when I leaned out into the hall, grimacing in pain, there were no guards there either. I hadn't been aware that they trusted me to this extent.

Their mistake.

I stepped one foot out into the hall, which was illuminated beautifully thanks to the openings in the walls that allowed the light of Inti to sweep in. Every step jarred my injured side, making me feel as if the healer had lied about the fact that I was doing better. Though I could walk, I felt nothing akin to my previous health and strength.

Meandering my way down the hall with difficulty, I poked my head into any doorway I passed. My plan was to pretend I was looking for the kitchens. I didn't know if I would get away with it, or if I would even find Zu in the meantime, but I knew I had to try.

As I passed room after room, I realized how truly massive the palace was, while most individuals in the village, like myself, lived in houses with only one, maybe two rooms. I knew, in this regard, I was also lucky, as my father had mastered the skills to expand our house beneath the surface of the Pacha Mama. Regardless, it was nothing close to the size of the palace where Zu had grown up. I could almost picture a young Zu with bright eyes, running through these halls with a smile on her face.

How different our lives had been.

What surprised me most about the palace, though, was that many of the rooms I passed were unoccupied. Actually, much of the palace seemed unoccupied. I passed several corners where the stones were worn, likely due to a guard pacing, only there wasn't a single guard in sight.

My heart clenched.

Were they already at the sacrifice? Was I too late?

I shook those thoughts from my head. Inti was still in the sky; I still had time. They wouldn't deviate from the established ritual.

Despite my own reassurances to myself, I couldn't seem to quell the deep-rooted fear in my gut and the unease taking up residence in my stomach. Where was everyone? Why was there not a single guard, nor signs of the healer who had just left my room a few moments before?

Despite my positive self-talk, passing more and more empty rooms and halls solidified my fears. It was likely that the sacrifice was about to begin. I was too late.

This would be the end of our story.

Thirty-One

AZUCENA

This was it. This was the end. After I was forced to dress in the typical, sacrificial wear, my hands and feet were bound in front of my body. In Sipan, we didn't make sacrifices very often, but I do remember the one after the death of my father, as the young woman who was supposed to be sacrificed had come to the palace and remained with us for several sun-cycles preceding the sacrifice.

Back when my father was emperor, the sacrifices occurred twice each solar-path—one on the shortest night of the year, and one on the longest night. Both were to ensure the bounty of the harvest. The sacrifices had always been of individuals between thirteen and sixteen solar-paths. And though the position was supposed to be a voluntary one, my parents had long suspected that those "volunteering" had been convinced by their parents to do so—to gain the gods' favor.

That aside, the tributes were treated well before their death—allowed to live in the palace and eat and drink as much as they desired, until the sun-cycle came for them to be drugged with coca and alcohol and led up the mountain to die in Inti's temple.

The young woman who had come when I was a child had been no different. At the time, I had been young—too young to know any better—and I had befriended her when she arrived, only for my mother to break the news several sun-cycles after her mysterious disappearance that she had gone to Hana Pacha to help the gods care for my father.

I was devastated, and my mother had known. I was never one for friends, not real friends anyway, and the fact that my time with my first one was cut so short—I had never really recovered. Thus, my mother, knowing my pain, had begun to lower the number of sacrifices from twice per solar-path to only once—praying the gods wouldn't be angry.

If you want to know my opinion, the gods hadn't seemed to care at all and during the eight solar-paths of my mother's rule, because nothing terrible had happened.

So, when my mother had gone to Hana Pacha, I had forgone the ritualistic sacrifices entirely. She could take care of father, and father could take care of her. Yezema had protested the stopping of tradition, as had many of my other advisors, but I was reeling from the death of my mother, the last thing I wanted to do was befriend another young villager just sun-cycles before I sent them to their death.

The older I had grown, the more resentful of the gods I had become. Why did the gods need help anyway? Weren't they gods? Couldn't they just snap their fingers and get things done?

But apparently, Yezema did not feel the same way, as I was about to become the first sacrifice to the gods in the six solar-paths since my mother's death.

It didn't matter though; it was too late for me. As soon as Inti left the sky they would begin to lead me up the mountains—to the holy peaks where I would be imbibed and left to die.

I let out a sigh and leaned my head back against the rough stone. I had spent too many solar-paths with my eyes theoretically closed to my own actions and those of my people. I had thought, because I was keeping the dungeons from overflowing, that I was doing good. The reality couldn't be further from the truth.

My stomach growled, protesting that I had done nothing but

split breakfast with Eztil that morning. That, and it still hadn't recovered from the several sun-cycles of low rations on the long journey here.

I just hoped they fed me before forcing me to eat the coca leaves and alcoholic chicha that would help the god of death, Supay, find me quickly.

I rested my chin on my chest. Might as well pray to the gods now so that they would have my place prepared for me in Hana Pacha. Maybe I would get to see my parents again. I hoped they were proud of me.

I swore I must have drifted off and started dreaming because I heard a voice that sounded just like Rurac's.

"My empress."

My heart rate increased and my brow furrowed. His voice sounded just how I remembered it. Strong, gruff—

"Zu, you have to wake up."

My eyes snapped open to connect with Rurac's brown ones. Before I could stop myself, his name tumbled from my lips. "Rurac. I missed you." I hadn't meant to say that second part.

He seemed taken aback by my words as he began working on the knotted rope that held my ankles together.

It seemed to be taking too long, and I had the sudden thought that this was my time to confess everything to him before I died.

"I know you lied to save me," I clarified. Although I could see the bright colors illuminating his aura now, I didn't have to glance at them to know how he felt about me. Not anymore.

The look on his face instantly morphed into regret, then desire. "You don't hate me?"

My ankles were free and he moved to the ropes on my wrists. "No, I don't." My voice was too airy, too light . . . had they already given me something to slow my inhibitions?

Rurac noticed too, his gaze coming up to search mine as the second rope fell to the floor. "Are you feeling all right?"

"I thought so." I stood and brushed myself off looking around the small room I was in. It tilted a bit, but I shook my head and everything straightened. "Where are we?"

He shrugged. "I have no idea—this is your palace. I just happened to look in this room and see you."

We both made our way to the door, and I poked my head around the corner. I pulled back. "I don't know either. Despite what you might think of me, I don't spend my sun-cycles cataloging the numerous rooms in my palace."

His lips turned up in a smirk. "I would never. Though you might consider housing some of the villagers who don't have a home in the future . . . if we get out of this." He grabbed my hand in his and I felt warmth run through my body, despite the constriction in my chest. "I guess we just run for it then. Are you ready?"

I nodded. "We need to get back to the yanakuna rooms. Nania can help us from there."

His face was filled with questions. "I don't know where those are."

"I'm not sure either," I admitted, shame clouding my voice. "But I think if we head to the kitchens, I can get us to the dungeons from there and the entry to the yanakuna hall is there.

"All right. Stay quiet and follow my lead." Rurac visibly winced as he leaned around the corner.

"No, I'll lead us." I pointed to my nose. "I've got this." I pulled him into the hall, relishing the way his hand felt warm and heavy in my hand. I knew that we needed to discuss more about what had happened on the edge of the cliff several sun-cycles before, but there would be time for that later.

I wasn't lying when I told him that I didn't recognize these halls, but as I passed a few hallways, I did begin to recognize the part of the palace we were headed toward. It was the area where all my advisors had lived before I had dismissed them (except Yezema). Now, it was used to house visitors when I had them—which, to be honest, wasn't often. And considering Yezema had moved into my rooms . . . well it was likely this entire hall was empty.

We hardly saw anyone, which was either a blessing, or an indication our luck was about to run out. At one point, we did hear the sound of footsteps coming our way, and we both pulled back against the wall as they drew closer. We stared into each other's eyes as Rurac pulled me into his chest.

My heart was about to explode.

"Do you trust me?" Rurac whispered.

I nodded, and before I could blink, his lips were on mine and he spun us, pushing me up against the wall.

I couldn't deny it, the feeling of his lips on mine felt like home. Like the thing I had been searching for my entire life and finally found. My heart calmed, despite the precarious situation we were in. My body had been missing this—no, craving this.

As quickly as it began, it was over, and the footsteps were fading away. Whoever it was hadn't even turned the corner.

"Um . . ." I searched for something to say—a way to bridge this valley of awkwardness between us.

"We better hurry," Rurac said, his eyes seeming to dart anywhere but mine.

I wanted to discuss it more, but I knew now wasn't the time, so I took the lead once more, leading us down corridor after corridor.

As the hallway began to widen, indicating we were coming close to the common areas of the palace, I pulled him against the wall, ensuring both of us were pressed flat before peering around the corner.

I spotted two guards who were standing further down, near the door where they allowed the peasants to enter each sun-cycle. Apparently, my pending sacrifice hadn't changed the tithe schedule at all.

"What is it," Rurac hissed under his breath, nearly intelligible.

"Two guards," I breathed back. He nodded, his lips pressed together in a thin line.

I tried to think of what to do—some way to get around them. But based on the actions which had brought me into this situation in the first place, I had nothing. So, we remained there, pressed against the wall.

"We can't just stay here," Rurac said at last, his voice barely audible.

"Do you have any ideas? Because I'm out," I quipped in return, trying to push away the memory of our kiss just a few short moments before, my arms and legs trembling. It was now becoming clear to me that I had been given something while I had been tied up. Likely some sort of muscle relaxing herb to keep me subdued, and all of this activity was stretching my capabilities.

He pinched between his brows, his lips moving, but no words came out. When his eyelids shot open again, I could see his resolve, obvious in their depths. "When I go around the corner, you need to run." Rurac's eyes bored into mine, waiting for my silent promise.

"I'm not leaving you," I whispered, gripping his hand tighter and leaning closer to him.

It didn't matter though, because Rurac pulled his hand from my grip easily, and before I could reach for it again, he was around the corner, gripping his side and limping out of my view.

"Excuse me." His voice was even and loud, probably for my benefit. "My healer said they would return with some bandages, but they haven't been back yet. Can you lead me to them?"

There were some hushed sounds as the guards conversed, then, "He will take you."

"Oh," Rurac moaned, but I could tell it was fake. "I think I'm going to—"

I heard the unmistakable sound of a body hitting the stone. I grimaced.

"Ugh," one of the guards huffed. "You take this arm, and I'll take the other. We will just carry him."

There was shuffling. "What does this man eat? He's heavier than a puma."

Despite the perilous situation, I couldn't help but grin as I pictured the guards struggling to carry Rurac's massive form.

The two of them continued grumbling as their voices faded from earshot. I waited an extra few moments to ensure I wouldn't run into them, then I dashed around the corner, heading past the kitchens to the hall that held the entrance to the dungeons.

Well, I tried to dash, but I probably looked more like a baby deer shortly after birth. Regardless, I was able to make it down the hall, around the corner, and press open the door to the yanakuna quarters without getting caught.

Letting out a breath, I leaned against the wall and allowed myself a moment to breathe. I didn't dawdle long though, because I didn't know if all the servants were loyal to me, and I didn't want to risk it.

My heart clenched at the fact that Rurac was back in captivity, but at least I knew he was alive, and that was more information than I'd had before.

And I was sure, now that I was free again, Eztil, the guards, and I would be able to come up with a plan to free him.

I pushed myself forward, down the few dark remaining paces to the first door, where we had been lodging. I pushed it open, excited to surprise Eztil with my return.

But the minute both empty beds came into view, my shoulders slumped.

Eztil was gone.

Thirty-Two

AZUCENA

I sank onto the bed, my legs nearly giving out beneath me. My natural instinct was to go and try to find Eztil, but I knew that if I was caught, Rurac's sacrifice would have been for nothing. On top of that, my legs still felt weak.

My only hope was to signal Nania.

Developing a plan, I moved back toward the door, cracking it a bit but staying out of sight, should anyone walk by. It was a bit difficult with my weak legs, but I brushed them off and told myself there would be time for feeling weak later.

It took much longer than I anticipated for another yanakuna to pass by, and I figured this must be a lesser-known entrance to their living area. But the moment one did, I called out, moving my body entirely behind the door and out of view.

"Excuse me."

I heard the yanakuna stop in her tracks.

Here went nothing. "Can you call Nania for me?"

"What for?" I didn't recognize the feminine voice that called back. Hopefully that meant they hadn't worked close enough to me to recognize mine either.

"She borrowed something from me, and I need it back," I fibbed.

"What did she borrow?"

This woman was nosy, but then again . . . I didn't converse with yanakuna other than Nania very often. I scrambled to come up with a lie that she wouldn't second guess. "A potion. For my female troubles."

There was a pause. Then, "I'll fetch her."

"Thanks," I replied, relief threading its way through my voice.

I stood there, my white knuckles gripping the door and my legs vibrating with weakness for what seemed like an entire solar-path until, finally, I heard the quick steps of Nania coming my way. I pulled back from the door just as she moved to push it open.

"Empress!" she nearly shouted as she went in to hug me. Normally I would push her off, but after the events of the last few sun-cycles, I allowed it to happen. "We thought you were gone forever."

"Me too," I replied as I removed myself from the embrace to look at the empty space behind her. "Where is Eztil?

She let out a sigh that I immediately knew wasn't good news. "Sit down, you're shaking."

I did as she commanded, my fingers splayed on my chest as I fought for breath.

Nania took the spot next to me. "He went into the metropolis."

My jaw slackened. That was not the answer I expected. "So, he's okay?"

"More than okay," she promised, laying her hand on one of mine. "He realized we were fighting a losing battle, so he went to go rally the villagers. He swears most of them are still loyal to you. I'm just sad that it has been in vain."

"No—" I spoke a little more harshly than I had intended and readjusted my tone before speaking again. "Not in vain. I'm still not free. I escaped when they weren't looking. We still need to overthrow Yezema. Is she still in the dungeon?"

Nania shook her head sadly. "I'm sorry, Sapa Inca, but when

you didn't come, they thought it was just the few rogue guards trying to overthrow—"

I gulped and hung my head. "So . . . ?"

"We had to adjust our plans." She dipped her chin. "We now have to hope the villagers come through for you."

I was pensive for a moment. Would it be enough to rally the villagers in my favor? I wasn't sure. "Go on."

"I don't think I can get word to Eztil before, but he promised when he left to have the villagers in place during the ceremony. He was confident that you still had many supporters in the village. The three remaining guards who are on our side, and weren't captured earlier, will be in place as well, and one of them will give the signal."

"Then we too should find a way to make it into the ceremony," I surmised, looking around the room.

"Absolutely," Nania agreed. "Maybe we could dress you as a yanakuna?"

I shook my head. "I'll be recognized. But you forgot the bigger issue. Without a sacrifice, there won't be a ceremony."

"You're right."

Just as I was about to tell her to let me head back to be tied up, she said, "I'll go."

My jaw dropped open. "What?"

"We need the tribute to be someone who is in on the plan, but also someone who can be drugged. We need you to be aware when the attack happens so you can seize control as soon as Yezema is dethroned. Also, we look alike." She motioned her finger between us, and for the first time I realized she was one of the few yanakuna that stood near my height, and our hair and skin were similar shades. Though our faces were different, from the back, no one would be able to tell that she wasn't me.

"But that's not fair to you," I argued, not liking the mental picture the thought of her being drugged produced.

She lifted her chin, her eyes, which I noticed for the first time were a curious shade of hazel, meeting mine. "Life isn't fair,

Empress. It wasn't fair that you got kidnapped all because you were planning on dismissing an advisor."

I sighed. "I know, Nania, but had I been a better empress—"

She shook her head. "It doesn't matter now. And even if it did, I think you were already on your way to becoming a great empress. You just needed a little more time to heal and grow."

Her words hung in the air, permeating the small room. I gave them a few moments to sink in before I disturbed the silence once more.

"You're an amazing woman, Nania."

"You too, Sapa Inca."

"Zu," I corrected, and she raised her eyebrows. "If you're really about to take my place as a sacrifice, you absolutely must call me by my name. I insist."

"Okay, Zu." A small smile played on her lips.

I rose from the bed, my legs still quaking. "We need to get you back to where they were holding me before they notice I was gone."

She nodded. "And we need to move slow, so I don't run out of breath before we get there."

My lips quirked up at the corner at the mention of her breathing condition. "Of course."

Thirty-Three

RURAC

Within a few moments of leaving Zu's side, I was once again back in my normal quarters, the same healer as before, peering at my wounds and frowning.

"It doesn't seem to be bleeding."

"It felt like it was," I fibbed. I didn't want to say anything that would make them undermine the story I told the guards.

"And you passed out?"

I nodded furiously. "I felt lightheaded. I missed my breakfast tray."

"Is that so?" The healer searched my face, likely trying to deduce how much of their trust to grant me.

"Yes, I believe I slept through it."

"All right. Well, I will send for an early dinner tray. Make sure you eat everything."

"I will."

The healer hurried from the room, a cloth bundle of their tools clutched to their chest, as seemingly unhappy to be in my presence as I was theirs.

Now, I had a decision to make. I could wait for the dinner tray, eat, and then try to find Azucena. Or, I could skip the dinner tray and run to find her now.

The rumble in my stomach chose for me.

I leaned back on the bed, wondering just how long I should wait when there was a knock on the door and a young man entered, a wooden tray balanced on his hand. Good thing I hadn't planned to run right away, I would have most certainly been caught.

The yanakuna placed the tray in front of me before bowing and taking their leave. I wanted to tell him to cut that out, that I wasn't any higher in life than he was. But there wasn't a chance. He was there one moment, and replaced by empty space the next.

I dug into the tray with gusto, savoring the spiced meats, yucca, and corn. I told myself to slow down, that this very well could be my last fancy meal for a very long time, but my raging stomach wouldn't allow my movements to slow. Within moments, I had wolfed down everything, an empty slab of wood staring back at me.

With my body's basal needs satisfied, everything that had just transpired between Zu and I sunk in.

It hadn't been until her body was under mine and my lips were on hers that I realized just how much I had missed her the past few sun-cycles—since I forced her to leave me for dead in the forest. And now there was a chance that we weren't going to make it out of this alive.

I grimaced as I remembered the way her eyes had come alight when she saw me. She had forgiven me in an instant, and the resolve in her voice when she said she trusted me after I had been the one to betray her trust . . . I didn't deserve her.

Especially if I couldn't get us both out of this situation alive.

I couldn't fail her. Even if I died, she had to go on.

With that in mind, I began to formulate a plan. One that no one in this fancy palace would see coming.

As INTI BEGAN to sink beneath the hills and the shadows began to grow long in my room, I pushed my plan into action. It wasn't the best plan I had ever devised, and it had lots of unknowns, but anything was better than sitting and hoping Azucena escaped but never knowing for certain.

At this point, because she hadn't returned for me, I assumed the worse.

Just as before, the door was unguarded and I poked my head around the doorframe to confirm the hall was empty, before slipping out of my room and beginning my journey past all of the empty rooms. Even though they said they didn't trust me, it sure seemed like I had a lot of freedom. *Ah, well, not my problem,* I thought with a shrug as I began to make my way down the hall. In any other situation, I would probably marvel at the brilliant stonework in this palace, and its impressive size compared to my small home, but there wasn't time for that now.

I couldn't be sure that I was following the exact same path through the halls as earlier, because when I had been with Azucena, I was far too distracted by the fact that I was in her presence to note the exact route we had taken together. But I remembered the first few turns, and by the time I arrived at the portion I didn't remember, I was able to follow my nose toward the kitchen, just as she had.

Now this was the part where I had to hope that the gods were looking out for me and were ready to give their assistance. But one look around the same corner I had stood on the other side of that morning confirmed that the gods must have been busy helping someone else today.

There were still two guards.

Brushing my hands down the front of my shirt, which by this point was threadbare and had seen better sun-cycles, I let out a deep breath and prepared to give the plan my all.

I stepped out from behind the corner and began walking calmly toward the two guards stationed in the wide entry hall.

Their eyes followed me, but they didn't shout or call for anyone, which meant they likely didn't recognize me.

If I had been sneaking past them, this would have been the moment I felt relieved.

But no, I needed a disguise to wear to the sacrifice. One that would give me access to Azucena no matter what had happened to her earlier.

And there was only one way to get one.

If the guards were concerned with how closely I was walking to them, they said nothing—at least, not until I was within arm's reach.

"What are you—"

Before he could finish, I bashed my fist straight into the side of his head and he dropped to the floor in a colorful heap.

Pain burst through my knuckles, and I was pretty sure something inside my hand was broken. But there was no time to worry about that now. Without hesitation, I took advantage of the other guard's surprise, and just as he opened his mouth to yell, I delivered the same punch to him.

While I hit him hard, I had apparently used most of my power on the first guard, as this one didn't crumble to the floor, and he fought to regain his bearings.

Thinking fast, I spun, dipping down low to grab the spear the first guard had dropped when he fell. Barely able to suck in a breath, I maintained my spin and swept the second guard off of his feet using the spear.

"Ack!"

His yell was cut short as he tumbled to the stone floor, but I knew there was still a chance someone had heard. I needed to move faster. My plan would be messy, but I had no other choice.

Although I had never killed a human before, I knew it was probably the only way to truly disable the guards. There would be no way to enact the last part of my plan with one of them being able to possibly expose me. It was simply too risky.

With a grimace, I pictured the guards as deer and I stabbed

the pointed end of the spear through the first guard's throat. Then I turned to the second guard, yanking his tunic over his head quickly, before he could regain consciousness. Once he was without his tunic, I repeated the motion with the second guard, my arms aching from the force needed to break through both skin and muscle.

I nearly gagged as the second one choked.

I had killed animals before, but that was different, and for some reason, this felt even more gruesome than I had anticipated.

Once I was sure the second guard was dead, his clothes placed safely around the corner of the hall, I picked him up beneath his shoulders and began dragging him back the way I came—to the nearest unoccupied room.

It was a struggle, taking every ounce of my strength especially as the unhealed injury in my side barked in protest. But I accomplished it, brushing off my hands in pride—only to realize I still had another guard to move.

Panting, my side aching, I bent over, hands on my knees, trying to find my strength. I pictured Azucena's face in my mind and the way she had looked when I found her earlier—tied up and drugged, a loopy smile occupying her lips.

That did it.

With renewed resolve, I began the process of dragging the second guard around the corner and into the room with his friend. Once they were both out of sight, I gripped my aching side and returned to slip on the clothes from the first guard. I had chosen his both because he had died first, and because he appeared to be the closest to my size. That being said, the clothes were still a tight fit, making it hard to pull my shoulders and arms through the arm holes. It was a frock-style uniform at least, meaning my legs weren't subject to the same confinement.

Once I was dressed, I grabbed the spear I hadn't used to take with me, tossing the other one out of sight. While I briefly debated taking both, I knew that blood on the end would draw immediate and unwanted attention my way.

Passing through the atrium, I headed the opposite way of the kitchens, knowing I needed to find some other guards to fall in with before someone noticed how little I actually knew about how to be a palace guard.

Lucky for me, as I rounded the corner, I could hear voices—one that was eerily familiar.

"Is the girl prepared for the sacrifice?"

"Yes, Sapa Inca."

"Shhh, not yet. You know I cannot take the title until it is confirmed that she is dead."

"Sorry, Sapa Inca."

My gut clenched and all the breath left my chest. Zu had gotten caught again. It had been too much to hope that she had gotten away during my distraction earlier.

Cautiously, I peered around the corner to see the same aged woman who had been among those who had found me by the cliff's edge. With her was a bulky guard who was nearly my size, and they both sat on a stone bench lined with straw cushions. I wanted to stay and listen, but I knew there was no way I could hide here.

Shifting to the shadows on the other side of the hall, I stood tall, my shoulders back, and walked in front of the door, holding my breath until I reached the other side. For a moment, I was worried their silence indicated they had spotted me, but then their conversation started up once more and I knew they had passed this obstacle with success.

I traveled further down the hall—this one was much more ornate than the ones where I had been staying. After the atrium, the halls had narrowed, but now they widened once more, and when I came to a double-wide doorway, somehow I knew that I was about to walk into the throne room—the one where peasants, like my father and myself, had visited once to pay their tithe and request an audience with the Sapa Inca. Images flickered in my mind from my previous visit, but nothing solidified, and they eventually dissipated like smoke into the evening air.

I stopped just before the doorway, ensuring my uniform was as natural-looking as it could be, despite its ill-fit, my back ramrod straight, and the spear gripped naturally in my hand. The last one was the hardest due to the bundle of nerves wreaking havoc on my insides.

After one last breath, I took a step forward, entering the throne room.

I fought to keep the surprise from showing on my face. The room was beautiful, with colorful paintings and gold painted onto all the walls. My eyes caught specifically on a puma painted on the wall opposite from where I stood, a young boy sharpening a spear painted just in front of him. I wasn't sure if it was the way the boy stood, or the fact that his back was turned to the puma, but I knew immediately that this was the Quipu Azucena had told me the end of. A little shocked that she hadn't mentioned that it was painted on the wall in the palace, I turned to find a large stone seat on opposite side of the puma painting, which had also been gilded to shine in the low evening light.

In front of me, there was a short line of peasants, likely the last of the sun-cycle, waiting for the woman I now knew as Yezema to return. I felt bad for them as they shuffled their weight from foot to foot, impatient after likely having spent all daylight hours awaiting their turn.

There wasn't time to follow that thought any further though, as I quickly noticed the two guards standing by the door I had just entered, as well as the set of two on each side of the throne. I needed to think fast.

If I had been anyone else, I would have just said I was there to replace someone, calling out a common male name. But as it was, I didn't even know what the common names were these sun-cycles—I had been so removed from society for the past ten solar-paths.

Although the gods had made me fight two guards, they were apparently not that angry with me because before I could truly embarrass myself, a voice behind me said, "You're replacing Ekkeko."

I spun to spot one of the guards motioning to the other one standing across from him by the door. I didn't say anything, I just went and stood beside him, ensuring my stance matched those of the others in the room.

The one who had spoken to me narrowed his eyes. "I haven't seen you guarding the throne room before."

"New promotion," I lied quickly, kicking myself for not having asked Azucena more about how the palace was run during our time traversing the forest. Then again, I hadn't really planned on impersonating a guard when we arrived at the palace either.

It was sufficient however, because while the skeptical look remained on the man's face, he turned back, facing forward, leaving me to stand and try my best not to draw any attention to myself.

It wasn't long before the woman I had heard conversing swept into the room, draped in massive colorful robes, taking a seat on the throne, listening to the various concerns of the villagers one by one. The man she was with stood next to the throne, his stance the same as mine. I couldn't speak for the villagers, of course, but I found the way Yezema looked at them with such disinterest appalling . . . Did they not recognize an uninterested individual when they saw one?

As that thought crossed my mind, I realized, without having met Zu, these people didn't know any better. Some of them may be visiting for the first time, and if they'd never known anything different...

I continued to stand there, my thoughts swirling as Yezema listened to complaint after complaint from the peasants. At first, it was easy—back straight, knees slightly bent, elbows stable. But as the moments turned into much longer periods of time, my limbs began to grow heavy, the spear clenched in my fist nearly sinking to the floor. How did the other guards do this for so long? Not to mention my side twinged from time to time, reminding me that my broken ribs had certainly not healed. I kept trying to flick my eyes to the side to see if the man across the doorway from me was struggling in a similar manner, but even this was more effort than it was worth.

Just as I was about to admit defeat and ask the adjacent guard about our next break, Yezema spoke to the final villager in line, dismissing them after their hefty tithe was paid. As she made her way down the steps, she spoke to the man who hadn't left her side during the entire exchange. "Prepare your men for the sacrifice and meet me at Inti's temple at star-rise." Then she left the room.

The moment she was out of sight, the men all visibly relaxed. Backs that were once straight as a tree relaxed, shoulders hunched over, and spears everywhere hit the floor.

The man next to me gestured to the empty doorway. "After you."

I hesitated, knowing that as a guard I should know this, but I didn't.

"What's wrong? Forgot the way?" he taunted, a sneer on his lips.

"Um, I just started today, I was stationed outside before, so . . ."

The man huffed his annoyance but apparently bought my excuse as he pushed past me. "They should've left you outside if you can't even remember the hallways."

I tried not to be hurt by his quip. After all, this wasn't really my job. But something about the way he said it made my blood heat and my heart quicken.

I didn't argue back, rather I just settled in line behind him, following his footsteps as we headed down the hall, through the atrium where I had killed the guards, and to a dark room that must've been located near the kitchens due to the delicious smells that wafted into the small space.

"Wait here. We will need a larger number to head up the mountain for the sacrifice."

I nodded mutely as the rest of the men from the throne room

filed into the room. Some immediately sank down on the floor, resting their tired limbs, while others merely rested their spear against the wall by the door before finding a place to lean. There weren't enough stone benches for everyone, but that didn't seem to matter. A jar of coca leaves were passed around.

Before I could wonder where they had gotten them, a dark arm was outstretched in my direction, a few leaves held between his fingers. "It's going to be a long night."

I had never had coca before. Only nobles could afford the bitter-tasting leaves, and they were the only ones seen as worthy of chewing it even if I could find enough trade to afford a few.

I startled as I realized that now, as a guard of the Sapa Inca, I too was thought to have come from a noble family. Not wanting to reveal my peasant status, I took the leaves from the hand and placed them on my teeth as I had seen the others in the room do.

Bitterness immediately flooded my mouth, and I fought the urge to spit the leaves out on the ground. How did people chew on this all sun-cycle? I felt my mouth salivating with the urge to spit the leaves, and I swallowed hard, begging my stomach not to revolt.

My eyes darted around the room, curious if anyone else was struggling as much as I was, but alas, they all seemed accustomed to the foul taste—likely having chewed the leaves since their teenage solar-paths.

The men began talking amongst themselves, but the conversations were of the personal sort, asking about family and plans for adding new rooms and features to homes—nothing I could comment on, having not known these men long at all. And they didn't seem to care to know me either, all of them pretty much ignoring my presence.

I have no idea how long we lounged there, waiting for more guards to join, but at some point, I began to feel invigorated, my energy seeming to restore to unnatural levels. It was either the coca or the gods, I wasn't sure, but I immediately found myself bouncing on my feet, ready to climb the mountain to Inti's temple.

My father had told me about Inti's temple as a young boy, but I had never visited it myself. I had been told it was one of the most beautiful places in Sipan. It supposedly had a view of both the palace and the village, as well as the carvings made by our ancestors.

I didn't have to wait long for our group to nearly double, and as soon as it did, we were collecting our spears before walking out the door and up the hill. As soon as we were under the cover of darkness, I discreetly spit the coca leaves off the side of the path into the bushes. Whether or not they were responsible for my energy boost, they weren't worth the foul taste.

The walk was brief, or at least it seemed that way, and before long, we were entering a circle of torches, with Yezema standing in the middle in a purple ceremonial garb, her eyes appraising each of us as we entered. Her appraisal seemed almost sexual, and coming from someone who was at least twice my solar-paths made me cringe.

I was situated in the middle of the group of guards, which made it easy to follow their motions as we all came to stand in a circle within the torches, gathered around Yezema.

I watched, the firelight casting an eerie glow on the woman and the stones of the temple, as we all took our positions. Once we were complete, Yezema nodded and shouted, "The gods await their tribute. Bring her forward."

Four guards, who hadn't been a part of our circle appeared, a woman clutched between them. At the sight of the dark curly hair, my heart clenched, only for my eyes to widen when I finally saw a glimpse of her face.

I didn't know who this woman was, but it wasn't Zu. Despite similar shades of skin and hair, the eyes and nose were all wrong.

Unfortunately, Yezema noticed at the same time I did.

"Who is this? This isn't the Sap—I mean Azucena Katia, as the gods requested."

The men looked around wide-eyed and I realized that most of them likely didn't know Zu's name, just her official title. That, or she had more enemies than I first realized.

"This is the woman you approved earlier." One of the men who had carried her tried to argue.

Yezema shook her head. "Did you even look at her face? The woman I saw earlier was the right tribute this . . . this is someone else!"

The guard opened his mouth once more, likely to offer another argument, but before any words could tumble out there was a large cacophony of voices.

I spun every which way, trying to see where the sound was coming from, only to realize we were surrounded by men and women alike, all of them dressed like peasants, spears and bows clutched in their fists.

Thirty-Four

AZUCENA

So far, everything had been going exactly as we had planned.

Until I spotted Rurac dressed in guards' clothes in the circle that surrounded my former advisor. He looked positively awful, I might add, his whole body leaning to one side as he tried to hide his obvious side wound, a bead of sweat rolling down his scrunched brow.

What was he doing here?

The villagers were already in place, all of them outfitted with extra spears that one of my loyal guards had procured from storage. Many of them brought additional weapons they'd had at home—items from short knives tucked into their belts to bows and arrows now held aloft. Eztil was also in place, with orders to remain hidden in the trees until the fighting was over, though I had a feeling he wouldn't be listening to those orders very well. I just hoped for his own safety he would.

Before I could think of some way to signal the villagers to spare Rurac, the order to attack rang out.

"ATIPAY!"

I couldn't tell you who shouted it, but all at once the sea of villagers we had collected swept in and began attacking the guards surrounding Yezema. Within moments, I lost track of Rurac as he disappeared beneath the flood of the crowd.

Eztil was right, although my enemies outnumbered me in the palace, with the help of the villagers loyal to me, they were the ones vastly outnumbered in the end.

Knowing that the villagers had their weapons and orders, I did the only thing I could do and started trying to find my way to where I had last seen Rurac.

"Watch out!" someone shouted in my direction too late, an elbow driving into my gut. The wind was knocked out of me just before the guard who elbowed me was killed, a short knife protruding from his neck, thanks to a villager. I gagged and turned away from the gruesome sight.

"Sorry, Sapa Inca!" the villager who had completed the kill yelled after me, but I didn't stop my search.

I ducked to avoid a flying spear, followed by dashing to the side to avoid another guard nearly falling on me. But all too soon, I found myself in front of none other than Rurac, who was lying flat on his stomach, face down, unmoving.

"Rurac!" I cried, falling to my knees next to his still body. I laid my hand on his back, holding my breath as I waited for it to rise beneath my hand. When nothing happened in the first few moments, I began to plead with the gods, ignoring the absolute craziness going on around us as I begged them to spare his life.

Before I could get too far into my prayer, beneath my hand, there was a flutter.

Releasing a breath, relieved he was alive but knowing it was better for him to stay down right now, I rose to my feet to glance around just in time to see Yezema attempting to slip her way past the fighting to sneak out of the circle.

"Oh no you don't!" I called out before launching my entire body weight in her direction. Unfortunately, before making my leap, I failed to properly gauge the distance between us (probably thanks to the drugs that were still in my system), so while I did manage to hit her, I only hit her legs, causing both of us to go tumbling to the stones . . . hard.

For the second time that evening, my breath was snatched from my lungs, and I struggled to catch it again. Lucky for me, Yezema seemed to be suffering the same problem, and she laid a hand on her chest, her mouth wide open as she attempted to suck in air.

When we both managed to catch our breath, and rise into sitting positions, Yezema glared at me with a look of pure murder on her face. "You absolute—"

"Don't you dare." I felt the anger bubbling within my chest, like a fire that had been fed for the first time—though I did regret that I had neglected to grab myself a weapon in that moment. "You're the one who tried to steal my empire from me! You drugged me, kidnapped me, and took me away from my home!"

At some point during my tirade, the rest of the fighting had concluded, resulting in most of the peasants of the village, and the remaining guards loyal to Yezema, staring at me with wide eyes.

"Ha!" Yezema spat with confidence, taking note of our attentive audience. "I'm not the one who turned my back on the villagers by demanding extra tithe to create a larger palace." She glanced around the circle of villagers who had gathered around us, shock evident on their features.

I knew I needed to stand for this next part, so I did before continuing. "I have not added anything to my palace since taking over for my mother six solar-paths ago. And I realize now that the tithe was too high. I will be lowering them going forward—starting immediately—so that the cold season is easier for everyone."

The crowd cheered, happy at my words, but before they could really rejoice, my disgrace of a former advisor cut in.

"You lie." Yezema narrowed her gaze and pointed her finger at me. "She makes false promises."

I shook my head. "I swear to you all, on the temple of Inti—where we are currently standing—that I will lower the tithe. Even though the tithe was too high in the past, you all know I used to offer benevolent extensions, and I never took your hands for late payment. Yezema however"—I walked around the circle, my gaze connecting with those of various villagers, most of which I didn't recognize—"used to send villagers, like yourself, to the holding cells for any reason. She would even remove limbs for late tithe payment."

"Y-you—" Yezema sputtered as she finally rose to her feet. "I mean, I only sent the worst of the worst criminals there. You know that." She tried to copy my tactic and make eye contact with some of the villagers, but I could see the colors of their distrust in their auras as they glanced away from her stare.

One of the villagers I didn't recognize stepped forward, holding his arm aloft where you could see the limb ended in a stump instead of a hand. "Sapa Inca is telling the truth. It is Yezema who ordered me to lose my hand!"

Gasps rang out through the crowd as everyone took in the missing appendage.

"Lies!" Yezema started again.

"Do not listen to her. She's the one who lies. The gods have told me so." I turned to where I had left Nania. "Even my own yanakuna can vouch for my way of leading Sipan."

Nania, though she had a glazed, drugged look on her face, quickly yelled the words to back me up. "Azucena is a fair Sapa Inca. The gods have always protected her rule. That is why she is here right now and not sacrificed to their service as her advisor intended to do against their will."

Heads were nodding now, and Yezema was quaking in anger as her plans crumbled around her. "Don't listen to them! The gods have told me that I am to be Sapa Inca!"

I tilted my head in confusion. "Then why am I the one still standing here calmly, and you are the one shaking in fear?"

I wasn't making things up this time. Whether it was due to the physical exhaustion on her old bones, or maybe the impact of hitting the stones hard, her limbs were shaking, visibly. The color blue was also present in her aura—something that I was beginning to think represented fear.

It was so silent; you could have heard a strand of straw drop. Mouths gaped open everywhere, and I could see the villagers mentally working things out and swiftly choosing my side. Finally, someone dropped their spear, the clank ringing out through the dark trees and bringing everyone back to the present.

Without missing a beat, I lifted my finger to point. "Arrest her!"

Two of the guards, who I had learned to recognize as my allies over the past few sun-cycles, rushed forward, reaching for her arms while two villagers stepped up to point spears in the direction of her chest. I searched for the last remaining guard on our side, Atiy, but he wasn't within sight. I briefly hoped he hadn't been hurt in the fighting, but I would have to look for him later.

Satisfied that her evil plan was ruined, I turned back to Rurac's limp body, only to find him holding his side and struggling to sit up.

"Rurac!" I dove to help him, but he motioned me away.

"I'm fine, just the ribs causing me problems." His eyes settled on Yezema. "Where is her right-hand man?"

I tilted my head to the side. I didn't recall Yezema ever being that close with anyone in the palace.

"A big man, like me," Rurac explained as he was struggling to draw in shallow breaths. "He was wearing a blue sash and a guard uniform earlier, but he may have changed before the ceremony."

The unoccupied guards and I glanced around, some of us inspecting the unmoving bodies lying on the stones. "I don't see him," I said, watching as my guards, too, shook their heads.

"I don't think this is over until we find him," Rurac grumbled, desperation in his voice as he searched the crowd without a hint of recognition.

"It'll be okay," I assured him before rising to my full height and addressing my people. "Villagers, thank you so much for coming to help me reclaim my kingdom." My voice was loud, hovering over the trees in the still, night air. "If you didn't hear, Yezema kidnapped me and tried to assume control of Sipan. She will be tortured and permanently imprisoned for her crimes. Anyone who wishes to stand with her, can, but you will also face permanent imprisonment at the hand of my loyal guards."

The silence settled over the circle, still illuminated by flickering torches. No one moved forward.

"As I thought." I surveyed the numerous faces, looking for one in particular. Once I found him, tucked near his mother who had also apparently come to fight, I motioned him forward with my finger. "I would additionally like to recognize Eztil before the gods for his amazing bravery in gathering all of you while I was disposed. There will be a feast in his honor in the palace tomorrow—all are invited."

A gasp rang through the crowd and one of my guards leaned forward to whisper in my ear. "Sapa Inca, I do not think we can cook that much food."

"I'll help," I whispered back. "I don't care about the cost. We will make it happen."

If the guard was surprised by my change in demeanor, and the fact that I had volunteered to do work in the kitchen for the first time in my life, he didn't show it, instead merely nodding to the others, including Nania, who had escaped her ropes and was standing to the side.

"For now, please return to your homes. Take caution as you make your way down the hill in the dark. If any of your loved ones are wounded, please help them down the hill to the palace. My healers will assist them there." The mass of people began to move, most of them smiling and chatting excitedly to one another. Once the area was mostly clear, I was relieved to see there weren't too many dead. Though several villagers and palace guards had been injured, most were able to hobble, with help, down the hill to the healers. The few unmoving bodies I did observe, forced me to fight back tears as their family members lingered nearby. It hurt that they had sacrificed their lives for me, but I knew they would be able to watch the impact of their sacrifice from Hana Pacha.

Once I was able to take a few deep breaths and compose myself, I finally turned back to the guards who still held Yezema between them. "Please deposit Yezema in a torture chamber, then come up here to collect the bodies and take them to the burial preparation room. I will pray that they are sent to the gods as yanakuna, in my stead."

"Yes, Sapa Inca," the guards replied before starting down the hill with Yezema trapped between them, leaving just Nania, Rurac, and I with the dead.

I embraced Nania, leaning in to whisper in her ear, "Thanks so much for taking my place. You were amazing."

"Anything for you, Sapa Inca—I mean Zu," she replied, a smile on her lips though the lines on her face revealed how exhausted and out of it she was.

I smiled back, just happy that she was finally using my nickname. "Come on, let's help Rurac down and then we can all rest." I moved to slip under his arm to take some weight off of his feet, but he brushed me off.

"I can walk myself."

I raised an eyebrow at him, uncertain. He was leaning to one side, whether he realized it or not, and walking with a limp. "Just let me help."

"No," he said firmly, turning toward the path. "I'll be fine."

My heart stuttered at his tone. One moment he was sacrificing himself for me, and now he was talking to me like that? My eyes caught Nania's, which were dancing with both mischief and concern as she looked between us. I knew I would have to explain everything about him, including my feelings toward him, to her later.

"All right, then." Taking one last glance around to ensure only the dead were left behind, I led both Rurac and Nania to the path down the mountain, taking each step with caution as my eyes adjusted to the dark after leaving the circle of torches. Rurac hobbled behind me, his arm holding his midsection and his breaths coming in gasps—he was obviously in pain. Nania walked behind him, slowly, thanks to the drugs. Rurac's large form blocked her from view for most of the path and I could only see her every so often when we passed one another when the path twisted.

Everything was fine until we stepped over the threshold to the palace, when suddenly, with a shout, Rurac lost consciousness, his large body collapsing to the floor with a thud.

Thirty-Five

RURAC

I was floating.

In space . . . maybe in time?

I was somewhere between the worlds however, that was for certain.

Or maybe I was floating through history?

I saw images of my father and I, first, and I almost didn't recognize myself—as a young boy that is. Regardless, the young boy with dark hair like mine darted between the trees, chasing a small animal while his father harvested the crops. I hadn't noticed as a child, but looking back I could see the tired lines drawn on my father's face—the fatigue of becoming both my mother and father overnight and being solely responsible for my survival.

Then I saw myself as an adolescent, learning to carve wood and cook potatoes—even as I argued with my father at every turn. The next image was me as an adult, as I mourned the death of my father and buried his body in the woods near my home.

Before I knew it, I saw Azucena as she came into my care, and although that was probably the end of my life, I couldn't help the smile which spread across my lips. Even in this moment, I found myself in awe of her beauty, impressed by her wit, and absolutely certain that she was the best empress for Sipan—even if I wasn't there to see it.

"We knew she was perfect when she was young. That's why we called her parents' home so soon."

The voice was masculine and deep, and I tried to turn toward it, but my eyes were blinded. He was so bright—like Inti when he crossed the sky each sun-cycle.

"Don't look," he admonished, his voice kind. I felt a weight on my shoulder, almost in the shape of a hand. "We have to send you back."

At his words, my limbs felt heavy, and I felt a nudge in my ribs. "But I'm tired."

His tone changed. "I know. But she needs you to keep her grounded."

"She's learned a lot on her own," I argued, though I couldn't figure out for the life of me why I was arguing. My heart wanted to go back—to her.

"She has. And she will learn even more with you by her side to support and comfort her in all that she does. Even the most powerful leaders need someone to come home to at the end of every sun-cycle."

"But my father?" The words were the barest of whispers as I glanced in the direction I had last seen his image.

"He will still be here, waiting for you, when it is time for you to return for good."

"All right."

The mist I was floating in seemed to intensify, and the light diminished as the weight on my shoulder disappeared and Inti shifted away.

"Don't forget what you saw outside the throne room—danger lurks still."

I frowned at his final words, but there was no time to think them through, as the darkness was suddenly all-consuming, the pain in my side renewed, crescendoing with every breath.

"Rurac!"

That voice was one I recognized. I shifted, a smile coming across my lips once more as that single word provided some comfort.

"Zu."

"Come back to me," she whispered.

She whispered other words too, but I couldn't make them out as I struggled to move my limbs, which were suddenly as heavy as the boulders we climbed out of in the sacred valley.

It seemed like an eternity later when I finally regained control of my eyelids, cracking them open and seeing her face hovering over mine.

"You're okay." She had a large hand clutched in hers—

Was that hand really mine? It looked far more pale than I remembered my skin looking. Tear tracks adorned her cheeks, though her eyes sparkled with happiness.

"Welcome back to the Pacha Mama."

I glanced around the room, realizing I didn't recognize the colorful walls, nor the clay ledge decorated with colorful lumps— no wait, were those llamas? Unsure why, my lips opened to ask that exact question.

"Are those llamas?"

Azucena gasped and then threw her head back and laughed. I tilted my head in confusion. "Well, are they, or aren't they?"

She shook her head, still laughing. "I can't believe you've been unconscious for three sun-cycles and the first thing you comment on is my clay llama collection."

I attempted to chuckle, but the pain in my side grew worse. "Actually, I said your name first."

"My nickname," she chided. "Then you commented on my llamas."

"Well, you do have an awful lot of them."

"I told you—they're my spirit guide."

I glanced over to them again before noticing the light outside of the windows. "Where am I?"

"My room in the palace." She sighed. "We brought you here after the sacrificial ceremony."

"Oh." I didn't know what else to say. I wanted to comment about what I had seen in my unconscious state, but something told me to hold back. So instead, I continued to glance around the room, taking immediate notice of the colorful blanket that covered me from the waist down. "What . . . "

"I bought them back—every last one we traded on the way."

"How?" I ran my hand over my mother's weavings, tears brimming in the corners of my eyes. I couldn't believe she had gotten this one back, as it was one that I had traded early on, when she was having her menses.

"I'm the empress, remember?"

"I remember that." I scoffed. "But I traded this before we even left the hut for our journey to the palace."

"I know. I tracked it down. This one was the most expensive, but you'd be surprised what some people will do for a little meat."

"You're right," I agreed with her, still aghast that she had gotten the precious blanket back. Before I could say anything else though, my stomach rumbled, and Azucena motioned to someone behind my head. "What was that for?"

Her gaze returned to mine, her hands settling to rest lightly on my chest and arm, where they had been when I had returned to Pacha Mama. "I sent for some food for you."

"I'm not hungry," I tried to fib, my gaze roving over Azucena's face before coming to rest on her lips. "At least not for food . . ." I struggled to raise myself to bring my lips to hers, realizing my body was still too heavy to move comfortably, so instead I whispered, "Kiss me."

Azucena leaned closer to me, but her lips were still a hands-width from mine. "Already trying to order the empress around now, are you?" she breathed.

"Mhm, it was a question."

"Didn't sound like it." Her lips shifted closer, but they still weren't touching mine.

247

"Please?" I whispered.

"That's better." She didn't even fully finish the second word before her lips melded with mine and the rest of the room sank away from my peripheral vision. It was almost as if I was back to the floating universe I had just spent several sun-cycles in, though my pain was there to remind me that it wasn't quite the same.

My arms finally responded to my mental orders and came up to tangle in her hair, pulling her to me. Although I was hungry and still in pain, I never wanted to let her go. But just as that thought passed through my mind, so too did the memory of the god's words about danger still lurking.

Against my better judgement, I pulled on her hair lightly. Listening to my movements, she removed her lips from mine, but kept her face near, resting her forehead on mine as she caught her breath.

I opened my mouth to ask about the man I had seen with Yezema, but Azucena spoke first.

"Rurac, will you enter a trial marriage with me?"

I don't know what I had expected to come out of her mouth, but it wasn't that. For a moment, I was so awestruck that someone as amazing as Zu had asked me to be in a trial marriage, that I didn't answer.

She sucked her lip into her mouth and began to talk rapidly. "I already told the people—while you were sleeping—that marriages were no longer restricted by class . . . so it's allowed. If you're not sure, we could just do it for a solar-path, see if we mesh. If not, we can go our separate—"

I raised my finger to press it to her lips. "You surprised me, Zu. But I want nothing more than to have a trial marriage with you. Though I can guarantee that it will last forever on my end, unless you want to leave after a solar-path."

Her shoulders dropped and I could almost see the tension leaving her body. "There's not a chance of that happening," she whispered, before leaning down to kiss me again. When we parted for the second time, she added, "You're stuck with me now, Rurac —for the rest of our time on the Pacha Mama."

I smiled, liking the sound of that, reaching up to guide her lips back to mine—

"Ehem."

Azucena immediately jumped up from the bed I lay on and spun around to face the owner of the masculine voice. She stood directly in front of him, so I couldn't see who it was at first.

"Atiy, come in. Rurac has awakened."

I couldn't explain it, but I suddenly felt cold, a chill working its way down my spine though I had been warm just a few moments before.

I heard footsteps as the man approached the bed. Azucena turned to me to explain, "Rurac, Atiy was one of the guards who remained loyal to me. Even during Yezema's attempt to steal the throne he—"

Her words were drowned out by a ringing in my ears as I saw his face for the first time.

It was the man I had seen in the room next to the throne room. The one who had been wearing the blue sash.

It was Yezema's right-hand man.

I opened my mouth to warn her "Azucena he's—" But it was too late, as he approached the bed, he pulled a short knife from his waistband. Azucena froze, but I could see the fear overcome her features.

"You know," he hissed, "I wondered how our carefully, laid out plan to sacrifice this one to the gods went so wrong, and I never could quite figure it out." He stepped closer, his knife pointed at me. "I even pretended to be on her side, so that I could interrupt any plan she came up with, yet she still managed to escape. All because of you."

My eyes rested on the knife, which was now just a few hands from my chest.

In that moment, though, something happened. I don't know if it was the gods helping nudge me in the right direction, but I suddenly felt relieved that the knife was pointed at me and not at Azucena, because in doing so, the man had made a terrible mistake.

He had underestimated her.

The only woman who had nearly beat me in a fight the first sun-cycle we met. Whose teeth marks were still on my arm in the form of a scar.

"That's where you are wrong," I corrected him, trying to keep the smirk from giving my plans away too soon.

His brows drew together. "I saw you together in the forest and I saw—"

I laughed. "I'm not saying you saw wrong," My eyes connected with Zu's over his shoulder, and I took note of how she was slowly stepping toward him, a glinting piece of jewelry clutched in her hand. "I'm saying you made a mistake."

In a flash of movement, Azucena jumped on the man's back, looping the necklace over his neck, before crossing the ends and pulling—effectively cutting off his air supply. As soon as he stepped one pace back from the bed, I stood. My legs were shaky, but I willed my weakness away. There would be time for that later —when my empress wasn't in trouble.

The man backed up, likely trying to hit his back into a wall to force her off, but I knew from when I first met her that Azucena wasn't an easy woman to fight. Regardless, I stepped forward, pulling the knife from his nearly limp fist to hold it at his throat. "Azucena managed to foil Yezema's plans all on her own. She didn't need me."

Atiy's eyes began to drift closed, and I caught him as he fell, allowing Azucena time to remove herself and her jewelry from him before he hit the stone floor.

I kept the knife, clutched in one hand, pointed at him while the other went to my side. The pain was still intense. "Are you okay?" I asked Zu.

She nodded, breathing heavily from the force it took to choke the guard. "I . . . can't—" she panted. "Believe . . . he was the one who was betraying me . . . the whole time." She moved toward the door, poking her head out to call in more guards, who were there in a flash to restrain Atiy as he regained consciousness. "Take him to the torture chambers. He will be dealt with as Yezema was."

"But empress—" One of the guards open his mouth, likely to speak in the man's defense, but Zu cut him off immediately.

"He has betrayed me, and he just tried to stab me with that knife. No more questions. He is to be disposed of. Permanently."

The men nodded, hurriedly restraining Atiy between them and dragging him from the room. The moment they were gone, Azucena rushed forward to enclose me in an embrace. I grimaced as her arm pushed on my side.

"I'm glad you are happy and alive my empress, but my side can't take this pressure."

"Oh!" she cried out, releasing me from her hold to move me back toward the bed. "I'm sorry, I was just so glad—"

It was my turn to cut her off as I pulled her down next to me, putting my arm around her shoulders and nudging her toward my uninjured side. "I'm glad too."

We sat there for a while, just holding each other, until Nania came in with a tray of food. I had to admit, though this was only my second time meeting Zu's yanakuna, I liked her already. Not only had she brought me food, but she had brought enough for Zu too.

"Thank you, Nania," Zu said before dismissing her.

The moment she was gone, we both dug into the food, both of us eating like we had gone without food for several sun-cycles. Once we had finished, we lay back on the bed, and I pulled Zu into my arms.

"Well, hopefully, that is all the excitement we will have for a while. I don't know if my heart can take anymore."

I chuckled, brushing a loose hair from where it had fallen in front of her face. I would never tire of holding her like this, of feeling her body pressed to mine. "I hope so too, but knowing you, I'm sure trouble will find us again someday."

"You're probably right," she agreed, leaning up to place a kiss on the bottom of my chin. But I didn't let her pull back, instead directing her lips to mine.

"It's like the Quipu of the puma and the boy. The fun is the journey, not the destination."

She raised her eyebrows. "You agree with the Quipu?"

"I do." I smiled. "Now, where is that healer? I need more healing immediately so I can go home." Azucena shot up, her eyes growing wide, but before her nerves could get the better of her, I added, "I need to move all of my items here."

She beamed, leaning back down to give me a hug. "Just do me a favor and wait a few sun-cycles. Fourteen, to be exact"

"Why?" I scrunched my nose, I was injured, but not that injured—at least I didn't think so.

"Because." She took a deep breath. "I sent men to fix the bridge, but it will take them some time to complete it."

I raised my eyebrows. "You fixed the bridge?"

"I did." She smiled. "It was the least I could do for the villagers who showed up for me in my time of need."

And just like that, I knew I had been lucky enough to be paired with the kindest, most beautiful, most amazing woman to ever rule Sipan.

"Azucena Katia, my Sapa Inca," I whispered, my hand going to the back of her neck.

"Hm?" she asked, smiling in that cute way she always did.

"Nothing. Just liking the way it rolls off my tongue."

Before she could say anything more, I pulled her lips to mine in a kiss.

Epilogue

AZUCENA

"Thank you so much for bringing this issue to my attention." I stepped down from the dais to stand in front of the peasant, my hands reaching out to grasp theirs. "I'm so sorry to hear that your crops didn't make it. Here's what I'm going to do"—I motioned to the guard next to me— "Amaru, here, will deliver you more seeds himself along with some provisions for the cold season. His family is from a long line of farmers, and he will help to check that your soil isn't the problem. If it is, he can help guide you to somewhere else that is suitable for growing, okay?"

"Yes!" There were tears brimming in the woman's eyes. "That sounds marvelous, Sapa Inca, thank you so much."

"Of course. Now, what did you say your name was again?" I discreetly checked the area above her head—more out of habit than anything else. I had learned that most of my villagers were trustworthy, and even though some weren't, it wasn't worth the risk of their child going hungry.

"Panti, like the flower." She wiped her finger under her eye to catch the tear that rolled down her cheek, and without thinking, I reached in my pocket to hand her one of my small, woven face cloths.

"No problem, Panti. If you have any further issues, please let me know."

"I will, thank you, Sapa Inca. You really are a gift from the gods."

I allowed Panti to kiss my hand once more before Amaru began to show her the door. He glanced over his shoulder, his gaze darting from me to the handkerchief still grasped in Panti's hands, but I gave him a small shake of my head to let him know it was okay that she kept it.

It had been almost a full solar-path since Rurac and I had begun our trial marriage, and he had moved from his small hut to the palace. It had been hard for him to say goodbye to the only home he had ever known, but as it had turned out, his friend Kuntur needed a place to begin his own trial marriage and had been happy to care for Rurac's home for as long as he needed. Which would be a while, if I had it my way.

I hadn't told Rurac yet, but I had already decided I wanted our trial marriage to become permanent. I just hoped he felt the same when I finally brought it up. Which I planned to do, immediately.

Nodding to another one of my guards and motioning toward the kitchen, he dipped his head, indicating he understood that I was heading for a snack and would return shortly.

I wasn't going to lie; it had been a bit difficult since Yezema was executed. I had never truly gauged how many people in Sipan had needed help and how many wanted to just be heard. Seeing as I was just one person, I had begun searching for a new advisor to take Yezema's place, but I hadn't yet found someone I trusted.

I had debated approaching Nania, and it was still an option, though I was afraid she was going to say no. But maybe I would find my confidence to ask her—just not this sun-cycle.

Plus, I knew for a fact Nania had her hopes set on a certain guard for a trial marriage of her own. Not that it would prevent her from becoming my advisor.

On my way to the kitchen, I passed Eztil, who was in his very own mini-version of the guard's clothes standing between the two door guards. I waved, and he waved back, a huge smile occupying his face.

Since dismissing Yezema, I had followed through on my promise to bring him to the palace as a trainee guard. However, I had much bigger plans for him, and once he was old enough, I planned to ask him to become my advisor and invite him and his mother into the palace. Just not yet.

Bringing Eztil on had been a huge inspiration to me, and I had decided to change things by hiring more guards who were experts at different tasks, instead of just the sons of the nobles. Amaru had been one of those hires, and when I brought him on, he had been ecstatic at the prospect of helping some of the lowest class peasants with farming, as needed. And he had proven to be an excellent guard during the moments in between.

Entering the kitchen (which was something I never used to do) I was greeted by the smell of roasting corn and spiced meat, and my mouth immediately began to water. Peering over the shoulder of Chaska, whom I had come to know as the head of the kitchen, I glanced at what was roasting over the fire. Chaska had been less than happy to hear that she had to cook for thousands of people, but once she found out what Eztil had accomplished (and I offered to help) she had eventually come to accept it, and I think she maybe even enjoyed it in the end because it had been the beginning of our friendship. Maybe.

Chaska just shook her head and pushed past me toward where we kept the clay plates. "I'll make you a dish, Sapa Inca." The pink in her aura revealed what her words did not. Though she seemed annoyed, she really did care for my well-being.

"Thanks, Chaska!" I called back before leaning over the fire to get a better look at the meat on the roasting rack. I had spent the last solar-path learning even more about my gift. Mostly thanks to Rurac, who I could ask about his emotions whenever I saw a color I didn't recognize, knowing he would answer honestly. Though he was still very gruff about discussing his feelings, and anything to do with spirit guides, he had deduced that the colors had some-thing to do with my gods-given gift that I refused to speak of, and had been very patient with my questions. And I, of course, had assigned him his own spirit guide without his knowledge. He would thank me . . . someday.

Lost in thought, gazing at the meat over the fire, I was startled when I suddenly felt hands on my waist. With a squeak, I turned, prepared to fight whoever it was off, only to find Rurac there, a wide smile on his lips.

"I'm sorry, Empress, did I startle you?" His eyes danced with mischief.

I crossed my arms over my chest in fake anger as I righted myself. "Yes, actually. And the punishment for startling me is quite steep, you know."

"Is it now?" He raised his eyebrows, his gaze darting from my eyes to my lips.

"Very." I smirked, searching the space above his head even though I could read him pretty well without my gift at this point. "I usually order many solar-paths of being a yanakuna, but for you . . . I might need an even more strict punishment."

"An even more strict punishment you say?" He raised an eyebrow. "And what would that be?"

"Oh, you know, I was thinking maybe you should be forced into an arranged marriage." I fought to keep the smile from my face, but it was impossible. "Perhaps one that included some responsibility to the empire."

Rurac was fully smiling now. "An arranged marriage, you say? To an empress?"

"Yes. Quite the punishment, I know."

"It is." He pretended to think about it for a moment, but I could see that he had already made his decision. "Well, if you think that's what I deserve as a consequence for my actions . . ."

"I do."

"Then I shall serve my punishment, for as long as you'll have me." He placed his large hand on my hip and pulled me closer, our ruse obviously over as his head dipped for our lips to connect.

"Even in Hana Pacha?" I whispered right before our lips met.

"Even in Hana Pacha," he whispered, before pressing his lips to mine.

THE END.

Please Review!

Did you enjoy reading Qoya? As an Indie Author, your reviews mean the world to me and the future of my author career.

If you could please leave a review on whatever platform you purchased Qoya on, as well as on Goodreads, I would be forever grateful.

Quechua Words

Yanakuna: Servant

Hana Pacha: The afterlife, world of the gods, or the sky

Quilla: The Moon Goddess

Qwui: Guinea pig

Sapa Inca: Emperor/Empress

Quipu: Story

Inti: The sun, also a god

Atipay: Attack

Inti Raymi: Festival of the sun

Mictlan: Land of the dead, equivalent to hell, also sometimes referred to as Hukhu Pacha.

Pacha Mama: Earth (Sometimes Kay Pacha is also used)

Atoq: Fox

Supay: The Incan god of death

Huayno: A traditional Incan dance

Acknowledgments

Edited by: Caitlin Lengerich

Cover by: Caroline Leger

Beta Readers: Kaye Walther, Holly Willett, Jeannette Davis, Heather Burt, and Dewi Boessen

Map by: @centaurmaps

Formatting by: Hope E. Davis

Also by Hope E. Davis

Fantasy Romance Novels

Modern Legends of Sidhe:

Demure

Bold

Resilient

Standalones:

Qoya

Mystery/Thriller Novels

Deceptive Perfection

The Fate of Ava Miller

Before Now

You Can't Run

Buy books and extras at hopeedavis.com/buy-books/.

About the Author

Qoya is Hope's seventh novel. When she isn't writing, she is busy traveling the world, trying new foods, or hanging out with friends. She is also an avid reader and is always looking for her next life-changing fantasy read.

A graduate of Metropolitan State University, Hope grew up in Colorado but currently calls the Netherlands her home. To find information about her other novels and be notified of her newest releases, follow Hope on Instagram @hopeedavisauthor, TikTok @hopeedavisauthor, Threads @hopeedavisauthor, and Amazon: Hope E. Davis.